UGLIEST

KELLY VINCENT

KV BOOKS LLC

This book is dedicated to the memory of Nex Benedict, an Oklahoma trans teen who didn't deserve to be bullied and harassed by his peers while adults looked the other way, implicitly—or perhaps explicitly—telling Nex that if he'd just "be normal" then everyone would leave him alone. Nex was brave enough to be exactly who he was. His death is an American tragedy and we must not forget him

PART I

GETTING OUR TOES WET

"I love seeing how happy you are, Nic," Mom said as we pulled into the parking lot at OAMS, returning for the spring semester at my boarding school. January 2nd, 2023—a new year that I had high hopes for. "You know I had my reservations about you leaving home so early, but you are doing so well. And especially with how the art thing is going."

"Don't jinx it!"

"Sorry, honey, I—" She slammed on the brakes after a truck turned the corner and nearly cut us off.

A big, red F-250 with an American flag sticker on the left corner of the back window, a MAGA sticker in the opposite corner.

Yep, there was no doubt where we were. One of the reddest states in the country. Good ol' Oklahoma.

Mom made an annoyed growl but didn't say anything.

I rolled my eyes. "I got out of Emerson, but Emerson came right with me."

There were no spaces anywhere close to the dorm. The truck suddenly sped up before whipping around to the next row.

"Nic, I don't see anything wrong with acknowledging that things are going well for you, despite the fact that there are still a lot of conservative people around you. This school was even willing to give you your own room. They are recognizing your gender identity." We crept along, both looking left and right.

She wasn't wrong. I was surprised about the room, honestly. Last semester, I had roomed with a girl named Sophia, but in November I came out as agender and asked for my own downstairs room, like one of my best friends here, Mack, who was a trans boy.

"Someone's leaving!" Mom said, pointing to a choice parking spot on the front row. She drove down the rest of the row and turned onto the front row.

For the sole purpose of getting away from my small town, I'd applied to the state's free math and science academy—The Oklahoma Academy for Mathematics and Science—and miraculously got in. It was on the campus of the Oklahoma Institute of Technology, in a suburb of Oklahoma City called Burnside, so it wasn't as conservative as my small town. The bullying hadn't stopped completely, but I'd found my people for the first time in my life. And I'd ended up with my best art teacher ever.

Just as we neared the spot, the truck whipped around the corner and into the space, rocking front and back from braking so abruptly.

"Well, that was rude," Mom said. Sometimes the obvious still needs to be stated.

Somebody left in the second row, so we went around and got that spot. I watched as Rachel got out of the big truck, a tall man pulling bags out of the second row of seats.

Rachel was basically my biggest enemy here, one of the many unchristian Christians I dealt with in Oklahoma—the ones that talked about religion a lot but were so hateful inside. She had a history with Mack—their families had formerly been friends, but when Mack came out as trans, Rachel's family lost their shit, and now Rachel was constantly harassing Mack. And since I was friends with him and in art class and art club with her, I was a constantly available target.

I had stood up to her at the end of last semester, but things were still bad.

When we got inside, there was fortunately no sign of Rachel or her dad. I'd dragged my giant suitcase and portfolio in, and Mom had the smaller duffel. She filled out some paperwork while the RA—my old one from when I lived on the girls' side of the dorm last semester—gave me my keycard and a snide remark about just doing "this" for attention. She pointed me to the second downstairs room, with that ever-present judgy look on her face. Her hair was pulled back into a pony tail, but she had enough makeup on to make it very clear that she was a woman.

That's why she hadn't liked me. I wasn't girly enough for her. If my little sister, Isabella, had been able to come with us, my old RA would have approved of her. I loved my sister to bits, but we couldn't be more different.

I headed back to my room and unlocked my door. It swung inside and I got my first glimpse.

This was positive luxury compared to the dorm room I shared with Sophia last semester. There was a whole living room. Small, but it had a couch. The walls were the typical industrial white, but the carpet and couch were both blue. I moved inside and saw there was a doorway to the small bedroom, with a twin bed and a small nightstand, and nothing more. Off to the side was a small bathroom with a shower, toilet, and tiny sink.

I was in shock. I hadn't realized it would be this nice.

"Knock-knock," a voice said.

I turned to see Mack, immediately jolted into a happy smile. "Hey!"

"How are you?" He was standing in the doorway, since he wasn't allowed in, wearing black cargo pants and a green t-shirt with a dragon on it. His grin lit up his brown eyes, and I was reminded how a crush doesn't go completely away, even when things don't work out.

"Good. Are you next door to me?" I pointed to the room that was to the right of mine.

"Yep. Just got unpacked." His wavy black hair had that windswept look it sometimes did, and a painful pinch of attraction hit me. I had to move on. "Did you change your earrings?"

"I did." He had two small silver hoops in both ears now, where he'd only had them on the left before, and both were gold then.

Mack and I had these special rooms because they didn't know what to do with us since we were both trans. I think they were worried about Mack's safety on the boys' side of the dorm, and since I'm not a girl—and they'd already let Mack have one room—I guess they thought I shouldn't stay on the girls' side anymore. Even though I didn't expect them to say yes when I'd asked, I wasn't going to complain when they'd agreed.

"Cool." I said. I realized I was still standing in the middle of the front room next to my luggage. I walked over to the doorway. "Did you eat already?"

"Yeah, we stopped at Arby's when we got to town."

"We stopped, too. The halfway McDonald's on the turnpike. Is it weird that I'm looking forward to the cafeteria food?"

Mack laughed, that easy smile he had making me happy. "Buffets are always appealing."

"True." I laughed. "Well, this is a dumb conversation."

He raised his eyebrows. "You know not every conversation between friends needs to be riveting, right?"

That actually made my heart pinch. He *was* right. "Okay, but what are you reading right now?"

Mack's smile widened, and this launched us into a conversation planning out our next book club pick. Mack and I were in a book club with our friends Jenna and Jacob. I'd befriended Jenna at the campus tour last semester, and Jacob and I had ridiculously sat next to each other in art class for weeks without speaking because we were both shy, until Mack brought him to our book club one Sunday. He fit right in. And then it turned out he was bi and Jenna was gay, so we were all LGBTQ in some way.

"Do you know if Jenna and Jacob are here yet?" I asked.

"No. Let me text them." Mack pulled out his phone and sent a group text. My phone dinged, which made me smile again.

I, Nic-freaking-Summers, had a friend group and a group text. It was unreal. My life was completely different now. Four months had changed everything.

"Oh, hi," Mom said from the hall. "Is this Nic's room?"

I poked my head out. "Yeah. Mom, this is Mack. Mack, my mom."

"Hi there," Mom said. "I've heard so much about you."

Mack quirked an eyebrow and looked at me.

I flushed and then shrugged. I'd never told Mom about

the hot week or so we dated before he broke up with me because he was asexual. She knew he was trans, but not about the dating or his being ace.

"Nice to meet you," Mack said.

Our phones dinged at the same time, and we both looked. "Jenna's upstairs," I said.

"I don't need to stay," Mom said. "Do you want me to help you unpack? Or do you want me out of here so you can hang out with your friends?"

"Give me fifteen minutes so I can get unpacked," I said to Mack. "Let's meet in the lounge."

"I'll text everyone," Mack said, turning to go. "Bye, Mrs. Summers."

"Bye, Mack," Mom said, stepping in. Once Mack was gone, she said, "I didn't know Mack was Latino."

"His mom is. His dad is white. And Jenna is white, but Jacob is Black."

"It's nice to see you with different types of friends." She looked around. "This shouldn't take too long, sweetie."

"I don't even know where the closet is." I dragged the suitcase toward the back and spied the closet next to the bathroom. "I think I can do it myself," I said.

"Okay. I'm going to head on out then. Give me a hug."

She put her arms around me before I had a chance to respond, and I remembered how much I appreciated her. I hugged her back nice and tight. She hadn't wanted me to come out as agender last semester, mostly because she and Dad worried about my safety in a state that hates us so much. But she was supportive, anyway, when I said I wasn't afraid. Not all moms would be like that.

"Have a good semester, honey. I'll see you on spring break. I love you." She smiled and wiped a tear from each eye and turned to go.

"Love you, too," I said, closing the door behind her. I wasn't good with the tears.

I hurried to unpack, impatient to meet up with my friends. Impatient didn't even begin to cover it. I couldn't wait to see the people who made me feel like I belonged for the very first time.

By the time I had my clothes put away and the luggage stowed in the closet, I was running late to meet everyone. I raced out to the lounge. It was packed with people and loud with the voices of so many. The couches were full, but I found Mack, Jenna, and Jacob at one of the tables by the front windows. Jacob had gotten the haircut he'd mentioned last semester, and his head was almost completely shaved.

"There they are!" Jenna called before I got to the table, waving at me. "I was wondering when you'd get here." She had on a nondescript long-sleeve green t-shirt. But it must have been haircuts all around, because her own spiky blonde hair was even shorter than when I'd last seen her. She had a wide grin as she jumped up.

I couldn't believe how happy I felt right now. People actually wanted me around. I was amongst a group, in an even bigger crowd, and I did not feel out of place. Emerson Nic would never have believed my new life.

But I wasn't going to think about it—I was going to live in the moment for once.

Jenna came around the table and suddenly gave me a hug. I went all stiff.

She let go. "Oh, are you not a hugger? Sorry!"

I tamped down the panic and decide I needed to get

better. Friends hugging was normal. "No, it's okay. I just wasn't expecting it." I put my arms out awkwardly.

She laughed and hugged me again. "You're totally lying, but I'm taking advantage of it."

I grinned and we finished the hug—not *too* awkward—and I slipped into the chair next to her, with Jacob across from me and Mack next to him. Jacob was wearing a ratty Marvel t-shirt with his standard loose jeans. I'd never seen him in anything but jeans, even last semester when it was still hot.

"How's your room?" Jenna asked.

"Man, it's like a luxury suite. Mack never told us."

He laughed. "I didn't want to make you all jealous. You can almost pretend like you're out in the real world in your first apartment."

"Who's your roommate, Jacob?" It suddenly seemed weird that I had no idea.

"Samson Simms."

"I don't think I know him," Jenna said.

"He's not bad," Jacob said. "Pretty quiet. Keeps to himself. He was in our physics class, Nic."

"Oh, yeah. The tall guy? He seems cool." I didn't really think he seemed cool, but I had so much energy that even my words were overexcited.

"Except when he does his lunges, he's fine. He grunts when he exercises. It's annoying—not even a particularly sexy grunt."

We cracked up. Jacob almost never said anything that even hinted at his sexuality. But it was funny how he'd been paired with a tall and athletic guy, given how small and non-athletic he was. I couldn't picture Jacob doing any sport, any more than I could picture myself doing one.

But then I noticed a book on the table. It was a copy of

Gender Queer, that book that conservatives went bonkers over and banned all over the place.

Jacob covered the book with his palm. "So, yes, Nic. I brought a copy of *Gender Queer*. My brother gave it to me. It's really good, and I thought the rest of you might want to read it, too."

He slid it across the table toward me.

"Me first?" I asked. I looked at Jenna and Mack, and neither protested, so I picked it up and started reading the back cover. It sounded amazing.

"So I also had an idea," Jenna said.

We all looked at her.

"I know we all hate book banning, especially because it's always the kind of books we want to read that are being banned."

Her blue eyes were lit up with excitement.

"What do you think about starting a TikTok on the books we read?" Jenna asked.

I looked at Mack and Jacob, and they both had thoughtful frowns on their faces. I was thinking no way, at least for me. Me on TikTok? I couldn't see that.

"Not something I'd ever thought of," Mack said, "but it could be cool. Why not?"

"Yeah," Jacob said. "I'm not sure I want to be on camera, but if you want to, I'm all for it."

They all looked at me and I said, "I'm with Jacob."

"There's always the option of voice-over," Jenna explained. "I've been on BookTok for a while. I've done a handful of reviews myself, but usually I just watch other videos. But I'd love to be a part of it. Except I'm too busy to really produce a lot on my own. Maybe Mack and I can be the ones on camera and you two help?" She raised her eyebrows at Mack, who said, "Sure."

She looked back and forth between Jacob and me and said, "Then you two could either do voice-over reviews or help film or whatever."

Talking on a video that went out to the whole world sounded intimidating, but I should try it. Branch out a bit. Nobody would pay attention to it, anyway.

"Didn't Schmidt ban TikTok?" Mack asked, referring to the Oklahoma governor.

"Only for government and ... oh—" Jenna said. "And government-funded things like public schools. Yep. Good call."

"We can still do it," Jacob said. "We just have to drop off the school network. It's not banned by our cell carriers."

"Good point," Mack said. "What else should we read? I assume we're keeping the book club going."

Jacob nodded, and Jenna said, "Definitely. I have a list."

"Of course you do," I said, making everyone laugh.

While she opened her list up on her phone, she pretended not to smile and totally failed. We went over her list and picked one for the Sunday after next.

"That's only for the book club," Jenna said. "We may also need to read more for BookTok. I have a different list for that. Or possibly we can cover books we've read in the past."

We went through that list too, and she assigned books to all of us—with our agreement, of course. In the end we each had three as a starting point.

"Awesome," Jenna said. "Jacob, you should do *Gender Queer* for our first review."

His dark brown eyes went wide. "But I don't want to be on camera."

No way was I going on camera, either. I had moved beyond my comfort zone enough for the moment.

"You could hold the book and film it in your hand, or

someone else could hold it," Jenna said. "Maybe I can do a smiling Vanna White with the book while you talk."

Jacob narrowed his eyes. "Maybe."

Jenna raised a finger. "Another thought. You and Nic could do a review together. That could be kind of fun."

Alarmed, I said, "I'm not going on camera, either!"

Jenna and Mack laughed. Mack said, "I could go first, if you want. I've read some other books I can talk about. I'm sure I can find one that has been banned."

"Yeah, same here," Jenna said. "Let's do that, until these chickens get braver." She looked pointedly at Jacob and me, but you could see the smile in her eyes.

Eventually, the downstairs RA came through the room telling us all we had fifteen minutes before curfew.

"Back to the grind," Jenna said to us.

"I know." Mack sighed and ran his hand through his hair, making it even cuter. "This semester's going to be tough."

"Did you overload yourself again?" I asked. He was an overachiever, like most of the kids here.

He nodded. "When does your art mentorship start, Nic?"

That made me grin, and my stomach did several flips. There were so many things that were good right now, and it was a little overwhelming. "I have my first meeting with her on Thursday, and then the first in-person thing is Saturday."

On Tuesday, Jacob and I took our seats at our customary table in art class. We were in the second row on the right side, and Rachel was in her regular spot in the front left.

Rachel still intimidated me. She'd spent all last semester actively bullying me, constantly mocking me and so on.

She'd especially attacked me when I came out as agender, all because of her family's history with Mack's. She hated him for being trans, and since I was friends with him, she wouldn't leave me alone. But at the end of the semester, I finally stood up to her and told her off in front of everyone. Of course, then I cried, which was idiotic, but it was still good overall, because everybody supported me and said Rachel was being horrible.

I watched her to make sure she wasn't paying attention to me, and quietly said, "So I finished *Gender Queer* last night."

But then Rachel turned around right after I said it, making my stomach drop. She glared.

"Did she hear me?" I muttered to Jacob.

But maybe it wasn't a glare? I was still so bad at reading people. I'd spent all last semester thinking Lily was against me, too, and she never had been. Over winter break, I'd secretly hoped Rachel would finally get over Mack "betraying" her by just being who he was.

But she was still looking, and she looked mad.

"I have no idea. But she's a whack job, I swear," he whispered. "But I don't think she heard you."

"I hope not." I watched her face the front again, her long brown hair swinging with the turn. Would I ever be able to really read people?

"But it was pretty good, huh?" he asked.

Huh? Oh, the book. "Yeah. Are you going to do the review for TikTok?"

"Possibly, but I'm not going on camera. I'm not sure how we'll do it. I need to talk to Jenna about what the options are."

I shook my head. "I can't imagine being on camera." I hated having my picture taken, and this seemed worse. I'd had enough experience with people hating me because of how I looked. The no-makeup was the biggest problem, but I mostly wore jeans and unisex t-shirts, too. "I guess I could talk if nobody can see me."

Jacob nodded just as Ms. Mangal clapped her hands at the front of the room. She was an Indian-American woman who usually dressed pretty artsy, including usually wearing a bunch of metal bracelets. She was the best teacher. "Okay, everyone. Welcome to spring semester. There are only a few of you I need to talk to about a semester plan—Lily, Nic, and Jacob, I'll come get you when it's your turn. We'll talk for a few minutes to lay things out. You can work in your sketch-books for now, and everyone else, work on your next projects."

She approached Lily, a girl I had dismissed as "normal" last semester because she was conventionally pretty—slim, delicate-looking, and blonde—and I had this thing where I thought anyone who conformed was somewhat evil. But Lily turned out to be really nice, and I'd revised my world-view. With mixed success. I was actively trying to keep from slipping back into my judgmental ways.

She and Ms. Mangal went to sit at one of the back tables to talk. I tried not to listen, but I was nosy. Lily was going to stick with her marker style, but Ms. Mangal wanted her to do one in grayscale only. Her normal style was to do portraits of people, and maybe the occasional dog, in rainbow colors. So, not natural skin and hair colors, but she still managed to make them look real. It was so impressive. She and Ms. Mangal picked some of the images she was going to work from.

I looked through my sketchbook, thinking of ideas. I glanced over at Jacob's sketchbook. I already knew what he would be working on, too. He was making a comic about a

Black superhero. He was writing it and everything. I wasn't into superheroes, but Jacob's art looked professional. He was especially good at creating fight scenes that sizzled with movement.

Then Ms. Mangal called me back there to join them. Lily smiled at me but didn't say anything. I sat down across from her.

"I wanted to talk to you both about the mentorship," Ms. Mangal said. We'd both won spots on an art mentorship with a big local artist named Clee, which started this Saturday. She explained how we'd get there—either dorm staff or Ms. Mangal herself—and some of the other logistics.

With every word, I got more and more excited. This was going to be incredible. I still couldn't believe I'd gotten selected for it. It was such an amazing opportunity— Saturday studio time plus a virtual mid-week meeting. There were only five mentees in the program, so we would get a lot of Clee's time. Even though this would make me even busier than OAMS already did, it would so be worth it.

"That's it," Ms. Mangal said, taking a sip of tea from the colorful mug she always had within reach. "I'm so happy you both are doing this."

When she said that, Lily and I smiled at each other again and she left to go back to her seat.

"So, what do you think, Nic?" Ms. Mangal asked. "Sticking with ink?"

"I think so."

"Okay, that's great. You can do three major ink pieces again this semester. I would like you to do one in color, however. You can pick which one."

A sense of dread filled my chest. Color? I'd never used colored ink before. What if I couldn't do it?

Ms. Mangal smiled and touched my arm lightly. "Don't

worry, I'm sure you'll do a great job. And if not, it's fine—not every single piece of art an artist makes has to be incredible. You always learn from failures. It's just a matter of putting the work in. You know that."

I flushed. I wished I wasn't so freaking easy to read. I needed to learn to keep my emotions off my face. If only I could be as hard to read for everyone else as everyone else was hard for me to read. "Okay."

"It's not radically different from working only in black," she explained, cocking her head to the side. "You'll need to practice before doing the final piece. And we can talk about options—you could still do shading in different black marks, rather than mixing colors. The color could be more of an accent. I'll show you some options when you get to that one."

"Okay." That did make me feel better.

"Would you like to do another acrylic painting for your second medium?"

"Sure." Probably fruit and flowers? Ugh. Why did they always teach painting with still lifes?

"I'd like to see you do another still life for that." She must have read the unhappiness on my face, because she added, "I know they're boring, but it helps you develop your skills and instincts."

I knew she was right. But still. Boring.

Maybe I could put a dragon in the background, peeking over the bowl of fruit or whatever. That could be fun.

"Okay, do you have any ideas for pieces, or do you want me to come up with prompts for you?" she asked.

"I don't have any specific ideas right now." I could always do more dragons and fantasy stuff, but I didn't have to. "It was fun to come up with something based on your prompts."

"Okay, great. I've got some ideas here. I'd like to see another self-portrait."

Oh, boy. So many artists did self-portraits, and I'd never understood the urge. Last semester's went okay. At least it didn't get me in trouble. The one I'd done last year at Emerson that was supposed to be me pulling off my real face, showing a demon-style face beneath it, got me in all sorts of trouble. The school freaked out and thought it was a threat of violence, and my parents sent me to a terrible shrink. I learned my lesson, for sure.

Ms. Mangal continued. "You can have some leeway on this—it can be a headshot only, or full or partial body, and you can choose to include props or setting, or stick with a simple background."

"Okay." I tried to forget the Emerson portrait, but I had no idea what I would do this time.

"Another one I'd like to see is a historical figure in a situation from a different time period, even modern. It should be a little incongruent, but there are so many directions you could take this."

No ideas came to me on that one, but it could be cool.

"And finally, I'm leaving the last one completely open. If you can't decide and want some ideas, let me know and I can give you a list of some more prompts."

"Okay," I said. My stomach was getting fluttery imagining picking something. I shouldn't be nervous, though, I'd never been short on ideas. "I'm sure I'll do something with dragons."

"I'm shocked," she joked. "But seriously, you can do anything you want, but I'd love to see you do something you've not done before, to stretch your abilities."

I nodded.

"I still remember your intriguing spotted leopard," she

said, referring to a drawing I'd done of a leopard, but instead of regular spots, I'd made them celestial objects—stars, suns, stuff like that. It had turned out great. "Something like that could be really fun."

"When are you meeting with Clee?" Ms. Mangal asked.

My stomach flipped, a mixture of excitement and nerves. "Tomorrow night."

"Great. You're going to have such a good time working with her and the other mentees."

"I'm really looking forward to it."

"Clee is great. So why don't you go ahead and start brainstorming for your projects—you can do them in whatever order you want."

I had no idea what I would do yet, but I was already looking forward to it.

Ms. Mangal raised a finger. "And I almost forgot, there's the art contest through the Artist Society. I'll share the link with you so you can see what the options are. But you should definitely submit something."

That was the art club I was a part of—on the board of, actually—and I definitely would be entering. This was going to be another great semester.

At least I hoped so. What if I couldn't cut it with Clee? What if Rachel wasn't done harassing Mack and me? Things were looking up, but looks could be deceiving.

Thursday night, the four of us met downstairs in front of the dorm front doors to go to dinner. Jacob and I started telling Jenna about *Gender Queer* because it was her turn for it today.

She covered her ears. "No spoilers!"

We laughed, and Jacob said, "This book can't really be spoiled. You have to read it to get it."

I nodded in agreement, just as Mack showed up, book in hand.

Jenna took it from him and smiled. "Now I can be one of the cool kids."

We laughed again and pushed out the front doors.

"I'm genuinely excited to read this," Jenna said as we stepped into the parking lot.

"Yeah, you will like it," I said.

Mack and Jacob had gotten ahead, talking about their superhero show they both obsessively watched on YouTube.

Jenna started reading the first page, and as we approached the first row of cars heading toward the cafeteria, I had to grab her arm to keep her from running into some car's trunk.

"Oh," she said, looking up. We laughed.

She grimaced and closed the book. "I guess I should wait."

"That might be best." I realized I'd just touched another person willingly, without even really thinking about it, and I hadn't disintegrated with discomfort.

But now I had a question in my head I'd been wondering about since my first physics class this semester. I needed help in there. Jacob and I were in the same class again, but this time Jenna's roommate—a Black girl who was a total physics genius—was in there, too. Maybe she would help me, but I was too chicken to go up and ask for help. She would hold court in the girls' lounge even before study hours, and definitely during. "I think I need help with physics. Does Tiana tutor anybody? Or how do you, like, book her?"

"I know that she does help people casually, but she also

takes on more official tutoring clients who pay her. You have to meet outside of study time for that, though."

"Oh." I needed that level of help, but the money might be a challenge. And so would time.

"Do you want me to ask about it for you? How much and stuff?"

"Yeah." I could ask my parents for help. I mean, they obviously would if they could. I thought things might have been getting better for them financially after a really rough year last year. Our allowances were back up a little. Isabella now got enough to pay for her monthly craft box. Last year I supplemented it from my own allowance, in exchange for her cleaning my room. The cleaning part hardly ever really happened, but I let it go.

"You big chicken," Jenna teased, bumping my shoulder as we finished squeezing past two honking-big pickups.

"She intimidates me." I wasn't entirely sure why, except that she seemed so confident and inherently cool because she was both very smart and really good at basketball, apparently. I admired smart people, although I could not possibly care any less about basketball, but it made her cool in a lot of people's eyes, and apparently I absorbed that.

"She's really nice, actually," Jenna said. "She's also very tidy, so she's the perfect roommate."

We stepped up onto the sidewalk from the last row of cars. Mack and Jacob waited for us to catch up so we could all go into the cafeteria together.

After we scanned in, we split up and agreed to meet in our regular section. I went for pizza and got my Coke, so I beat everyone to the table. I was still thinking about physics and how I hoped Tiana could help me. But then I realized I'd forgotten napkins, and when I got back to the table with them, Mack was there.

"Isn't your meeting with the artist tonight?" he asked.

"Yeah, on Zoom," I answered.

Jacob and Jenna got there at the same time, Jenna with soup and a Caesar salad and Jacob with one of his trade-marked deli meat salad monstrosities.

To Jenna and Jacob, I said, "Mack was asking me about my meeting with Clee. It's tonight at seven, but I'm nervous."

They nodded and Jacob took a bite of his monstrous salad. This one was like his others—he started with a big pile of lettuce, tomatoes, and carrots, and plopped on a crazy amount of those small slices of turkey and ham, and it literally looked gross to me. It was through making fun of his salads that I'd finally learned the lesson that it was fun for a group of friends to tease each other on low-stakes things—even when you were the target. This kind of light-hearted teasing was not what I'd endured back in Emerson.

"It sounds awesome, Nic," Mack said. Jenna agreed.

But it was sweet that Mack had remembered the meeting. I knew he did care about me, and I felt like I was really getting over him. I just hoped I never fell for an asexual guy again. I would forever be scarred by the fact that my first kiss was with someone who hated it.

Well, maybe "hated" was too strong a word, but I know he didn't like it at all. He basically said that when he told me he was asexual, completely stomping on my heart. He did feel really bad about it, because he'd sort of led me on in his experiment to figure himself out. He said he felt closer to me than anyone else ever, and he thought that maybe that was attraction. But it turned out it wasn't. Rejection hurt no matter what.

"Do you know what you'll be doing yet?" Jacob asked me.

It was good to have that stupid thought train interrupted. I don't know why I was thinking about this. I really wasn't so hurt anymore.

"No." I needed to focus on the now and future, not dwell on the past. "I think she'll explain everything tonight."

We started eating and were quiet for while, but then Mack said, "I think we should do our first TikTok tomorrow, assuming you finish the book tonight, Jenna." He looked at her.

"I should be able to. Or at least right after class tomorrow. But yeah, we can all talk about it on the video, even if you don't all want to be on camera." She looked pointedly at Jacob and me.

We both gave her sheepish smiles. I took a bite of my pizza, instead of answering.

"You should think about it," Jenna said with raised eyebrows.

I laughed as I realized something. "You know, I think this is my first peer pressure situation."

Everyone laughed and Jenna put her finger to her lips and said, "Shh, you're not supposed to talk about it."

"Oops, my bad," I answered, zipping my lips shut.

"You don't have to be on camera, Nic. I think it would be a badass video with all four of us, though. And it will establish us as a group account."

"Where are we going to film it?" Mack asked.

"I'm not sure," Jenna said. "I mean, what are our options? Nowhere in the dorm works. Maybe outside?"

"We could get a library study room," Mack said.

Jenna cocked her head. We couldn't do anywhere in the dorm because there was nowhere all four of us could go with any privacy. Nobody could go in my or Mack's rooms, and we couldn't go on the girls' or boys' sides of the dorm, or in the gender-assigned lounges. That left the main lounge, which always had people.

Jenna nodded confidently. "Let's do the first one outside and see how it goes. Otherwise, we can film several at once at the library. I did look into the ban and it appears to be specific to the networks, not physical locations, by the way."

"That sounds good," Mack said. He put all the toppings that had fallen off his burger back on and took a bite.

"It will have to be before dark," Jenna said. "So, pretty soon after class. But I'm thinking that if you two really don't want to be on camera, we could start by showing the book propped up against the dorm wall while you say your parts, and then we can cut to Mack while he speaks, and then to me."

"Okay," Jacob said slowly. "What am I supposed to say, though?"

I was thinking the same thing, my stomach jittery. Then I remembered I was meeting with Clee tonight and I got doubly anxious. I didn't know what the time commitment would be for the mentorship. I had to figure out what I wanted to say about the book. And then I had all my regular homework to do.

"Whatever you want," Jenna answered. "We're basically doing a book review, so you can talk about any aspect of the book or the ideas or whatever. Let's think about what we want to say tonight. Maybe peruse BookTok for some ideas."

"Why don't you send us some good accounts to follow?" I asked. She had been on BookTok for a while, but mostly as a consumer, not a creator.

Jenna nodded as she collected romaine on her fork. "Will do."

"So I wanted to tell you all about something," Mack announced. "Over the break, I found this amazing blog by a trans woman who posts every day about all the anti-LGBTQ+ legislation that's coming up. She's a journalist, but she knows everything that happens in the political world affecting trans people."

"So, like, everything in one place?" Jenna asked. "Isn't that kind of depressing?"

Mack nodded and looked up. "Yeah, but it's also powerful. She's really thorough and knows her stuff."

"I should read that," I said.

"I'll send it to all of you," Mack said. "It's on Substack, and I actually paid for a monthly subscription, which gives me full access, but she still releases some info for free, I think. But I can keep you up to date if you want."

"That would be great," Jenna said. Jacob nodded in agreement.

"Have you learned anything specific?" Jacob asked.

Mack leaned forward, elbows on the table, and nodded. "Yesterday she released a post naming the five worst states to be trans in. Good old Oklahoma unsurprisingly made the list, at number five."

Jenna shook her head. "Where was Florida?"

"Only three, actually. Guess where Texas was?"

"The worst?" I asked.

Mack nodded. "Yep. Alabama and Arkansas were the other two."

"So what were the things that got Oklahoma on the list?" Jacob asked.

"Well, obviously it was many things, but one is the bill that's in play to make gender-affirming care illegal for anyone twenty-one and younger. But also, there are no protections for trans people, so it's legal for anyone to discriminate against trans people for being trans, like with adoptions, health care, and everything." Mack paused.

"There's even a defense that's commonly used in murder trials called the LGBTQ panic defense, where the murderer claims that the victim's trans identity or sexual orientation caused the murder. It's been banned in many states, but it's still allowed here."

"I think I heard about that. Didn't they use it in the Matthew Shepard trial?" Jacob said.

Mack nodded. "Fortunately it didn't work there. But yeah. It sometimes works. A couple days ago Kentucky introduced a bill that literally said that a trans student using the right bathroom for their gender identity was an 'emergency,' and there's a crazy provision that lets any cis person sue the school if they find out they were in a bathroom the same time as a trans person—up to two years after being in the same bathroom. Like, literally just being in the same room."

"Ugh," Jacob said.

I exhaled heavily. I wanted to be transported to a different world that didn't hate me.

"You know what?" Jenna asked. "I think we can talk about these issues on TikTok."

We all agreed.

I didn't know how to feel. Everything was so awful outside my little world. We had a plan to talk about it on TikTok, and I would be nervous until it was over, even though it was also exciting to be engaging with the wider world, which so clearly needed help.

On top of that, I had all my other stuff going on. I was really hoping working with Clee would be amazing. I'd get my first hint tonight.

～

Later Thursday evening, I logged into Zoom for my first virtual meeting with Clee. I got the message that the host would let me in soon.

My stomach was all fluttery from a combination of nerves and excitement. I couldn't believe this thing was really about to start. I tapped my fingers on the desk.

When I was in the meeting room, I saw a woman about my mom's age. She had high cheekbones and straight black hair, pulled back from her face.

I turned my camera and microphone on, and Clee smiled at me. "Hi, Nic! How are you?"

Her smile was infectious, and I said hi back but was feeling shy.

"It's so great to finally meet you—kind of face-to-face," she joked.

I smiled in return but didn't know what to say. Where had shy Nic come from? Where the heck was OAMS Nic? I needed them back.

"So, for today, I just wanted to meet you and tell you how the mentorship will go, and talk some about your art and your goals."

I nodded.

"But first I'm going to give some overview info, because I tend to forget this if I don't get it out of the way. The weekly Zoom calls are an hour each. You will send your in-progress work for the week by the day before, and I'll review it with you. Then we'll look at the completed version Saturday."

This sounded rather terrifying, but I also knew I would learn so much.

"I'll explain more about the Saturday sessions later. But now, I'd like to start with quick personal intros." She told me about growing up in Tahlequah, a town east of Tulsa. She went to college at the small college there, but then did her

MFA—that was a master's of fine arts—at Yale. "I came back to Oklahoma after working a few years in New York. Even though I don't always feel welcome, it's my home and I feel grounded here."

I wondered why she didn't feel welcome. I was pretty sure she was Native American—maybe she was discriminated against for her skin color.

Whatever it was, I still couldn't believe she'd come back here. I wasn't going to do that. Once I left, I was going to stay *gone*.

"Also, the first few years in New York, I was trying to make a name for myself, but it's so competitive there. My practice completely changed when I returned. I went back to my roots and reconnected with other Native artists here. I love the community."

I'd been nodding along, but then she paused and said, "So tell me a bit about what makes you tick. And what are your pronouns?"

"Oh, they/them. Okay." Now I was stalling because I didn't know where to start. "Well, I'm a junior at OAMS. I grew up in Emerson, outside Tulsa, and have always done art. My favorite is fantasy art, but I've also had fun doing other projects for my art teacher, Ms. Mangal. But I love dragons the most."

"I do remember your dragons," she said. "What got you started taking art seriously?"

"Well, you know, we all went through the macaroni art stage, but gradually it got to the point where people were telling me my drawings were good, and I loved that."

Clee laughed. "I have some of my niece's macaroni art on my fridge at this moment. So what about mediums?"

"When I had a choice, I always worked in pencil before Ms. Mangal's class. I didn't have any real skills in other mediums, although I had done some stuff in colored pencils, and charcoal. But once I got here, I started working in ink—well, mostly with pen, not brushwork—and I really love it. I still need to get better, though."

"The pieces you submitted were a lot of fun. I'm a fan of incongruity. Are you going to continue working in ink in the short term? And what about your longer-term goals?"

"Yeah, I'm sticking with ink in Ms. Mangal's class. She wants me to do one in color."

"Oh, nice. That will be fun."

"Yeah, though I am intimidated." I was getting comfortable talking to her. "But also, one thing I want to get better at is making pieces look alive. Sometimes mine are just so ... static."

She gave a quick nod. "We can definitely work on that. But honestly, it's one of those things that comes with practice. And confidence. I think that if you keep practicing, it will suddenly be there in all your work. It's like finding your style. It emerges organically."

"Okay." I hoped she was right.

"So do you want to work on ink with me?"

"Yeah, but longer term, I'm interested in watercolor combined with ink. I know most fantasy art is done with bold colors, and I like it, but I'm really interested in more gentle and subtle work, even depicting intense fantasy scenes in watercolor."

Her eyes lit up. "Unconventionality again. I love it."

"Do you think I could work in watercolor with you? Or is it too soon? The only painting I've done is a single acrylic still life last semester." That boring bowl of fruit.

Clee rested her chin between her thumb and forefinger. "Let me guess—a bowl of fruit?"

I laughed.

Still smiling, she said, "The watercolor one is a good question. Watercolor takes some time to master. If you think you could spend time outside of class working on your watercolor skills in addition the ink work you'll be doing for me—I can give you 'homework.'" She made air quotes. "If you do that, then I can work with you while you're here. Think about it and we can talk again on Saturday. Otherwise, you can stick with ink, staying with black or experimenting with color. I know you are busy at that school."

"Yeah, my classes take a lot of time." That was no joke. But I felt this desperation at the idea of squandering the opportunity to learn from Clee. "I could swing more time in the studio."

I had to make that work. I absolutely had to. All I had to do was keep my grades up enough, not perfect. Bs would suffice.

"Sounds great. Actually, one of the other mentees is a watercolorist. She's fairly new to it but has solid foundations, so you could learn from watching her if you want. But think about the extra work, and let me know on Saturday. Whatever you decide, we can grow your skills. If you need to be cautious and not overextend yourself, that's fine."

"Okay." But if I did watercolor, I'd have less time to spend with my friends, even if I scaled back my studying for my other classes. I was making Bs and As now, so I couldn't scale back too much, or I'd risk getting kicked out. And second-semester physics was going to be even harder. I could not get kicked out—that would ruin everything.

It still struck me that a year ago, losing time away from friends wouldn't have even been a factor. My only friend at Emerson had moved away over Christmas break, so there was nobody to spend time with. How weird—and great—a turn my life had taken.

"Okay," Clee continued, "let me tell you more about how the mentorship works. Let's start with the Saturday sessions in the studio. They run ten to four. There are five students taking part this semester. Each Saturday, you will all spend some time working together on a collaborative project that you will complete by the end of the mentorship. The sky's the limit on this, and you will choose a theme and your medium—or mediums. A lot of time mentees do a collage of some sort, and almost always mixed media. You can see the previous students' work at the studio."

My stomach twisted. A group project? That sounded intimidating, and I usually hated those in regular classes. What if all the other artists were better than me? I already knew Lily was.

I reminded myself that I wasn't supposed to think like that, but it wasn't like my brain ever did what I told it.

"For most of the time, you'll be free to work on what you want, so it could be the group project, or your own work." She explained that we'd all have thirty minutes with her individually every Saturday, and there'd be a group critique at the end of each day with two or three people going, so I'd have to go every other week.

Ugh. I felt queasy. That was even more often than Ms. Mangal's critiques.

She wasn't done. "As far as the work that you do goes, I am happy to give you prompts if you want, or you are free to come up with your own projects, but I do want you to clear them with me first, just so I can ensure you are challenging yourself and growing your skills. And they need to be distinct from your school projects. At least separate pieces, if not entirely different concepts."

I nodded, still anxious about the frequent critiques. But the freedom to do whatever I wanted was excellent.

Clee continued explaining a few more details. She'd provide lunch for us the first Saturday, but after that we'd have to bring our own. There was a fridge and a microwave, and we were free to eat whenever we wanted. I wasn't sure what I'd do for lunches.

Soon, we wrapped up, and I was left with a decision to make about doing watercolor or not. I thought I'd kick myself later if I didn't do it. But could I give up that time with my friends? And how in the world would I keep my grades up? I honestly didn't know where I'd land by Saturday.

"You all weren't kidding—this book is amazing." Jenna held *Gender Queer* Friday after class. We were all standing on the lawn in front of the dorm, getting ready to film the first TikTok.

Our dorm was a long white brick thing, like most of the buildings on campus, and it was right behind an identical one, which was basically where we were standing.

The sun was already starting to get low in the sky, and it was cold, but there was really nowhere else for us to film, except for rooms at the library, which we hadn't booked yet.

"So how are we doing this?" Mack asked.

Everyone was looking at me, and I had no idea why, but it heightened my already over-active nerves.

"Am I going to be the one filming, or something?" I asked, my voice cracking on the *or*.

Then we all looked at Jenna.

"Okay, let's do this." She flipped the book in her hands. "We're going to take turns talking about the book. We don't have to say a lot, but give our opinions, but we should try to not say the same things. Who's going on camera?"

No freaking way was I going on camera. The panic started kicking up dust.

Mack and Jenna raised their hands. They both looked at Jacob until he said, "Okay, fine."

Then they looked at me. "I can't. You know I can't." I hated how high-pitched I'd gone. Chill out, Nic.

Jenna nodded. "No, that's totally fine. But you're going to still talk, right?" She looked around and said, "We have to convince them to talk, you all."

Mack and Jacob looked at me, both with their eyebrows raised.

I nodded. Even that was scary, but I knew I should participate. I didn't want to miss out on everything. I might regret it later if I didn't participate at all.

Jenna smiled at me. "Then we should start with you, Nic, and you can hold the book in your hand and talk about it."

Even talking without appearing on camera was so intimidating. My pulse was racing.

"No, wait!" Jenna said. "I have an idea. This would be really different. You can be the first one to talk, but maybe Mack is on camera holding the book while you talk, and then Jacob takes the book from him on camera and Mack talks, then I take the book on camera and Jacob talks, and I guess I'll finish up by talking while still holding the book."

"That seems complicated," Jacob said.

"Sounds interesting, though," Mack said. "Let's try it."

Jenna pulled her phone out and opened up TikTok. She gave the book to Mack and he took a couple steps away.

What was I going to say? Panic, panic, panic.

Jenna looked at me. "I'll hold the phone for you." She stood next to me.

"I have no idea what to say," I said with a grimace. "Maybe we should practice?"

"Let's try to be authentic. That's how BookTok is. But we can always re-film each person's part until we get it right. But just talk about what you thought of it overall, and how it made you feel. It's actually most relevant to you, out of all of us."

"Yeah, that's true. Give me a minute to think." I needed to calm myself down, or my voice might shake or something embarrassing.

I tried to tamp down the panic and come up with some talking points.

"It's really okay, Nic," Jacob said. "We can do several takes. Take a deep breath."

"Okay, I'm ready," I finally said, not really ready, but knowing that I never would be, so I might as well go ahead. Rip off the Band-Aid or whatever.

"Get ready, Mack," Jenna said.

Mack stood with a silly smile on his face, arm out to the side, with his palm flat and holding the bottom of the book. He kept it upright with his other hand. "Wait a minute."

He plopped down in the grass and sat cross-legged, holding the book upright in his lap.

"Three-two-one," Jenna said way too fast.

"Um," I started, a long and drawn-out sound, and then froze in horror at how stupid I sounded.

Jenna folded in laughter and then patted me on the shoulder. "We can do this as many times as we need, Nic. I will definitely be editing this, so I promise you don't need to worry so much. We can edit out the beginning or any other spot where you falter. Let's try again. Okay? Three-two-one."

"So," I started, on edge again. But I gathered my thoughts. "Everyone knows this is one of the most banned books in the country. We all know book-banning is stupid, and smart people seek out banned books to read because nobody should tell you that you can't read something, and if they do, you know you really *should* read it."

Okay, that wasn't bad. I remembered how much I liked the book, and how much I related to it.

"*Gender Queer* is a memoir about someone who spends much of their life confused about their gender identity. Sorry actually they use different pronouns. E, em, and eir. Like they/them, but without the starting consonant. So e are confused but hate the female characteristics of eir body. I can definitely relate to that as an agender person, myself. If you want to see what the journey to understanding can look like, Maia is a great guide."

I stopped talking and Jenna stopped recording. "Great job, Nic!"

I flushed like I always did at praise.

Mack dropped his arm with the book and started to hand it to Jacob.

"Mack, go back," Jenna said. "It would be fun if you would look into the camera and say 'My turn,' and then hand the book to Jacob, who'll hold it while you talk."

This seemed very convoluted, but we all did as Jenna instructed and in the end, I could imagine the video looking cool. Jacob pretended to be reading it while he was on camera and Mack was talking. Jenna held the book with arms straight out, one hand on top and one on bottom, while Jacob talked, and for her own turn, she held it up and moved it to emphasize her points.

Jenna promised to edit it that evening after dinner and post it.

I had been checking out BookTok myself recently, and most BookTokkers are solo, so we were already different.

Now we'd just have to see if anybody would ever watch our videos.

This was nerve-racking, thinking about strangers all over the world watching our video and hearing me talking about being agender.

All the way to dinner, I worked on convincing myself that it wasn't that big a deal. There were so many people on TikTok, and I wasn't even on camera, so no one would even know it was me unless they already knew.

I even wondered if I'd like it if a bunch of people watched the video.

This was uncharted territory for me.

PART II

AN INITIAL ATTACK

Saturday morning I got downstairs right before nine thirty, my backpack full of art stuff, ready for our first mentorship session with Clee. Lily was sitting at one of the tables along the front windows, head down, drawing in her sketchbook.

She was wearing jeans and a simple t-shirt under a red puffer jacket. Just fairly regular clothes, reminding me that there were probably more points that we had in common than differences between us.

I knew I should go over there, but I was intimidated. What if she was mad for being interrupted?

The slightly more socially aware part of me knew I should still go say hi, and the longer I waited, the more I would look antisocial. I steeled myself and went over and pulled out the chair opposite her.

She looked up and smiled when she saw it was me. "Hey, Nic. Are you excited?"

"Yes. Also nervous, and I didn't know what to bring, so I have a bunch of random art stuff."

"Me too! I mean, she's doing this for free, so I wondered if she would give us art supplies. I guess we'll find out soon enough."

"Yeah." It was so frustrating that I spent almost all last semester thinking Lily had it out for me. All because I believed Rachel. *She* did have it out for me—Rachel was the problem, the damaged person—but Lily was nice. "Do you know who's driving us this time?"

She shook her head. "No idea."

Soon enough, Ms. Mangal came in and smiled and waved at us.

We both jumped up, backpacks in hand. It made me feel better to know that Lily was as excited and nervous as I was.

Lily let me have the front since I was taller, and we were off. Ms. Mangal's car was a small red hatchback, so it actually was nice to have the extra legroom in the front seat.

After we got out of the parking lot, Ms. Mangal asked us what we'd heard about the mentorship. She said Clee sometimes changed things up, even though she'd been mentoring for a while.

We told her what we knew, and I wondered if Clee and Ms. Mangal were friends. Then Lily and Ms. Mangal started chatting about TV shows. I didn't keep up with TV, especially since coming to OAMS.

Soon we were in downtown OKC, and Ms. Mangal parked on the street in front of a warehouse, doing some skilled parallel parking I could never have pulled off.

We were in front of what looked like a warehouse. We climbed out and she led the way in through a nondescript door. Once inside, it was warm and cozy, as there was a sitting area with some worn upholstered chairs and nice art covering the walls. Ms. Mangal continued down a hallway, past several rooms, some with the doors propped open, some not. I peeked in the open ones, and noticed that they were all art studios.

Lily was looking around with similar interest.

"What is this place?" I asked. I couldn't imagine how awesome it would be to have my own studio like this.

"The Bricktown Fellowship program hosts artists for a year, and this is their studio space. This is Clee's second year, the last one for now. She's the last room on the right." She motioned ahead and we followed her.

"The nice thing," Ms. Mangal continued, "is that there's a community room all the fellows and former fellows can reserve for outreach initiatives like this. She books it for Saturdays, and voilà, we have this program."

"Oh, neat," Lily said.

We finally reached Clee's door. Ms. Mangal peeked around the doorframe and I heard a voice from inside call, "Geetha!"

Then Clee met her at the door and they hugged.

Now I knew Ms. Mangal's first name. Felt weird, as always. After they finished hugging, Clee looked at us, still smiling. "Lily and Nic, I presume."

Lily grinned and said, "I'm Lily."

Then I said my name and waved awkwardly, like an idiot.

"I'm so glad to meet you! A couple of the other mentees are already here, so I'll take you back. We're just waiting on one more." Today Clee had her hair in a long, thick braid and wore a colorful bead necklace. She was also wearing baggy paint-covered overalls, and I realized I wanted to embrace being an artist to that degree someday, too.

"I will see you all later," Ms. Mangal said. "Ms. Patton will be picking you up after the mentorship. Look for the school van." She looked at Clee and they shared a smile before she turned and headed out.

We followed Clee back into a large room with art everywhere, kind of like I'd always imagined any good studio. There were several large tables in the middle area, shelves along the walls, a couple ceramics wheels. And a lot of other stuff. Two teenagers sat at one of the tables, looking at us. One girl, one boy. At least I assumed, which probably I shouldn't have.

"Hi, this is Lily and Nic," Clee said, pointing to each of us in turn, and then she motioned to the other two, introducing them as Devin and Addison. Then to us she said, "Feel free to take a seat. I'm trying to keep it two to a table."

The other two watched us head to the table next to them. Devin was wearing a black t-shirt and had a septum piercing, the first time I'd ever seen one in person. Addison had on a long black dress with a multi-colored striped sweater under it.

"Where are you guys from?" Devin asked.

"We both go to the Oklahoma Academy of Math and Science, in Burnside," Lily said.

"Oh, really? So you're a couple of nerds, then?" Devin joked. "Do you have to pay for that?"

Honestly, I was surprised that I could tell he was joking. Last year I would have assumed he was trying to insult us, but I would have also been confused about him insulting someone as cute and normal as Lily.

Lily laughed. "Something like that. And no, it's just a public school except that you have to apply to get in, and they cover room and board since we have to live there."

"How does it work?" Devin asked. "I heard they're opening up for arts next year and my younger sister was thinking of applying."

"Yeah, supposedly they are starting it up for art, music, and theater," I said, curious how that was going to work out. "She should apply. We're actually on the OIT campus, so it's almost like being in college." OIT was a decent-sized tech college and we had the run of the campus when we weren't in class or locked up after curfew.

"That's cool. I might want to ask you some questions about that. Anyway, I'm from OKC, but Addison here is actually making a trek." He looked at her.

"I live in Lawton, but my brother is here so I'm able to stay with him Friday nights."

"That's cool," Lily said. "I wouldn't be able to come if I wasn't at OAMS. I'm from Woodward."

"The panhandle?" Devin asked.

Lily nodded.

"Where are you from, Nic?" he asked.

"Emerson, outside of Tulsa." I was still nervous about talking with this many people I didn't know. Also, my brain was starting to sow doubt. What if these other kids were way better than me? And Devin was very charismatic and outgoing. I hoped he didn't turn out to be a jerk. I wanted to like him.

Clee brought in Briana, a small girl with perfect straight, blonde hair. Clee pointed her to the table next to ours. "Okay, let's get started! I would imagine you have been introducing yourselves already, but let's do it again for everyone's benefit. Names and where you're from should be good for right now, but you should talk more after I leave you."

We went through everyone. When it was my turn, I had a stroke of courage and mentioned that I used they/them pronouns. Briana frowned when I said that, and I instantly thought she would be one of the nasty people.

My stomach roiled. I did not want to have another bully.

This was supposed to be a good experience—was it going to be ruined by another hateful, unchristian Christian like Rachel?

No, I shouldn't be so quick to judge. People like Rachel went above and beyond in their bullying, like some of the people back at Emerson High. But I had finally realized last semester that it was only a relatively small proportion of people who had been like that. Most people just ignored me. Plus, however this girl turned out, the other two seemed pretty great.

Briana said she was from a small town south of Norman, but I didn't really get a read on her.

Clee started by explaining that today we would begin the group project. She pointed out a couple large canvases that had collages, one with a lot of paint and another with a lot of significant textured parts.

She tented her fingers. "So, what I'd like for you to do is talk to each other about the kind of art you already do—including media—and what you plan to get out of this program. And then try to come up with some ideas for the project over the next hour." She explained what she was expecting. "Please make a decision by the end of the day so you can start working on it next week. In the afternoon, I'll meet with each of you for about fifteen minutes to plan out your individual projects."

Of course, Devin started us off. "Briana, why don't you join us over here so we can talk more easily?"

Briana sat at Devin and Addison's table.

"What kind of art does everyone do?" Lily asked. "I do marker portraits in bright colors."

Everyone looked at me. "I mostly make fantasy art. I used to work exclusively in pencil, but I've branched out to ink, just black so far, but I'll be working some in color this semester."

· Devin said, "I also do fantasy art, but I'm a painter now. I work in acrylic, and I'm hoping to start trying oils soon. My mom's a painter and randomly decided I can't do oils until I turn seventeen," he said, laughing. "My birthday is in a couple months, so we'll see how it goes then."

Addison went next. "I'm also a painter. I've worked in acrylics for a couple of years, but I've branched out into watercolors, and I'm still learning, but I love it. I do landscapes mostly."

"Hi, I draw scenes from the Bible," Briana said in a quiet voice. "I use colored pencils. I really want to illustrate books for kids."

My first thought was that it wasn't a surprise that frowny and judgy Briana was religious.

But then I reminded myself that being Christian didn't automatically make someone a nasty person—something I had to remind myself often.

But also, disregarding Briana's actual religion, I didn't get illustrating things from the Bible. I was picturing cheesy illustrations, which had already been done a million times. Those few times I'd been dragged to Sunday school when I was little, they made us color in biblical scenes, which everyone did in between bouts of making fun of me when the teacher wasn't looking. That was totally what I was thinking of. But for all I knew, Briana did stuff like those gruesome works the "old masters" painted a few hundred years ago, like those with beheadings and whatnot.

Unlikely, but it made me smile. People had been surprising me lately.

Then I noticed the quiet had been going on a while and now everyone was looking at me.

Anxiety pierced me and I glanced around and said nothing.

Devin said, "So. What do you guys think about our project? We've got fantasy, religious, landscapes, and portraits. How can we combine all that? We probably should go with a collage style like the other students did, but I'm definitely open to other ideas."

Then I thought of something. I hesitated, but then got my nerve charged up. "So, I'm a big fan of incongruence in art. The first thought I have is that landscapes often feel big and majestic and watercolor is usually fairly subdued. And then, you guys haven't seen Lily's portraits, but they're so vibrant and beautiful." I glanced at her and saw she was blushing a little, but I continued, "She does this thing where she uses all bright rainbow colors that aren't realistic, but somehow does these portraits that feel real, even though they're impossible."

Man, that was a lot of spoken words from me. I flushed.

Lily tapped my chair with her foot and whispered, "Thanks, Nic."

"I kind of like that idea," Devin said. "The incongruence, I mean. Biblical scenes are always so serious, and putting a bright, multicolored person in there might be interesting."

"I don't really want to do a biblical scene," Addison said. "I'd prefer something fun."

Thank God I wasn't the only one who didn't want to depict something from the Bible. Ugh.

Lily nodded. "Yeah, I feel the same. I think I'd be okay if we did something Bible-related if it was historically true. Maybe we could find an idea that could be interpreted different ways."

It got quiet again, until Briana said, "Why don't you all

want to do a scene from the Bible? There are so many to choose from."

"I'm not Christian," Addison said. "Or Jewish."

"You're not?" Briana asked, surprised. There was that frown again.

"No, and it's not interesting to me and is never something I'd choose to depict in my art. We need to find an idea that means something to all of us."

Briana was looking uncertain. Maybe she wasn't used to people not pretending to be Christian to fit in.

"I agree with that," Devin said. "Let's keep throwing out ideas."

We carried on brainstorming. At one point, Devin noticed a whiteboard amongst the easels. He held up markers in triumph and rolled it over to us.

Clee came in after while and asked how we were doing, giving us some pointers. "I'm going to start meeting with each of you now. It will be short, so keep brainstorming. You'll have the last hour of today to finalize your idea with everyone back in here. Who wants to go first?"

Briana raised her hand, still looking unhappy.

Clee smiled. "Come on back, then."

After she was gone, Lily had another idea and we got going again.

I forgot to be nervous and suggested we mind map.

"Great idea!" Devin said.

I was loving this process. Devin and Addison seemed really nice and I liked them.

A few minutes later, Briana returned and Addison told her we were mind mapping, and then went back to meet with Clee.

When it was my turn, I was nervous, but it was fine until Clee asked me about doing the extra work in watercolor.

Despite obsessing over it, I'd never come to a decision. It was so hard to know what to do when the semester had barely gotten started and I had no idea what it would really be like.

So I sat there, panicked and silent, spinning on the stool. I looked around her studio and admired the dozens of charcoal sketches. There were also some of her watercolors and acrylics. She had a bold style that was unusual in watercolor, I thought.

Clee laughed. "Don't worry, you can think about it some more if you want. Let me know next weekend. We can start it whenever, if you decide to do it."

"Okay." Phew.

"So did you decide if you want me to give you prompts for your pieces?"

"I don't think so. I think I'm going to try a dragon in ink. I haven't actually done much real fantasy art in ink, so I want to try a few different things there."

"Perfect. I think I've got everything I need, so feel free to get back to the group project."

I headed back into the big room and joined back in the brainstorming, the watercolor option was weighing on my mind. I had no idea what I was going to decide. Time would tell, like with so many other things in my life.

Sunday afternoon I talked to Mom and Isabella on FaceTime, something we still did weekly. Nothing really important had happened for any of us, but I did tell them about starting the TikTok. I knew Mom didn't know anything about TikTok, but Isabella asked for our username, so I gave it to her.

Now, I was with my friends because Jenna wanted to do a review of Toni Morrison's *Beloved*, which she'd read in English last semester. I was filming her. She'd gotten her phone set up, showed me how to stop and start it, and jogged to get in front of it. We were standing on the lawn in front of the dorm.

"So, one of the things that I thought was most powerful about the novel is how it reminds us how trauma stays with us. If someone is going through something terrible, stopping the thing doesn't mean they can snap their fingers and be all better. The book was set after the Civil War, so there was no more slavery, but the characters had been enslaved people, and that experience didn't go away."

I glanced over at Jacob, wondering how he felt about a white person talking about what Black people have gone through. He rarely talked about being Black. I did know how hard it was to be the only one of something amongst other people, but every person's experience was different.

His face was pretty neutral, so I hoped he was okay. He kept things pretty close to the chest in general.

Jenna wrapped up by addressing how much she thought everyone should read the book, even though it was challenging, and the horrible things that happened were hard to take.

"Okay," she said, so I stopped filming.

Jenna walked over and took the phone from me. "That shouldn't be controversial."

We walked over to where Mack and Jacob were standing.

"Are you kidding?" Jacob said with a snort. "You spoke about the *Black experience*, which all these red states are cutting from the curriculum and libraries because it might make white kids feel kinda bad for a millisecond."

"Yeah," Mack echoed. "Not that they care how the brown

kids feel when they have to debate illegal immigration or when students create a mock slave-trade event to be funny or whatever, or really just *all the time* at mostly white schools."

I sometimes forgot Mack was Latino. But so many people would never forget. They were too busy judging him.

Jenna frowned. "You're right. This sucks so much. How can they enforce their hate on everyone? They're taking away all our basic rights."

"Everything *is* about human rights, you know," Jacob said. "They're trying to take us back to where we were when the Constitution was first written—where only rich white men had human rights, and when anyone else tried to get their own rights, the white dudes violently put that down."

I was really struck by the phrase "human rights." I'd never really thought about it that way.

"I wish it wasn't so true," Mack said.

Jenna's frown deepened. "I know."

"Everything's just getting worse and worse," I said.

Everyone nodded and we were quiet for a moment.

"Let's go to dinner," Mack said.

We all nodded and started walking toward the cafeteria, not saying anything.

I was feeling down. The reaction to our *Gender Queer* TikTok had been our intro into the world of online trolls. That video had some supportive comments, but a lot of it was hate filled. That book was inherently controversial. But so was *Beloved*. Basically any book that said anything important was going to make some people mad.

But that was why we were talking about these things, right? It had to be worth it.

~

In art class on Monday, I was looking through the thumbnails I did over the weekend, trying to pick one for the historical figure doing something anachronistic assignment. Thumbnails were really small and rough sketches to explore ideas and composition. My idea centered around Harriet Tubman, who had always been my favorite American hero. I wondered if it was weird for a white person to love her so much, but I guess whatever was in my head was fine. But would putting it on paper be a problem? Maybe I should ask Jacob.

I'd loved Harriet since I'd first found out about her. I'd only really come to understand what slavery was in sixth grade, and it totally destroyed me. I didn't understand how people could be so horrible to each other. But I took solace in the fact that some people fought back, and Harriet was probably the most important one. She knew what was right and what was wrong, and she just said a big fat No to the wrong things, no matter what was thrown in front of her. I'd read a couple biographies of her, and there was so much more to her than what most people knew. I think I kind of identified with her because she was so underestimated because she was a woman—and she used that to fly under the radar so effectively.

I had done several different thumbnails of her doing something that's only done in our time, and I worked on a few more. Some of them were silly, like the one with her working on a road crew laying pavement, and the one of her decorating a giant wedding cake. I had her roller-skating in another one. But I didn't love any of them because they didn't show the kind of power she carried inside. It was a quiet power. That's what I wanted to have. Incredible internal strength without the need to show off.

Everybody knew she was part of the Underground Railroad, helping enslaved people escape from the south. It was incredible—she escaped herself, and then *went back to get other people*. She could have been recaptured at any time, and the punishment would have been really bad. She was notorious, and hated by all the slaveholders, so they would have treated her especially bad if they'd caught her—but of course, they never did because she was too smart for them. And *then*, she was a spy for the North during the Civil War. She was shrewd and resourceful, and basically, nothing stopped her.

Even though she was born without even basic human rights, she changed America for the better.

America could use some changing right now, too.

I tapped my eraser against the paper and considered the thumbnails.

I felt Jacob look over.

"Sorry," I whispered. He was not a fan of the pencil tap.

"It's okay." He gave me one of his charming smiles, his freckles on full display. "What are you working on?"

Suddenly I was uneasy about telling him. "Ms. Mangal wants me to do a historical figure doing something anachronistic. I want to do Harriet Tubman, but everything I'm thinking of makes her seem unimportant, but she was so amazing, and I don't know what she'd do if she lived now, but I know it would be something important." I flushed because that had turned into some verbal diarrhea.

Jacob's eyebrows were raised. "She was a spy in the Civil War. You could make her like a James Bond-style spy."

"Yeah. That's a good idea. Spies still exist, but the way they go about it is different. And if I do that, it really celebrates her strength in a way that showing her operating a roller coaster doesn't."

I pointed at the roller coaster thumbnail and Jacob

laughed and said, "Yeah, I think you should avoid anything that shows her in a service-type role."

That was it, exactly why I didn't like the ones I'd done. "I couldn't figure out what was wrong with them. But there you are, being right again."

Jacob smiled. "Just don't make her a politician."

I stuck my tongue out in disgust. "I hate politicians."

"Exactly," he said.

But I was freaking out a tad. I could have made a huge mistake if I hadn't checked with him.

"Jacob …" I paused while he looked at me, curious. "Is it okay for me to do a drawing of her? Since I'm white? Is that, like, cultural appropriation?"

He cocked his head to the side. "It's fine. Why shouldn't white people like her? She was amazing."

I nodded.

He tapped his chin. "I think it's different when you're making money off it, or when you co-opt something that isn't your own culture for, like, your brand or whatever. But you're just celebrating an important historical figure in an assignment for a class."

"That makes sense. I guess it's important to be careful in situations like this to be respectful." I laughed. "Satire and parody probably aren't a good idea for something like that."

"Definitely. But you are safely in the respectful category if you do what you talked about."

"Yeah." This made me feel better. "So what are you working on?" I looked at the large piece of paper in front of him, covered in his own thumbnails for his graphic novel.

"This is the part in the story where Jace finds out where his nemesis is hiding."

"Is that your superhero's name?" I asked. "I never knew it."

"That's his real name. His superhero name is Black Bullet. I doubt you know the reference, but that's one thing they called Jesse Owens in college. He was the Buckeye Bullet because he was at Ohio State. And his real name was J.C., but a teacher dubbed him Jesse when he was a kid, so he went by that for the rest of his life. But J.C. is where Jace comes from."

"He was the one at the Olympics in Germany right before World War II, right? When Hitler thought he was going to prove how 'superior' white people were, and then Jesse smashed all the competition?"

Jacob nodded. "Busy proving Hitler wrong, though just like today, nobody cared about reality, only what people they admired said."

This made both of us frown in unison. We were quiet and stared at the table. How were you supposed to change someone's mind when they disregarded all the mounds of evidence refuting what they believed?

We weren't going to solve this problem in class today. But I was curious. "What's the J.C. stand for?"

"James Cleveland."

I nodded. It seemed important to know. And then the next natural question popped into my head. "What's Black Bullet's superpower?"

"He's very fast and can jump long distances, both along the ground and into the air."

"Just like Jesse Owens." Something was brewing in the depths of my mind, that way you can feel something but can't quite remember the word.

"You have to tell me about your mentorship, Nic."

"Okay, sure." But before I started, an idea appeared in my brain like an eruption. World War II!

"What?" Jacob asked. "You look very surprised."

I closed my mouth and smiled. "Harriet as a French Resistance fighter in World War II."

Jacob nodded. "That could work."

This amazing idea popped into my head, based on a book I read a long time ago about Virginia Hall, an American spy in France during World War II. The Americans wouldn't hire her because she had the wrong genitalia, so she worked with the British. And she was the most valuable spy there was because she was all business and helped get supplies to the French Resistance, while most of the male spies were screwing around with pretty women who'd go toddling off to the Germans for more attention and conversation.

"What about this: Harriet as a part of the French Resistance, walking out of a small forest like she was out for a stroll, a giant explosive cloud behind the trees, the result of the bomb she placed and calmly walked away from."

"I love it," Jacob said, smiling. "Where did you come up with that? It's very specific."

"I read a book once." I shrugged. "You know how it is."

He laughed lightly. "I think you read more educational stuff than I do."

"What are you talking about? You know lots of stuff."

"Maybe."

Ms. Mangal appeared on the other side of our table, coffee mug in hand. Or tea, since that was her brew of choice. "Hi, you two. I know what you're doing, Jacob, but Nic, did you decide if you wanted to do this one in color?"

Jacob and I looked at each other. Then I said, "I'm going to do this one in color. I have an idea."

"It's really cool," Jacob added.

"Great, I'm looking forward to seeing it. Let me know if

you need any help." Ms. Mangal smiled at us and wandered off.

"This will be great in color—if you can pull it off," he teased, winking at me.

"Oh, shut up, I'm a hotshot artist, didn't you know?"

He raised his eyebrows. "You are, actually."

I flushed. "Well, you're even more."

We smiled at each other for a moment, but then something passed across his face. He raised a finger. "One little thing, though—since you're doing color, you should talk to me before doing Harriet's skin. I can help you with that."

"Ugh." I grimaced. "I hadn't even thought about that. Skin is so hard. I've never gotten it right even when doing white people."

"Yeah, it's just hard because it's never a color-wheel color, or anywhere close. But I've worked on it many times, for lots of different shades, so I can help you."

"Thanks." Now I was scared. But at least I had the composition mostly figured out. Next came value—the idea in grayscale—and color studies, then the detailed line drawing. I'd never done color studies before, but that was okay. I was excited to see what I could do with this idea.

It sucked having physics first thing. Eight fifteen. I was still half asleep when I walked into the classroom Tuesday morning. Dr. Jones—the same teacher from last semester, who still didn't like me, just for being me. She still refused to call me anything other than Nicole. I guessed she had strict rules about gender. I didn't think most of the fundamentalists out there would approve of a woman getting a PhD in physics, but who knew where her worldview came from. People always made exceptions for themselves, anyway.

Like Rachel. She was supposed to be this great Christian girl, but she had so much hate in her for people she didn't approve of. So much for "love thy neighbor." This was actually common here—the most vocal Christians were the worst ones. I'd once heard someone say that in the South, everyone was performance-management Christians—it was all about putting on the right show, like going to the best church, and making a production of showing how perfect you were, and then judging noncompliant people in the agreed-upon way. These were the people who just used their religion as a weapon.

I got settled in my normal seat in the fourth row, thinking about the art club board meeting after school today, which meant even more of Rachel. I'd been roped into being the secretary for the board last semester, and Rachel was the president, so it was all bossiness here, judgment there.

Tiana, Jenna's roommate, walked in and sat in the front row. I'd love to be so smart. She had an energy drink in front of her, and I wondered if that was the secret. I realized Jenna must have forgotten to talk to her about possibly tutoring me, and I'd forgotten to ask Jenna.

I pulled my notebook out and stared ahead, dreading the lecture starting. I didn't need my self-esteem beaten down even more.

Jacob walked in and Tiana said something to him, and he laughed and said, "Yeah."

I was really curious about what she'd said, but I hadn't been paying enough attention, and it would be weird for me to ask him. I hadn't even realized they knew each other.

He was still smiling when he sat down next to me. "Morning."

"Morning." I covered my mouth for a big yawn.

"You sound—and look—so excited for class," Jacob said sardonically.

I sighed audibly. "It makes me feel so stupid."

"This class does seem harder than last semester. We can always study together."

"I know, but I think I need more help. Like, professional help."

"You should talk to Tiana. She's nice—and the next Albert Einstein."

I laughed. "With better hair." She had those tight braids close to her scalp.

"Definitely."

Dr. Jones cleared her throat and we all looked at her. "You'll remember Coulomb's law from yesterday," she said. Then she wrote the formula on the whiteboard. I did not remember, but I looked back and it was in my notes from the last class.

She started talking about electric fields and did some drawings with arrows pointing all over the place, and I still felt lost.

Maybe I was letting myself be intimidated. What would happen if I pretended like this wasn't hard? It could be a self-fulfilling prophecy for me, like when people are so convinced they can't do something, they actually can't.

I decided no way would I crash and burn. I resolved to pay attention, take good notes, and study hard. My time management would have to be good because of all the other things I was doing. But I could do it. When it came to getting tasks done, I always made it happen, somehow or other.

I looked up at Dr. Jones again and realized I'd missed the

last bit of what she was saying while I'd been planning my recommitment to trying hard.

Ugh.

She continued talking about the properties of an electric field, and it continued to feel fuzzy to me. The mechanics we studied last semester was easier—much more tangible. Like, I can picture a ball rolling down a hill. But an electric field is invisible. She was talking about how we represent it with short arrows pointing in the direction of the electric field in the different places around the electrified object, but they weren't visible at all in real life because they aren't really there.

I deflated again. I would have to talk to Tiana soon. Maybe she had tricks for making something so abstract easier to understand. I shouldn't be intimidated since two of my best friends insisted she was nice.

I hoped she could help me.

Wednesday night, Mack, Jacob, and I were in the cafeteria again. Jenna was with her dad.

"Oh, I forgot to tell you," Mack started. "My dad did find someone who can do a self-defense class for us, starting this Sunday."

"Oh, that's good," Jacob said.

"Is this going to be like karate or something?" I asked. Mack's parents and my parents were all worried about us getting attacked for our gender identities. Jacob and Jenna were along for the ride even though neither was really out as gay. Or maybe bi for Jacob. He was still figuring things out.

Mack cocked his head and shrugged. "I have no idea."

"We'll find out Sunday, then," Jacob said before taking a bite of his salad.

"How do we pay for it?" I asked.

Mack nodded. "Let me give you both my mom's phone number, and your moms can call her."

I twirled some spaghetti around my fork. For some reason, I was nervous about this. I wasn't sure, but it had to involve touching. I was still weird about touching other people.

I felt eyes on me and looked up.

Mack smiled. "It'll be fine, Nic. I mean, I doubt it will be like karate, but we'll all feel safer when we're done." He wadded up his napkin and dropped it on his plate.

"Okay." I took my bite of spaghetti. Still worried, but I wasn't sure why. "How much will it be?"

"I don't know. Let the parents figure it out. I don't think it's very much."

Jacob and I nodded.

I hoped it wasn't too much. My parents were still struggling, even though I wasn't sure how tight things were.

"So, I wanted to get your opinion on something," Mack announced.

Jacob and I both looked at him.

"What do you think of me doing a video on TikTok about the law that stopped gender-affirming care at the Oklahoma Children's Hospital?"

"On our new account?" Jacob asked.

Mack nodded. He had gotten screwed by a new state law that had gone into effect last October. He'd been getting his testosterone—what he called his T-shot—there, in Oklahoma City. Someone from the school drove him and it was easy. But then our piece-of-shit governor made them stop providing gender-affirming care to transgender kids. Mack was lucky that he had an aunt who was able to take him to Kansas once a month for his shot. He'd have to do it this way until he turned eighteen, but then, who knew if it would even be available for adults in Oklahoma by then. Or if Kansas would outlaw it in the meantime. Arkansas and Texas were both out, too. He'd probably have to fly somewhere. The politicians hated us.

"I'm okay with it," I said. "But we should see what Jenna thinks. She knows more about TikTok than we do."

"True," Mack said. "I could always start a new account. But since we're going to be talking about LGBTQ books, it seems to fit."

"Yeah, I think it's fine. As long as Jenna agrees." Jacob unlocked his phone and I heard a split-second of audio. "Oh, we have over fifteen hundred views on the *Gender Queer* video. The *Beloved* one is still at eleven hundred."

"That's a good start," Jacob said as I nodded.

Jenna said it was common for new accounts to get a decent amount of views, but that we'd have to work to keep our view numbers up. On Monday night, we'd done a review of *Phoenix Extravagant*, a fantasy novel with an East Asia-like setting that was about a nonbinary artist. We'd read it last semester in our book club.

"Oh, look, we have over a hundred likes on the *Gender Queer* one." Jacob started scrolling as Mack pulled his phone out, too.

I pondered numbers, nerves, and how I was kind of surprised I wasn't more stressed with the idea of so many people hearing me talk on a video. It really wasn't that big a deal. Sometimes I could be overdramatic, even in my head.

Mack grimaced. "Another troll."

My stomach twisted. This part is what made me nervous. "What'd they say?"

"Some nonsensical things about freaks, with lots of typos," he said.

"That's impressive given how few characters you're allowed in a TikTok comment," Jacob said. Mack laughed.

Tension was mounting in my core. I didn't want to have more people hating me or thinking I was a freak than I already had in real life. Maybe I shouldn't take part in any more videos.

"Nic, you are so easy to read," Mack said. "Why do you care what some random jerk thinks?"

"Oh, come on, Mack," Jacob chided. "You care, too. It sucks."

Mack frowned. "I don't want to, though."

"I was trying to do the same thing in physics yesterday," I said. "Trying to convince myself to not be intimidated and just assume everything was fine and I could do it fine. To manifest confidence."

"How'd that go?" Mack asked.

"About as well as you'd expect," I snarked.

Everyone laughed.

"Maybe if we keep posting and supporting each other, we'll stop caring about the trolls," Mack said. "I mean, so many people on social media don't really care about these things. They're just being assholes for the sake of being assholes."

"Good ol' assholism," Jacob said wryly.

My stomach was still a ball of nerves, but it was less bad to know that I wasn't the only one stressed about it. And it was interesting to be experiencing this stuff with other people, instead of alone like it always used to be.

Our phones all chimed at the same time. I looked at mine—a message from Jenna, who spent Wednesday evenings with her dad.

—Are you all still in the cafeteria? I'm back early—

"Nice. We can ask her about my video idea," Mack said. "I'll text her."

I was curious to find out what Jenna thought. I thought it would be awesome for Mack to talk about the bullshit. I was curious about what he'd say—would he talk about the law only, or would he talk about the bigger picture? All these politicians with nothing but hate in their hearts ruining people's lives.

Thursday evening, the four of us were on the lawn in front of the dorm, which ran up to the back of our dorm's twin, used by the university. We were getting ready to film our third video, which was Mack's. It was going to be about some of the anti-trans laws that had popped up in the last week, and then he'd talk about his personal story. We'd talked about it and decided that was okay. We were still defining who we were as a TikTok account and what exactly our content would be.

So only Mack was going to be on camera for this one.

He was standing there, his back to the big parking lot next to the lawn between the dorms, in his jeans and t-shirt with a light, olive green jacket over it, while the rest of us had winter jackets on. Jacob and I were on either side of Jenna, who was bringing up the TikTok app.

"Are you almost ready?" Jenna asked Mack. "Let's get this done. It's freezing. I hate January. My favorite blanket is calling my name. I can hear it here, all the way from my room." She held her hands up on either side of her mouth and shouted, "Jenna! Jenna!"

Jacob and I laughed, but Mack said, "You guys—you all

are wusses." We could all see his breath dissipating above his head.

Then he smiled. "But yes, I think I'm ready."

"Okay, on three." Jenna held her phone up. "One, two, three."

"Okay, everyone," Mack started. "I wanted to talk about some of the anti-trans laws that red states have been trying to pass. But first, I am going to say, gender-affirming care saves lives. This is a fact. So these laws are based on hate, pure and simple. But let me start with a really bad one in my own state.

"The Oklahoma legislature introduced a bill last week that would ban all gender-affirming care for anyone under twenty-six. This would force adults now receiving gender-affirming care to detransition. Kansas and Kentucky both have new bills under consideration that will force detransitioning on people up to age twenty-one and eighteen, respectively, and Missouri has one that would ban gender-affirming care and force detransitioning on minors, and also make helping a minor receive gender-affirming care criminal child abuse, like Texas did.

"I could go on, because there are already over twenty-five anti-trans bills in play, and we're not even halfway into January."

He stopped for a second to take a breath after he said that, and I could see him clench his jaw. He was pissed.

He continued, "The legislatures are just getting started this year, and there will be more to come. Last year brought us over a hundred and fifty anti-trans bills, and experts think there will be more this year."

Mack blinked a couple of times for impact, still looking mad. "These laws are so dangerous. Anyone who's looked at the real data knows that gender-affirming care saves lives.

It's being completely misrepresented in the right-wing media. Gender-affirming care for minors always starts with hormones, and almost never goes beyond that while they're still minors. Not being cisgender is already hard enough, because society is constructed entirely around the gender binary."

He took a deep breath and looked off to the side. He was quiet long enough that Jenna stopped the filming and asked, "Are you okay?"

He looked back at the camera. "Yeah. I was going to talk about the other stuff."

"Okay, I'll start filming again," Jenna said. She pressed record and said, "Okay, go."

"I can tell you about my own experiences with these laws." He narrowed his eyes slightly. "First of all, I used to live in Texas, and as I mentioned earlier, there is a Texas law that punishes parents for helping their children get gender-affirming care. I had been getting that care, so my parents got in trouble."

He stopped and looked off to the side again, his jaw clenching.

I still couldn't believe that laws like this existed. They sounded like the kind of laws the Nazis put in place, punishing people for just existing. I knew it was hard for Mack to talk about this stuff, because it was so awful for him. He must have been terrified for his parents.

He started again after a big breath.

"To get around it, they transferred custody of me to my aunt in Oklahoma, until I'm eighteen. I had to stop treatment during all this switching around while my family figured things out, but once I moved to Oklahoma, I started getting my monthly T-shot at the children's hospital in Oklahoma City. I had finally started feeling more like a normal person, or at least what I've always assumed a normal person felt like, because I was no longer constantly confused by my body and how people responded to me. It was such a relief." He closed his eyes, obviously remembering that feeling.

I wondered if I'd ever do anything medical. It was hard to know.

Mack's lip curled as he started again. "But last October, the piece of shit that's in the governor's office for Oklahoma, Schmidt"—he spat the name—"passed a law that would fully defund any hospital that provided gender-affirming care to minors, which basically meant the children's hospital in Oklahoma City, which I think was the only one in Oklahoma providing it. But it wasn't the only care they provided, so they couldn't compromise all other children's health care just to stand up for what was right. Schmidt made it so that they wouldn't be able to provide care for cancer and all the other things they do if they also provided gender-affirming care. But just like when cancer is something that has gone wrong with the body and it needs to be fixed, gender-affirming care fixes something that has gone wrong with a body, too ...

"And these people claim to be the party of family values."

He closed his eyes again, a grimace on his face. "So my T-shots were no longer available, and basically, every trans kid in Oklahoma had their treatment abruptly cut off. Detransitioning is even worse than never having started transitioning in the first place. Because once you start, you know how right it is, so you know exactly what you're losing when you have to detransition. It's an invitation to suicide. Schmidtler's shriveled heart got what it wanted."

Mack tented his fingers in front of his face and lowered

his eyes for a moment, before looking up again and continuing. "I am lucky that my aunt is able to take me to a clinic in Kansas to keep getting the T-shot. But it means time away from school and costs a lot more, and it's a whole lot more work for my aunt."

I wondered what his relationship with his aunt was like. He'd never talked about her at all, except how she took him to the clinic and everything.

"And the thing is, I am lucky. Most kids here probably aren't able to do that. And also, Kansas is now trying to ban it, as I mentioned, and that would stop my shots again. I'll be eighteen soon so I may be able to keep going, but I don't know." He shook his head. "Can you stop filming for a second, Jenna?"

"Yep." She dropped her hand with the phone. "Were you going to say more?"

"I think so, but I'm trying to organize my thoughts."

"Do you want to run things by us?" I asked, shivering as an ice-cold wind hit us.

"Actually, I'll just say it. I'm ready." Mack nodded firmly.

"One, two, three," Jenna said in a singsong voice.

"The worst thing about these laws is that all these politicians are basing the decisions on completely inaccurate facts about gender-affirming care. They aren't doctors and know nothing about medical care. They think it's dozens or hundreds of top surgeries a week on minors, or something completely insane." He rolled his eyes in disgust.

"This is not accurate at all. Very few teenagers actually qualify for top surgery, as there are so many requirements to meet. But also, when we point out that gender-affirming care saves lives, all these evil politicians cover their ears and sing la-la-la, because what they are actually trying to do is erase us. Maybe they think more suicides among trans kids is good, because then there are fewer of us."

He pointed at the screen. "Just remember this. There are people who are starting to call this a genocide. I think it's not truly to that level, but it's not completely off base, either. They want us gone, not here, which basically means dead."

He closed his eyes and put his hands up to cover his face.

"Okay, I'm stopping filming," Jenna announced. "But are you okay?"

I was wondering the same thing. Was he crying?

We all rushed to surround him and Jenna put her arm over his shoulders. "That was really good, Mack. You explained things well."

"Yeah, good job." I patted his shoulder, too. I wanted to do more, but I still felt weird about touching him, about touching people in general, really. Last semester's crush was a complicating factor.

"Let's go back inside," Jacob said quietly.

Mack dropped his hands and his gaze landed on me. "I'm going to stay out for another minute."

"I'll stay with you," I said, because I thought he wanted me to. In some ways, he and I had more in common with each other than the others. To Jacob and Jenna, I said, "You two go on in."

Jenna said, "I'll try to get the video edited and posted tonight." Then she and Jacob headed toward the dorm front door.

"You know what worries me the most?" Mack asked me, his slightly red eyes directed right at me.

"The fact that Kansas is one of these states?"

"Exactly. I wouldn't have to only make it to eighteen, but to twenty-one. I mean, I'll be long gone from this state." He wiped his eyes. "I will never live in a red state after I can get out of here. But I worry about other people here. Not everybody can go to college, or just up and move like the red state refugees who are popping up in blue states."

I nodded. "I know. I still haven't decided if there's anything medical I want to do, but obviously I'll wait until I'm somewhere safer if I do."

He ran his hand through his hair.

I exhaled heavily, which blew my visible breath into his face. "Sorry."

He smiled weakly.

"Let's go inside," I said.

"Okay."

We walked side by side into the foyer. We were still good friends, and I loved that he trusted me enough to share even more of his fears with me. I think having him be normal about things probably made it easier to forget the crush.

Things were still good in my life, and this TikTok thing was cool because we were doing something important. And I was doing it with a group of amazing kids who were all my friends now. I still couldn't wait to see what happened next with these videos.

I was working alone in the art studio Friday night. We were allowed to work in here outside of school hours if we let the front desk know where we were going and had the security guard let us into the building. It had become a bit of a Friday night tradition for me, which was great, though leaving afterward to scramble back in the almost pitch dark was my least favorite part.

But for the moment, I was working on two more color

studies for the Harriet Tubman piece, which was going to show what a total badass she was. I'd finished the rough earlier in the week and done three value studies. The last one I did turned out perfect. Harriet was slightly over from the bottom left corner, facing the viewer, her whole body showing. She wore a nondescript jumper-style wool dress that ended below the knee over a loose white shirt, all from 1940's France (thank you, Internet). She carried a basket that had a cloth over it, like she was innocently coming home from the market, like a reimagining of Little Red Riding Hood.

Then there was some space behind her where I'd drawn some grass, and then a forest in the distance, stretching from the left to the right, filling most of the top, with one opening indicating the end of the forest, and a large cloud from an explosion behind it. The city was on the other side of the forest, and she had done her revolutionary duty and was walking away, feeling no remorse for doing her part to help the good guys.

I'd done the value studies to figure out what to emphasize. I wondered how dark to make the forest, but I decided if it was too dark, having Harriet and the explosion be super light wouldn't make total sense. I picked one that was a good mix.

For the next color study, I used a medium forest green and thought about Harriet's clothes. They should be drab to go with the war. Women in France in World War II were definitely not wearing colorful prom dresses. It was a time when you didn't want to draw any attention to yourself, which was how I felt about being trans nowadays. Some people wanted to flout it because they knew who they were and weren't afraid of backlash. That was fine for them, but felt too risky to me. Besides, I felt like being agender wasn't the most important thing about me—I'd rather people think of me as an artist first. Why did gender have to matter in everything? Does the barista at the coffee shop really need to know my gender to take my order or make my latte?

Obviously not.

But back to Harriet's clothing. I needed a light, dull color —probably a gray or cream, and maybe some other washed-out colors. I got to work.

My phone dinged. Jenna had been sending funny videos all evening, so I didn't look right away. But then there were more dings, so I thought I should look.

When I did, I saw a text from Mack. He must be back from Kansas. His aunt had taken him this morning for his T-shot.

—*There are now five states that are trying to criminalize being an affirming parent to a trans kid. They are trying to set it up so the state can take kids away from their parents and give them to non-affirming foster parents while the real parents go to jail*—

Oh, man. Why did everyone hate us? I felt queasy.

—*Everything is so horrible*— Jenna responded.

—*Where are the bills?*— Jacob asked.

—*One is still Texas, of course*— Mack said. —*Then also Missouri, Mississippi, Indiana, and Wyoming*—

I shook my head. These politicians had no idea how hard it was to be LGBTQ, to be marginalized and persecuted just for being different. They were monsters.

The school had made me start back with the counselor every week on Thursdays now. They'd decided I needed counseling back when I came out as agender last semester. It was basically conversion therapy lite. And this semester they were making me miss art class for it. I hated them. It was totally pointless. I mostly sat there quietly, waiting for the forty-five minutes to be up. The counselor thought I was being stubborn. I was like, no, I'm being me.

But I needed to focus and get back to my drawing and not think about how crappy the world was.

I gave Harriet an incredibly faded red jumper dress over her dull gray shirt. She wore scuffed-up brown lace-up ankle boots and looked scrappy in the best way possible. She would fit in with the villagers, innocently bringing home the bread and salt she was allocated.

Little would anyone know, but she'd departed this morning with a completely different basket, picking this one up from other French Resistance operatives after she'd planted the bomb.

—*Why do these idiots care so much about all of this?*— Jacob texted.

This increased the turmoil in my stomach. Because, really—why? It made no sense. I wondered if I should respond. But I was feeling sick from it already, and thinking more about it would make me feel worse. I really did need to get more work done.

I needed to put the phone down. I rolled the green pencils back and forth on the table and then selected a medium shade. Once I'd done a quick coloring of the forest, I went back over it with darker greens and browns for the trunks you could see at the front of the woods.

Jenna responded to the text. —*I know, they don't care about protecting kids from angry white dudes flush with power after buying their big manly AR-15s, but they're in so much danger from being in the presence of a trans or gay person. Like being gay and being in the same room as a kid is "grooming" them. No LGBTQ+ person has ever converted an otherwise straight, cis kid to be gay or trans, but we have an interminable list of dead and maimed school kids killed by white cis, straight men, but God forbid we take the guns away—*

—Parents of kids who commit suicide after being denied gender-affirming care should sue the state governments— Mack said.

Tears pricked my eyes. I knew all this stuff, so why was it getting to me right now?

I took a deep breath and started working on the explosion, which was really just smoke in dark grays against a light sky.

Before coming to OAMS, I'd been unhappy and bullied, and I wasn't myself, but everything was small. Now I felt like I was part of a bigger world, but it was hunting me and everyone like me. It was so much worse than I'd thought it was back then.

—You there, Nic?— Mack texted.

Now I had to answer. *—Yes. I agree with you all, I'm just trying to get some stuff done. I'm in the studio.—*

—Well, keep at it— Jenna said.

I would. After finishing up the explosion, I compared the two color studies, and definitely the second was better. But something was off with the smoke. It might be better if it was the explosion that was showing, rather than only the smoke aftermath.

I did some research and found some good explosions to model, so I did the third color study with the adjustments.

After that, I packed up and walked back to the dorm, hurrying past the darkest areas. Once in the building foyer, I ran into Sophia, my roommate from last semester. We'd had a rocky start because she was kind of a snob at the beginning, but she'd opened up near the end of the semester and was supportive when I came out as agender, which surprised me at the time.

"How's your luxury apartment?" she teased.

"The constant supply of bonbons is nice," I said.

She laughed. "I must admit that it's kind of nice to have my own room."

"Yeah, I know what you mean. Living in a small room with another person when you've had a whole room to yourself your whole life is difficult." It was so odd how I was having this relatively mundane conversation without great awkwardness.

"Definitely," she said. "Did I see you guys filming some stuff outside?"

"Yeah, we've started a TikTok account and are doing book reviews and stuff like that." I shouldn't have been surprised that she'd comment. She was big on TikTok, with thousands of followers on her videos about biology. She loved to talk about Darwin and evolution.

"Awesome," she said. "Let me know if you ever want to borrow my tripod. You can film a bunch at once or something. And I'm happy to share what I've learned. You know I've been on there a while. Not on BookTok specifically, but on other areas."

"That would be great. Jenna's the only one of us who's ever posted, but she doesn't have a lot of experience making videos. She's been more of a lurker."

"There's a lot of stuff you learn by trial and error, but if you want to skip that awkward step, let me know. I'm staying here this weekend." She pulled out her phone. "Give me your username."

I gave her our username and watched her type it in lightning-fast. My belly flipped at the thought of someone I knew watching our videos. What would she think? We were amateurs.

"See you later." She waved and headed upstairs while I

went down the hall, still worrying she'd think we sucked. But she knew we were new, so maybe she'd help us out and wouldn't judge. Her videos were really impressive.

We were a bunch of noobs with a ton to learn. I just hoped we'd learn fast.

~

The following morning, an RA dropped Lily and me off at the mentorship warehouse. We were the first to arrive. Clee greeted us as we passed her studio, and then we went into the large back room and sat at the same table as before.

Devin arrived, wearing a blue and white shirt that a rockabilly singer would have worn, carrying a roll of canvas. "You all ready for today? What pieces did you bring?"

"I did another portrait," Lily said. She unrolled the paper she'd been carrying. It was bright colors like her others, but this one was something I'd never seen before from her—or anyone, really.

"The Simpsons!" Devin exclaimed.

Lily's portrait was amazing because it looked like the Simpsons would look in real life instead of in cartoons, but she still used all those bold colors she was famous for—so the Simpsons solid yellow coloring wasn't there, but they were still totally recognizable. Her technique involved mostly vertical stripes of different colors—reds, blues, greens—all colors you really wouldn't see in real people. For this one, she did use more of the Simpsons yellow than in her normal work, but only enough to get the impression across.

Just then, Addison came in, and Devin said, "Addison, look at this!"

Her eyes widened and she said, "Wow."

Briana walked in then, a portfolio under her arm, and headed toward her table.

"Briana, you should look at Lily's drawing," Devin said.

I looked at Lily and she was blushing pink as anything.

Briana walked over, with hesitation, and said, "That's really pretty." She smiled at Lily and sat down at her spot at the table with Devin and Addison.

Pretty was such an odd word for Lily's piece. Briana could have been uncomfortable because it wasn't realism? I had no idea.

"Let's finish sharing the work we did over the week," Devin said. "I'd love to see everyone's stuff. Briana, come back and let's look at Nic's."

Now it was my turn to blush. I turned my piece over. It had turned out good, but my stomach was still tangled with anxiety. It was a dragon sleeping, with a smaller one curled up on her back, also snoozing.

"Nice," Devin said. "I'm always up for an adorable dragon drawing. Even if dragons are lizards and the mother-baby bond isn't really a thing." He grinned at me, obviously teasing.

I pretended to be offended. "Shut up, it's fiction and I can do what I want."

Everyone laughed, and Addison and Briana said nice things, and then we all migrated over to the other table.

Devin unrolled his canvas and showed us a beautiful, delicate painting of a cleric crouching down, investigating herbs. A very peaceful image, which surprised me coming from a guy. I'd imagined battle scenes or the really sexist stuff of artists like Frank Frazetta. This served as yet another reminder that you can't know everything just by looking at someone, which I should freaking know.

"Is that a magician?" Briana asked.

No judging, Nic.

Devin shook his head. "No, it's a cleric looking for healing herbs."

Briana nodded. "Don't we have to do the critique today? I'm really nervous about that."

Lily and I laughed, and I said, "Yeah, it's scary, but it's not as painful as you might expect. I think everybody here is nice."

"I've never done critique, either," Devin said.

"Same," Addison said.

"We do it in our class, but like Nic said, it's actually okay," Lily added.

"Okay, please everybody be nice to me," Briana said. She smiled shyly.

"Don't worry," Devin said. "I think we're all pretty safe, because all of us are good. But I am really here to get better, so if someone sees a way I can make my art better, I'm all ears."

"That's basically the right way to look at it," Lily said. "We're just trying to help each other."

Briana nodded. "Here's my piece for this week." She held up a large piece in colored pencil that was hyper-realistic—I had never met a real person who could get that level of realism with colored pencils. I assumed it was a Bible scene, but I had no idea what. It was a bunch of people working in a field in old-timey clothes. And it wasn't silly or childish like I'd thought last week. It was simply a realistic portrayal of a historical scene, whether real or made up.

I felt really bad. I'd judged her so harshly. I thought that while, yes, she was religious and I hated religion, she just hadn't been exposed to much outside her limited worldview. She hadn't even been openly rude to anyone, just surprised or uncertain. Maybe she wasn't so bad. If her religion didn't take her directly to hate, don't pass Go, then I had no right.

"That's amazing," Devin said. "So realistic! You should see my sloppy attempts at colored pencil." He shook his head, and I had the same thought.

Addison shared a watercolor landscape of a field of flowers, with a barn and rolling flower-filled hills in the background. We all admired it.

Everyone's work so far seemed so professional. I was starting to doubt myself again. Still, everyone seemed to like my piece, even though I thought everyone else's was better. Fortunately, Clee came in before I could go down that mental rabbit hole.

"Okay, everyone, let's get started. Keep working on your group project while I do the individual sessions. Are you ready for a large board for the project?"

We had explained the project vision to her last week, so she knew what we were doing. We had a sequential-art-inspired idea.

"Yeah, that would be great so we can start sketching things out at the right scale," Devin said.

"You can pull whatever you need from here," Clee said, walking over and pointing to a stack of huge canvases leaning against the wall.

Devin hopped off his stool and the rest of us followed him to the canvases.

"Who wants to meet with me first?" Clee asked.

We all looked at each other. Then Devin said he'd go, so they left for Clee's studio.

"Who's going to make a decision about the canvas since Devin is gone?" I joked.

Everyone laughed. We flipped through the canvases and then Lily said, "Maybe we shouldn't pick yet. Should we thumbnail first to decide exactly what each panel will be, so we better know the shape?"

Briana and Addison looked confused.

Lily and I explained thumbnailing and they both agreed more planning would be a good idea.

We'd decided to show a dragon fighting a medieval knight, which we convinced Briana was kind of David and Goliath inspired. But there'd be another creature coming from a third direction that Lily would be doing. Like something from another dimension that was unusually colorful.

We weren't doing collage, but instead a multimedia sequential art piece, where we'd all stick with our mediums. Addison and Briana would do backgrounds, and Devin and I would add ours over those. There were some logistics to sort out, but we'd make it work. Then Lily was going to do her magical creature.

We'd be showing the knight's journey starting on the left and moving right, the dragon's journey starting on the right and moving left, and Lily's creature coming from the top. Then when they met, we'd show the fight sequence in the middle panel and then more panels going down, like a big plus sign. We'd figure out the fight panels later.

So we got together and thumbnailed as a group for the next couple hours. I again met with Clee last because I was still chicken.

We talked about the sleeping dragon I'd brought in. She said it was charming and strong. She pointed to a couple areas that were too dark—I still made that mistake, probably because dark fit my worldview so well. Even if it was changing. Clee gave me some pointers on avoiding it in the future.

Then I told her I did want to do the watercolor work, and she told me that if I needed to take a week off at some point, I could, which was a relief. She said she'd send me some photos I could choose from for the first piece, and that she'd give me a pan set of watercolors to start with.

"I'm looking forward to seeing your paintings. What's your next ink piece going to be?" she asked.

"Maybe a huntsman of some sort, sitting by the fire and roasting whatever he's killed. But making sure it has a fantasy feel, not like some backwoods modern guy. No camouflage Carhartt."

"That could be fun," Clee said, smiling. "It also gives you the ability to make the background as detailed as you want. Work on your planning and thumbnails and starting the watercolor, and you can send them to me Tuesday if you want some feedback before we meet on Thursday."

"Okay, I can do that." I was still nervous about everything, but also excited. But probably more nervous, actually. I wanted to get better no matter what, but it felt like a huge risk to try a new medium.

But how else would I know the medium I most liked? Starting with ink had been scary, too, but it had gone fine. I'd focus on doing the work and try to not think about it. Sometimes you just had to power through things.

The four of us were at dinner Saturday night, and I was telling everyone about the group project on the mentorship. I looked up and saw Sophia standing behind Mack and Jacob, who were across the table from me. She had on a worn Old Navy t-shirt with a flag on it and her hair was pulled back in a pony tail. She waved. I'd forgotten about her offer to help us.

"Oh, hey," I said to her, then to the rest of the table, I

said, "I forgot to mention that Sophia said she could give us some tips to help us get our BookTok account going."

"Oh, I love your videos, even though biology really isn't my thing," Jenna said. "All your stuff about evolution is really interesting. They're way more interesting than Mr. Jensen back at Burnside High."

Sophia laughed. "I hope so."

Everyone else knew that she was big on TikTok, even if they hadn't seen her videos.

"So we'd love your help," Jenna said. "I've been on TikTok the most out of all of us, but I don't really know what I'm doing."

"Whatever, Jenna," Jacob said. "You know what you're doing."

"Yeah, I've seen what you've posted so far," Sophia said. "Your videos are way better than most people's when they first get started. They're interesting and not overly long. But I can still give you some tips. If you have time right now, we can talk about it."

"Sure," Jenna and I said at the same time.

Sophia sat down next to Jacob and she started going over some of the basics. "What are your long-term plans for content?"

We explained, then Mack gave more info. "So, LGBTQ issues and banned books are definitely the focus, I'm also wanting to address the various specifically anti-trans and more general anti-LGBTQ laws that are popping up all over the place. So it is diverse."

"I'm not as familiar with BookTok," Sophia started, "and I wonder if you really want to be there if you're going to talk about LGBTQ issues more generally. I think it could work if you focus on those kinds of books, because the laws tie into both book banning and LGBTQ themes. It just depends what your focus is."

"Yeah, I think we're not sure where to focus," Jenna said. "The original vision was book reviews of banned books, but I liked Mack's video."

"I think you can keep it open for now and see where you go. I can do some research to help you identify the best hashtags to use, because those can be crucial."

"That would be great," Mack said. "We've struggled with picking the right ones."

"Yeah, definitely look at other videos like yours to see what they use. You should also come up with some kind of hashtag—or several—that represent you as a group, so it's easy to search for your videos. You'd add it to all your videos. Maybe different ones for the books versus the law videos."

"That makes sense," Jenna said. "Thanks for explaining all this."

Sophia nodded, tapping her fingers on the table in front of her. "Sure. The beginning can be really important. If your views are too low or people stop watching too fast, TikTok can start blocking you, basically no longer showing your videos."

That sounded crazy. Why should they be deciding that?

"We have a lot to learn," Jenna admitted, fiddling with the sleeve of her yellow puffer jacket.

"I actually think what you've done so far is good, but you need to step things up." Sophia raised on finger like she was counting. "The first thing you should do is to make sure to start with a powerful hook. You need to grab your viewer in less than two seconds. A good way to do it is to start with an interesting question. Or say something edgy or controversial. You want to make sure you don't lose people who would be interested just because you have a slow start."

We all nodded, all ears.

Sophia held up two fingers. "Second, you need to post a lot. Record several at once and then you can post them later. Ideally you want one a day, but I know that can be hard. At least three to five per week, every single week, no matter what. And you don't always have to post as a group—you could easily post individually to your group account to keep your numbers up."

Jacob exhaled. "Every day is a lot."

"Yeah, especially at first. Take advantage of the fact that there are four of you. But make sure to post together a lot, too, because that will be part of the appeal of your account." She held up three fingers. "And the last thing I recommend is keeping a spreadsheet to keep track of everything—all your ideas and then the recorded and posted videos. I even track the captions and hashtags in my sheet." She leaned back in the chair.

"This is great, Sophia," Mack said. "We really appreciate your help."

"Definitely," Jenna echoed.

Jacob and I looked at each other. He looked as overwhelmed as I felt.

Sophia smiled big. "No problem. I like to help. Are you all headed back to the dorm?"

We took our trays to the return area, and headed out.

"I'm going to go for a walk," Mack said. He waved at us and veered off to the right. I watched him go, again wearing only a light jacket. The reflective part of his running shoes shone from the streetlight he'd just passed. I didn't know how he wasn't freezing all the time.

He constantly took these long walks. He'd invited me a

few times last semester, but mostly they were his mental health thing.

Sophia fell into step with me. "Did you hear about the water leak?" she asked.

"No, what happened?" I asked.

We stepped into the parking lot. "There was a huge leak from the ceiling in my room that somehow was related to a roof leak from that crazy rain we had last week, even though it didn't flood the rooms above me, which makes approximately zero sense, but okay. They forced me to move in with Kylie, the only room left with just one girl. So much for enjoying my own room."

"That sucks!" I started working my way between two cars. "Are they going to fix it so you can go back?"

"I don't know. But Kylie isn't happy about it, either."

"What happened?" asked Jenna and Jacob after they fell back to walk with us.

I explained.

"I never realized we were that full," Jenna said.

"Yeah, apparently there's only my old room that's unoccupied now, and it's uninhabitable," I said as Sophia shrugged.

We all went single file between two silver cars, eventually making our way to the dorm.

"I'll let you all know about the tags," Sophia said to all of us. "In the meantime, keep on filming."

If she could figure out how we could get more views, that would be really nice. I might have to get braver and go on camera eventually.

Maybe that wouldn't be horrible? I felt ... less scared than before. Would I really do it?

∼

Sunday afternoon, Jenna, Mack, Jacob, and I were gathered on one side of the school's auditorium stage facing a beefy woman who was going to be our private self-defense class teacher. A lanky teenage boy stood next to her.

"Okay, kiddos, let's get started," she barked.

I watched the security guard—a familiar face from Friday nights in the studio—leave the auditorium.

Mack's dad had found the instructor, and all of our parents pitched in to cover the class.

"I'm Peggy," she announced. "This is my nephew Tristan, who will be helping us with the class." She motioned to the boy, who looked about seventeen and bashful. "I don't know you, except that you're a group of friends who felt like they needed more confidence and know-how in staying safe. So give me some info about yourselves."

I was already feeling uncomfortable. This was going to involve touching and who knew what else. Jacob was tense and unmoving next to me, while Jenna was on my other side —true to form, she was bouncing on her feet, totally unbothered.

"Yeah, we are a tad ... unconventional, let's say," Jenna started. "It would be a good idea if we could defend ourselves if we ever needed to."

Peggy tented her fingers in front of her. "Okay. Tell me your names." She pointed at Jenna, who started us off. I sounded like Emerson Nic when I said my name, then Jacob went, and Mack finished.

"Got it," the woman said. "So we've got five sessions together. Usually I teach this class to women and girls, as there is absolutely no emphasis on fighting for anything other than survival, and I work under the assumption that you have less strength than the person or persons you are trying to stay safe from. But there is otherwise nothing 'girly' about self-defense." She made air quotes around girly.

We all nodded along. Mack's neck looked a little pink, and I wondered if Jacob was embarrassed. I wasn't sure if what she said was better than just saying it was gendered.

Peggy continued. "So Tristan's main job here is to play the attacker in some of the demonstrations, but there will also be some pairing off for exercises, especially starting next week."

Today's class was all about getting away from an attacker. She said that, usually, men who attack women are looking for a quiet woman alone, and they want to avoid attention. So we had to practice yelling—like, making a scene, instead of avoiding a scene at all costs like girls are socialized to do. This was actually really hard for me, I've always been weird about yelling in front of people. Would I ever get past all my weird things?

At first it was just, "Stop! Go away! Leave me alone!" but then Peggy told us cussing was fine and Jenna's eyes got big and she smiled.

Then Peggy introduced the next step, which still required making a scene, but for this she had Tristan don a heavy black padded suit, and we had to back up to him as if he had grabbed us from behind. Then we had to yell something and then karate chop him—well, the suit—in the crotch region.

All this role-playing was awkward, but eventually we had each other in stitches, especially when Jenna started doing a bad British accent and telling her attacker to "Bloody sod off!" I don't think anyone knew what that actually meant, but even Tristan was smiling.

"That's the most basic thing there is," Peggy said. "If you can disable the attacker for even just a second, it can be enough time to get away, and get yourself in a safer space, like with other people around. But there are some other good tricks for getting away if they have you in a stronger hold."

She demonstrated several with Tristan, including where to hit to get the attacker to drop their hold. For this one, she had us pair off. I immediately sidled up to Jenna, because as weird as I was about touching people, it would be easier with her than anyone else. The first trick was to suddenly bend your knees, to throw them off balance. She also had us slam our foot down on the top of theirs. And then there was a well-placed elbow jab.

We were supposed to practice the motions in our pairs, but without any force, obviously.

Jenna started off as the attacker, so she had me in a chokehold, her whole body against my back. I was so uncomfortable with all this contact, almost as uncomfortable as I was with hugs from people I didn't know very well. Or even people I did know, honestly—the only person I could hug without getting uncomfortable was my sister, Isabella. Although Jenna's hug when we got back this semester wasn't terrible. Maybe I was going to eventually get over the touch thing. Just not today.

"Are you okay, Nic?" Jenna asked me quietly.

"Yeah." So I went through the motions we were supposed to be practicing and did my best, but I was so unsettled by all the required touching that I couldn't pay full attention. I hoped I'd remember what we were learning.

Then it was my turn to have her in a chokehold, and I was reminded of how much I disliked my breasts, all smashed up against Jenna's back. I wished I didn't have them. I wondered if Mack was still going to be able to get his top surgery, and if I should try to get it. Not now, but later.

"Try to focus on where Jenna is hitting you, Nic," Peggy said.

I flushed and tried to focus, and we continued, but my mind was still all over the place.

After we finished with that part, Jenna squeezed my shoulder. She must have known how uncomfortable this all made me, but she also wanted me to learn everything, so she wasn't going to let me off the hook.

"Okay, great job, everybody," Peggy said. "That's enough for today. Practice any of those moves between now and next week. Next week we'll review everything from today and get into some new techniques. I'd also recommend wearing loose shorts if you have them."

Jacob's eyes went wide when she said that, and as soon as he saw me notice, he looked down.

"Thanks, Peggy," Jenna said. "Do you need help getting stuff to your car?"

We helped her take the padded suit and some other things in a giant duffel to the car. Then we headed back to the dorm to grab our wallets so we could go to the Indian restaurant we'd been planning to go to.

I wondered how much the self-defense stuff would help me. Which Nic would emerge in a bad situation—Emerson Nic, or OAMS Nic? I really didn't know.

A little while later, Mack and I waited for Jenna and Jacob in the foyer, and we chatted about ideas for more videos.

He started, "I think we should tie specific LGBTQ+ elements of books we review to the various anti-LGBTQ+ laws being passed—even if it's something as generic as, 'He wouldn't be able to go by those pronouns with this law.'"

I nodded, impressed by this idea. "That would be awesome—it would connect books and anti-LGBTQ+ laws together, and make it more logical to talk about either separately, too."

"Oh, hey guys," Sophia said, coming out of the stairwell.

"We're going out for Indian food if you want to join us," I said, surprising myself with my social skills.

"Oh, that would be cool," she said. "I need to get my wallet. Let me run upstairs."

Jenna appeared just after Sophia started up.

"Sophia's coming," Mack said.

She nodded. "Where's Jacob?"

I realized there was a lot going on—people coming and going, plans changing spontaneously—and I wasn't freaking out or even uncomfortable. I was so different from when I was in Emerson. It still shocked me.

I suddenly doubted myself. Should I have invited Sophia? I was comfortable with my group now, but adding another person might mess the dynamic up.

Jacob and Sophia both showed up at the same time, and we left.

"Mack, explain your idea about TikTok," I said.

He started telling us about it, and everyone loved it. This way we could still do books, and not every review had to tie into legislation, but it would be a great way to keep people up-to-date on the laws, because a lot of people had no real idea.

"I love this," Jenna said.

We stepped into the parking lot and started crossing.

"I'd love to talk about Maia Kobabe's discomfort telling people eir pronouns," I said. Sophia looked confused. "That's the author of that book *Gender Queer* that conservatives went bonkers over. Kobabe uses ey/em pronouns."

Sophia still looked a little confused, so I explained more. "Like they/them, without the 'th.'"

She nodded in understanding.

I continued. "In the world of the book, it's still eir option, but in some places ey'd be breaking the law if ey gave them."

"This is genius," Sophia said, holding her hands up in excitement. "I had no idea all the stuff politicians are doing until I started looking into it after watching your video, Mack. It's crazy."

"I know!" Jenna said. "This is the whole reason we need to make these videos. Most people don't even know what's happening."

We worked our way past a row of cars.

Mack said, "Yeah. The politicians are rabid for LGBTQ people, but most people—even people in the reddest states —don't care that much about LGBTQ people existing. But that's the problem—they *just don't care*, so they either don't vote or vote for these horrible people, and there's nothing to stop the fanatical, lunatic politicians from decimating people's rights. Most people aren't bothered because it doesn't impact them."

It was so depressing. Suddenly I had a burst of rage. "Why do they hate us so much?" I nearly yelled, making everyone look at me. I took a breath. "Sorry. But why is it that you give some power to a small, hateful, privileged white man and suddenly he's going after people who aren't like him using his warped interpretation of Christianity that's actually about as love-thy-neighbor Christian as a mass shooting?"

Jenna snorted. "Okay, it's not funny at all, but that was very astute, Nic."

I felt my face flush, despite the cold. I took another deep breath to calm myself.

Mack patted my shoulder, which messed with me because he almost never touched me, and I was again feeling the pain of his rejection after we'd kissed last semester.

I wanted to cry. We filed between another row of cars.

Jenna came over and put her arm across my shoulder. "I don't know. But I think it's true. Power corrupts. I don't know how to fix that."

She squeezed my shoulder and I felt a tad better, even though this had been a weird day full of touching. Maybe that's what triggered the rush of emotion.

Jacob broke the silence that followed. "And you know what's extra crazy about it? They don't even know what they're doing. They make these laws and then the state supreme courts tell them they're unconstitutional. Making laws should be one of the most important jobs in the country, but we elect people that have no experience doing it, or even working in government, and they have literally no idea how to do the job. It's weird."

"Oh my God!" Sophia said. "I just realized—you have to have a law degree to be a lawyer, right, but not to be a lawmaker. I never really thought about how crazy that is. How can you make laws if you have no idea how they work?"

Everyone agreed.

"*That* should be your hook," Sophia said. "It's perfect."

Jenna and Mack nodded thoughtfully. "I think we can make that work," he said.

We finally made it to the other side of the parking lot. The rest of the walk was on sidewalks. We talked about more mundane stuff, and my burst of emotions quieted down.

My mind went back to Jacob's face when Peggy asked us

to wear shorts. What was that about? I'm sure his legs looked fine—he was a little skinny, but who cared about that? Maybe I could reassure him.

Jacob and I happened to fall into step a bit after that.

"What's up?" he asked.

Apparently I'd been looking at him weird. "I was wondering something. How come you never wear shorts?"

He laughed, but it didn't sound quite right. "It's the middle of January, Nic."

"I know, but last semester ..." I trailed off because I realized he must not want to talk about it and I'd missed the cue. I felt like such a loser suddenly. "Sorry."

"It's okay," he said quietly. "There is actually a reason. When I was a little kid—when I was three—my legs were burned in a campfire accident. I was in the hospital for months. So my legs are covered in scar tissue, and it was such a point of interest to other kids when I was young that I just never let people see them anymore."

"Oh, my God, Jacob." I felt so horrible now. "I'm sorry I made you tell me."

"You didn't. It's okay. It's not really a secret, anyway. I told Mack once. You can mention it to Jenna if you want."

He obviously didn't like to talk about it.

"Okay," I said, still feeling guilty. I had questions, but obviously I'd never ask them. "You shouldn't feel like you can't wear shorts. We shouldn't have to hide our imperfections."

"Yeah. How's your drawing going?" he asked. "Did you work on it Friday night? I really should go into the studio with you Friday nights. But sometimes I go out with my other friends."

"It's good. You should come with me some time. It's nice and quiet."

I still sometimes forgot he had his other group. It was Tiana and the three other Black kids at the school.

"Maybe I'll check with you next Friday. When do you usually go?"

"After dinner. Sometimes I wait a bit, but not too long."

We all usually hung out Saturday nights, but for some reason we didn't on Fridays. Mack would go on one of his long walks, and Jenna told me once that she chilled and read.

"Cool, we can talk at dinner," he said.

"Yeah."

After that we walked in companionable silence. I was still reeling a bit from Jacob's revelation. I tried to remember if I'd ever teased him about the jeans, or just thought about it. I was pretty sure I'd only thought it.

I hoped that was right. I wondered if I should apologize in case I had, but from my new and improved social skills, I knew that the opportunity had passed and bringing it up again would actually just be awkward.

Instead, I decided to tell him about the mentorship yesterday, and then Jenna fell back to walk with us and we talked about physics homework. Jenna also had Dr. Jones, just at a different time.

Once we got to the restaurant, I suddenly felt nervous about knowing nothing about Indian food, but I shouldn't have been. Everybody was nice. And then it turned out Sophia had never had it either, so we all shared a bunch of different things to figure out what we liked. I remembered chicken korma for future reference.

It was a nice way to end the day, before we had to get back for study time. The semester had barely started and it was already back to the grind.

This school was intense, and I still wasn't sure I was

going to be able to hack it with physics, and the mentorship, and now TikTok. But I was going to try my best.

In my last class on Monday, one of the administration staff popped into the room and said, "Nic, please see Ms. Patton directly after class."

I about had a heart attack when she said my name. Everybody turned to stare at me as I turned what must have been a rather fluorescent variant of beet red.

What would the dorm mom want with me? Was I in trouble? What had I done? I hadn't done anything wrong. She'd never given me any trouble before. I couldn't stop obsessing.

The instructor started back up and I checked the clock. Twenty minutes left.

Well, I wasn't going to learn any more chemistry today. I spent the rest of the class obsessing, and then when we got out, I went to the dorm front desk. Mack was standing there, his brow furrowed in an expression that looked as worried as I felt.

"You, too?" he asked. Kids were streaming in the dorm door and heading to the stairs.

I nodded, words failing me. The only other time I'd gotten in trouble was at Emerson, when they decided my creative self-portrait was either a threat of violence or a cry for help.

For the record, it was neither, and I still loved it.

"Any idea?" he asked.

I shook my head in silence. I really had no idea.

Just then, Ms. Patton emerged from the direction of the

main lounge. "Hi, guys. Follow me. We'll go to my room for some privacy."

Mack and I looked at each other and fell into step with her. My heart was pounding like crazy. He grimaced at me, and I deepened my frown and looked at the back of Ms. Patton's head as we walked through the lounge. Her chestnut hair was wavy and bounced as she walked, almost like she was in a shampoo commercial. She took us down the hall on the boys' side of the dorm.

She opened the last door and held it open, her hand splayed on the door. "Come on in."

We went in and were basically in the living room area, like our rooms had. We awkwardly and silently sat down on the couch, a stiff blue utilitarian job. I was so nervous that my hands were shaking.

She shut the door and sat in an ugly olive green chair next to the TV that was opposite the couch.

How could a chair be that ugly? My stomach roiled.

Ms. Patton leaned forward and tented her hands, light glinting off her bright pink nail polish. "The Board of Trustees has made a couple of decisions." The subtle downturn of her mouth betrayed her discomfort.

I wanted to throw up. This was going to be bad. But what was it exactly?

She looked at us. "First, you both need to start using the student bathrooms in the classroom building."

Mack blinked, surprised and unhappy. This sucked. But my heart was beating fast because this was just one thing.

Ms. Patton took a deep breath. "They have also decided that you both have to move into the girls' side of the dorm. You will no longer have your own rooms downstairs."

"What?" Mack said. "Why?"

"They have decided that they will not recognize gender other than the gender you were born as."

"You mean the gender we were assigned at birth on our birth certificates," Mack said in disgust. "Neither of us was ever that gender."

Ms. Patton pursed her lips. I couldn't tell if she agreed with this or not, but it was obvious she didn't enjoy telling us.

My mind was spinning. How could they just change their minds? We'd gotten this approved. We'd jumped through the hoops. I couldn't calm my thoughts. There were going to be some girls who wouldn't want us sharing the communal bathrooms with them.

I couldn't believe I was going to have to move back upstairs. I'd gotten used to having my own bathroom.

That was a stupid thought. That wasn't what mattered here. I couldn't focus.

I might be speechless, but Mack's brain was clearly functioning because he asked, "Where will you put us? I thought the dorm was full."

Ms. Patton nodded. "You two will be sharing Nic's old room on the second floor."

"What?" Mack asked. He looked at me in shock.

My eyes were wide and I thought I was going to throw up. How could I share a room with him? Didn't they know we'd sort of dated last year? Why would they put us together?

"But," I started. "You know that uh ... last semester ... we, um—"

"I think I know what you're trying to say, and they aren't concerned. I'm sorry," Ms. Patton said.

Mack looked at me again, utterly horrified at the idea of sharing a room with me.

Ms. Patton was looking at a spot over our shoulders and not actually at us.

"I know this is not welcome news, but this is how it's going to be. The room was recently fixed up after the flooding, so it smells like paint, but it should clear soon. There are two other rooms on the fourth floor that are out of commission, so it may be that if we get one of those fixed up, we may be able to separate you. But you will stay on the girls' side."

"Whose idea was this?" Mack asked, sounding very suspicious.

"The Board of Trustees decided on it together." Her face was still neutral, but I suspected she knew. I didn't know what he was getting at, though.

"Uh," I started stupidly. "When ...?"

"You will have to move in after classes tomorrow, before study time."

Mack put his hand to his forehead. I could feel the stress coming off him. I guessed that he was thinking the same thing about how crazy it was that they were putting us together.

"I'm sorry about this," Ms. Patton said. "You are free to go. We will have your new card keys tomorrow."

We stood up in unison, my head spinning in actual dizziness, so I paused and Mack bumped into me.

"Sorry," we said at the same time. Then I made it to the door and we were in the hall by ourselves.

"This is a disaster," he said, strain in his voice I hadn't heard since the night he'd told me he was asexual and killed our little romance.

"It is," I said. But I was numb.

"I'll see you later." He looked down the hall. "Going for a walk."

"Okay." How in the world was this going to work?

PART III

ONE THOUSAND

The next day, I went to my room after class and loaded up my suitcase. I thought crying would have been appropriate, but I was all cried out already.

Mack was probably in his room, packing like me.

Last night, I'd immediately called my parents, who promised they'd try to fix it. I went to dinner with Jenna and Jacob, but Mack said he couldn't go. They were upset for us but didn't know what we could do. I cried the rest of the evening once I was back in my room.

Then this morning, I'd talked to Sam, my best friend from Emerson. She'd moved to Glasgow, Scotland, in the middle of sophomore year, but we'd stayed good friends. I'd even visited her in Scotland last March. She was sympathetic but didn't have any advice.

It all rested on my parents and Mack's parents getting this decision reversed.

I rolled the suitcase to the door and went back to try to cram everything else into the duffel. In went my shower caddy and other toiletries, and then all my underwear and bras.

Bras. Ugh. It was so wrong that they were a part of my life. This was one more horrible thing.

I dropped the duffel next to the suitcase and fell onto the couch. I did not want to do this. I didn't want to share a room with Mack, of all people. I was afraid that being around him so much would make the crush feelings come back. And I'd been doing so much better.

I sighed and stood up, grabbing the suitcase and heading upstairs. At least when I called home, I got to talk to Isabella, who was super mad for me. Then, in art class earlier, Jacob had asked how I was doing, and I'd just shrugged. What was there to say? Plus I didn't want Rachel to hear. I was sure she was involved somehow. She'd smirked at me right before class started, so I was pretty sure she had something to do with it.

I opened the heavy fire door to the second floor, remembering my first day here back in August. Here I was, heading to the exact same room. Life was weird—in a really shitty way.

I tried to think about better things as I headed down the hall. I'd worked on my Harriet line drawing during class, but I kept messing up and drawing too dark when I meant to keep it very light. I was mostly able to erase to get it light enough, but it was still frustrating how stupid crap was affecting the things that mattered the most to me.

I scanned the card to open the room door. Mack wasn't there yet and the room was totally empty of personal stuff—only the bunk beds, desks, and dressers. I didn't want to just claim anything without talking to Mack, but I rolled the suitcase to the desk in the corner behind the bunk beds, the one I'd had before. I really wanted this desk again.

On my way down the hall, I spotted the bathroom door, beyond the stairwell. I didn't want to share a bathroom with girls, and I knew some of them wouldn't want to share with me. It was going to be horrible. And even more wouldn't want to share with Mack. He was probably already traumatized by the bathroom aspect.

God. How could people do this to us? I shook my head and stepped into the stairwell. How could you live your life fueled by hate and malice? Because putting us in the same room, on the girls' side, did nothing but harm to everyone it touched. It was obviously terrible for my and Mack's mental health. But thinking of all the girls here—it benefited none of them and only caused problems because some of them would be uncomfortable with or angry about our presence. The only point to something like this was to punish us.

And putting us together was even nastier. Also, weird, given how they thought about teenage sexuality—like we were all insatiable sex fiends. Ms. Patton implied that they did know that we'd kind of dated last semester but didn't care. It wasn't really a secret for anyone paying even an ounce of attention.

I turned into the downstairs hall where my old room was, and nearly ran smack into Mack.

"Oof, hi," he said. He was frowning and his black hair was mussed up. He looked stressed. He also had two big blue duffel bags with him, one on each shoulder.

"Hi." I backed up and moved over so he could get by. "Is that all your stuff?"

"Yeah, everything but my backpack and books. I'll come back for those." He shifted one bag that was slipping off his shoulder.

"I've got to make one more trip. Let's talk about who gets which bed and crap when we're up there."

"Okay." He said it slowly, utterly downtrodden. I think this was even harder on him than me.

He walked past me and I went back to my downstairs room and hefted my near-bursting backpack onto my back, tossed my sheets and pillow on the duffel, threw the duffel over my shoulder, and grabbed the three textbooks that didn't fit anywhere else in my other arm.

As I made my way up the stairs, I felt like I was loaded down with hundreds of pounds. The weight of all the hate in Oklahoma. It was too much.

Mack opened the door at the second floor and held it for me. I didn't say anything and he just nodded before going back down.

I dragged everything into the room. I put the books on my old desk—I was really hoping he wouldn't mind—and sat on the lower bunk.

There was a slight paint smell, and I turned and could see that there was a strip down the middle of the wall that looked freshly painted. That must have been where the leak was. They probably scrambled to get it fixed so they could move us in here as fast as possible.

Then I stared at the opposite wall, where Sophia's evolution poster used to hang. I could even see the thumbtack holes that had held it up. She was going to be shocked by this room reassignment, and also frustrated, because I knew she'd hoped to get this room back to herself.

But nope, because the hunt was on for trans kids in red states.

I closed my eyes and tried to forget about everything. But Mack came in before I got anywhere, and he dropped his backpack—as crammed full of stuff as mine—on the other desk and then sat down next to me.

"Nic, I am so upset." He stared at his black Converse

shoes. "I know they hate us, but why can't there be some good people to stop the extremists? Why does hate get to win here?"

He was so right. Things used to be more balanced. "My mom once told me that a few decades ago, Oklahoma was considered a Democrat state."

"Really? That's hard to imagine." He sounded tired.

"Do you mind taking that desk?" I pointed at the one with his backpack.

"No, it's fine. Which bed do you want?"

"I wouldn't mind the bottom, but if you want it, I can take the top."

"I don't really care," he said in what sounded like slow-motion. "What does it matter?"

"Yeah." This was horrible.

Mack fell back onto the bed and I rested my face in my hands, elbows on my knees. We sat like that for a while and then I heard Mack sniff, like he might be crying.

I lay back and looked over at him. He was staring at the underside of the top bunk.

"Can you imagine what a nightmare the bathroom is going to be?" he asked. "Is it just one big room?"

"I thought of that. Some of the girls are probably going to complain. So, there are two identical ones on the floor, and they have everything—two toilets, three showers, and three sinks. The showers have a simple curtain but they're not too small, so I think everyone gets dressed in them. That's what I did. I never saw anybody walking around in their underwear or anything."

He wiped his eyes and sniffed again.

Somehow we had to live together and still get all our work done, just like normal, when nothing was normal anymore. I really didn't know how this was going to work.

How could I stand being this close to someone I still had a crush on? Seriously, how would it work? I didn't even want to find out, but I had no choice.

Wednesday, late in the afternoon, Sophia stood behind the tripod that held Jenna's phone, adjusting something in the app. Jenna stood next to her while Sophia explained what she was doing.

We were on the lawn in front of the dorm, filming Jacob talking about a graphic novel featuring a trans superhero. Jenna had already done a review of an urban fantasy called *Magic for Liars*. I was standing off to the side and wasn't really paying attention to Jacob's recording because I was watching Mack. He was still uncharacteristically quiet, ever since we'd gotten thrown into a shared room. He was staring at the ground, messing with the grass with the toe of his black Chucks. As usual, he was wearing only a light hoodie, even though it was cold. If I was a huggy person, I'd go give him one.

I looked over at Jacob, who had a real jacket on and was bouncing on his feet, book dangling in one hand. "Come on, can we hurry? I'm freezing."

"Almost there," Sophia called from the tripod.

"We're just trying to find the right filter to make your goosebumps pop more," Jenna said, which made Sophia and Jacob laugh.

Mack was still staring at the ground, his Kindle in his right hand. I knew he felt wretched, and I was so worried. But I also felt bad for myself—they'd obviously punished us on purpose simply because of who we were—two trans kids.

But it was easier for me to focus on how Mack was feeling than to wallow in my own unhappiness.

I also still wondered what the school was going to do next. I didn't think they were done.

"Okay, that's good," Sophia said, stepping to the side.

Jenna prompted Jacob, who got into position, and they continued filming. He talked about how great the story was, but how the art was even better.

"The best part of this book has to be the fight scenes," he said.

Jacob and his fight scenes. He cracked me up. Of course he'd pay attention to those in other comics. I mimicked brandishing a sword, which made him smile on camera.

I looked at Mack again, who was staring off in the distance. I decided I should go over there to talk to him. I didn't know why we were all spread out like we were, like we owned this section of the lawn. I walked behind Sophia and Jenna and glanced over at the front door of the dorm. Rachel stood outside the front door with a few friends. She was watching us, but she was too far away to hear anything.

A chill went down my spine. It wasn't because of the cold air.

"Rachel's staring at us," I whispered when I reached Mack.

He rolled his lips in and nodded, not looking at me. I awkwardly patted his shoulder. I was so weird about touching, and this was the best I could do. But it didn't seem to make a difference, as he didn't react at all.

Sophia was looking at us while Jacob wrapped up his review. She looked sympathetic—she knew what had happened with our rooms. Everybody did.

Jacob came over to us while Jenna and Sophia talked about the video.

"What are you reviewing?" Jacob asked Mack.

"I actually don't think I'm going to do it right now," Mack answered.

Jacob and I looked at each other. It was obvious why Mack didn't feel up to getting on camera.

I wanted to do something to make him feel better, but I had no idea what.

Jenna looked over. "So you don't want to do your review now, Mack?"

"Let's save it for tomorrow. I'm hungry. Early dinner?" He sounded tired.

"Sure," I said, not remotely hungry, which was rather odd for me. Soon Jacob and Jenna agreed.

"I've got some stuff to do for world history," Sophia said. "I'll talk to you guys later." She grabbed the tripod and headed inside while we started toward the cafeteria.

Jenna was working on her phone while we walked through the parking lot toward the cafeteria.

"Oh, hey!" she said suddenly. "We have over three hundred followers!"

"Really?" I said. "How?"

"So, there's a thing called reader follow parties, where basically you post a video to get people to follow you and you follow them back, and then other people follow each other from the comments. I did a bunch of those."

Mack was still walking with his head down. We were almost across the parking lot with just a final row of cars to squeeze past.

"Huh," Jacob said. "What link are we going to put up when we get to a thousand?"

Once you had a thousand followers on TikTok, you were able to put a link in your bio.

"I'll make a Linktree," Jenna said. "We can link to resources and stuff."

"Cool," I said.

Once we stepped onto the curb, Jacob said, "I've always been convinced I could jump over those bushes if I wanted to." He pointed to this row of bushes running between the round side of the cafeteria and another short white brick classroom building and we all stopped and looked. Jenna and I laughed.

"That's random. Why don't you try?" Jenna asked.

"Another part of my brain thinks the first part may be overconfident."

I glanced at Mack, who still hadn't engaged at all.

"I'll try it," I announced, thinking maybe this would distract Mack from his thoughts and cheer him up a bit, which would be my good deed for the day. I wasn't into sports, but I had pretty good hand-eye coordination, and I was strong. It couldn't be that hard.

Jacob's eyebrows were raised as he looked at me, and Jenna looked equally surprised.

"Can you jump?" she asked.

"Sure." The bushes didn't look too tall, really.

Or maybe they did. The hair went up on the back of my neck.

"You'll have to get a running start," she said.

"Yeah." I was going to do this. It would be fine. I cracked my knuckles, which made Jacob laugh.

"Yes, visualize yourself gliding over the bushes," he said.

Even Mack was giving me a funny look, with wide eyes but a pained expression. He was surprised but not really engaged.

We walked over to the other building, as far from the

bushes as we could get. It was about twenty-five feet to them, and the cafeteria was about ten feet beyond the row.

I really had no idea what I was doing. I might have been in shock at my own decision. This was so not Emerson Nic. Where was this reckless energy coming from? Who knew. "Okay, I'm ready."

"Okay," Jenna said skeptically. She held up her phone, obviously planning to film this, which made me look around to make sure no one else was watching or filming.

Jacob also watched with a smile on his face, and Mack was looking at me, too.

I got into a sort of crouch, like I thought sprinters did before starting. A germ of doubt was growing in the back of my mind, but then decided I just needed to commit to this crazy idea, and took off.

I hadn't moved this fast in years. This was going to be a breeze. But as I got closer to the bushes, I didn't know how I was going to do it. When should I start the jump? I had no idea.

Abort! I was moving too fast and there was nothing to catch myself with, so I barreled right through the bush, all legs, tangling in all the dry branches, cracking sounds all around me as I crashed to the ground on the other side, sliding on my stomach and stopping only a couple feet from the cafeteria wall.

The base of the wall was dark from the dirt up against it. About five feet to the side was a rat trap box against the wall. Gross. Seeing how close I'd gotten to breaking my neck made my heart nearly stop, but then I could feel the hysteria building up.

There was cackling coming from the other side of the bushes.

I was lucky that there was grass between the bushes and wall, or I'd be covered in dirt. I did a quick scan to make sure I hadn't broken something. I shifted to start getting up, still about to lose my shit laughing.

I tried to gather my limbs and got onto my knees and looked back. The bushes were still there, but there was a big hole in one of them. I could see Jenna bowled over with laughter, Jacob with his head thrown back, cracking up. Mack's eyes were even wider than before and he had a smile on his face.

"What was that, Nic?" Mack asked, crouched down and peering through the hole.

I pushed myself off the ground, the heat in my cheeks fighting against the cold. I took a deep breath.

Everyone was still laughing, and those giggles finally exploded out of me. I was struggling to walk like a normal person as I went around to the end of the row of bushes and skulked back to my friends. Everyone was laughing at me, but this time was different from all the other times back at Emerson—we were laughing together and they weren't mocking me. This was a totally new experience.

"You want to give it a shot?" Jenna asked Jacob between gasps of breath. Her hand was on her stomach.

"No, based on new information, it appears that my brain *was* overconfident after all. Sort of like someone else we know." He looked pointedly at me, his grin endless.

"That may be the first time in my life someone has accused me of that particular character flaw," I said. I cupped my chin and looked skyward. "No, it definitely is."

Jenna shook her head. "Let's go inside before somebody asks us if we know what happened to that bush."

I looked back. It was truly mangled. I grimaced—I

would get in trouble for that if I got found out. "Don't share the video, okay?"

She laughed some more. "Just don't piss me off, and you're good. But I'm going to guard this precious footage until the end of time, or at least until a time I need something from you." She gave me a malicious grin.

That made us all laugh even more, and we hurried toward the cafeteria door.

I considered my state. I had several scratches on my hands. I ran one through my hair, coming away with a small clump of dirt. My right shoulder was already sore. I'd landed hard, so I was probably going to have several bruises, but I seemed to have survived without real injury.

One body part that was definitely going to be sore was my stomach, already aching from the extra work of laughing so much.

Why had I done that? Had I lost my mind? Was this the beginning of a long slide into madness?

Probably not, but I didn't know what it was. There was changing, and then there was changing so much that you were an entirely new person. At least it made Mack smile.

When I reached for the door, I noticed a small twig stuck to the sleeve of my jacket. I was a long way from Emerson.

Thursday evening I was in my room working on the drawing for the watercolor I was doing for my mentorship. This was going to be my first attempt. I was working from a picture of a peach on a blue table, on nine by twelve paper, so there was room at my desk.

Mack was at Sophia's old desk that was facing the wall behind me. I assumed he was reading for a class. I could hear him breathing and sniffing a little. I hoped he wasn't getting a cold. He was already going through enough.

I finished the drawing part of the watercolor peach. I'd work on painting it in the studio tomorrow. I was hoping Ms. Mangal wouldn't mind if I worked on it in class, too. The line drawing for the Harriet drawing was done, and I'd even started inking it, so far in black only. The in-class critique wasn't for another two weeks.

I was amazed when I realized I wasn't even nervous about that. Last semester, standing in the front of the class-room next to your art on an easel, listening to people give you feedback on it, sounded like hell on earth. But I'd gotten used to it, and people weren't mean. And they had nice things to say, too.

I put the drawing in my portfolio and propped it up against the wall at the back of my desk. Out came my physics book. I'd already read the sections we were working on once, but I was going to read them again.

I'd met with Tiana earlier today, after dinner, and she had agreed to tutor me twice a week, which I couldn't believe. She said she'd do it just because I was such good friends with Jacob. I hadn't realized they were that close, but I guess it wasn't for nothing that I was infamous for being oblivious.

Honestly, I wanted to get better about that, but how did you make yourself think of something when you weren't thinking of it? I did feel like I was getting better about judging people. I guess one self-improvement step at a time.

Tiana and I were going to meet for forty-five minutes each Monday and Thursday, right before mandatory study time. And since we were in the same class, she'd basically be helping me learn what we were working on.

She also gave me some tips, and one was not just to read

the textbook parts multiple times—which was pretty obvious—but to take notes and build upon the same paper notes on each pass. Basically, go deeper on each pass. So, not to get stuck in the weeds on the first pass, but rather to get a solid, high-level overview that time. And then get more on the next pass. I was going to follow her advice.

Mack sniffed again behind me.

Man, I was worried about him. Now I thought he might be crying.

We both worked in silence. My attention drifted as I was reading, but I tried to force my way back. If Tiana was willing to put time into me getting better, I should obviously put in the effort myself.

"Hey, Nic?" Mack said, totally jarring me out of my reading.

"Yeah?" I turned around to find him looking at me.

His mouth was turned down, and he said, "I think I want to make a TikTok about this."

"This?" I asked.

He waved his hand around, indicating the room. That's what I'd guessed—the eviction, move, and everything.

"Okay," I said. "We can film it tomorrow after school."

"No, I want to do it tonight."

My head rocked back in surprise. "Oh."

"Can you film it?"

"Sure." I'd have to figure out how. Maybe if he talked through everything, it would make him feel better.

"Okay. Right after study time."

I nodded and we both turned back around to our desks.

What was he going to say? And as much as I knew talking about upsetting things can help you process them, it can also make you more upset. I didn't know if I knew how to be the friend Mack needed. But I would try.

A few minutes later, after I'd made a trip to the bathroom—stressful because there were girls in there—we were about ready to start recording.

He raised a finger to emphasize the point he was going to make. "I'm going to start with Sophia's hook—the thing about how you don't have to have any idea what you're doing to be a lawmaker in this country. And just how idiotic and incompetent all these people are, and how they rely on false numbers to support their completely irrational conclusions."

"That sounds great."

He nodded. "Let me think for a minute."

I opened the app, navigating to the screen waiting to record.

He ran his hand through his hair. "Okay, I'm ready."

I held the phone up and got him centered on the screen. "Okay, go."

"Have you ever thought about the fact that lawyers have to have law degrees, but people who *make* laws don't?" His voice had energy again. "Okay, stop for a second."

I clicked pause.

"Was that good?"

"It was awesome," I said. "That's definitely a hook."

"Okay, let's do this."

I started recording again.

"The far-right politicians who are proposing all these bills against LGBTQ people, and sometimes even passing them, are literally so incompetent at their jobs that they keep passing laws that the state supreme courts are striking down, basically saying, 'You can't do that, dipshits.'"

We paused and he took a breath before continuing.

"Everything about them is incompetent, but you can't ignore their evil nature, either. They use utter junk science and don't even read the real reports about gender-affirming care for minors. Instead, they believe the other incompetent, lying assholes telling ridiculous lies, like that there are dozens of top surgeries a week on minors in their states. This is simply not the reality of gender-affirming care in this country."

We stopped for a second while he took another deep breath and messed with his hair again.

"Gender-affirming care saves lives, and these buffoons want to take it away because they believe that there's such a thing as binary biological sex, completely disregarding every doctor who says it isn't true. Even if you really believe that genitalia defines someone's gender, *intersex people exist*." He leaned forward as he said the last part, slowly and emphatically. "Biological sex is not binary—why would gender be?"

This was really good. But then he started going into his own story.

"As a kid I was confused by gender expectations, and I dealt with it mostly by ignoring gender. My parents helped with this because they didn't force gendered toys on me or anything. But when I hit puberty, I was no longer confused—I knew it was all wrong. I became depressed and was really struggling. I hated school because gender was so enforced there, and I did start having a lot of suicidal thoughts, which is so common among trans kids. People act like we're doing this for attention, or to upset people, or some stupid shit. Who would want to have feelings completely disconnected to their body? It's stupid."

He paused for a moment and I stopped recording.

"Okay, I'm ready," he said, so I started the video again.

"My mom was really good at pulling the truth out of me, so they eventually got me started on gender-affirming care. And it was amazing. I finally started feeling like everything about me wasn't all wrong. It was good for a while, but then Texas created that law that basically said parents were abusing their children if they got them gender-affirming care."

He closed his eyes. Then he opened them and spoke again. "My parents' oldest friends reported them to the authorities. To make a long story short, my aunt in Oklahoma had to legally adopt me to keep them out of trouble. This is *insane*." He said the last part with such force I almost flinched.

Then he talked about how Oklahoma effectively banned all gender-affirming care for minors last semester, forcing him to leave the state to get his monthly shots. He had me pause again.

"Are you okay with me talking a little about you?" Mack asked. He raised his hands. "Not too much detail, just stuff that's relevant to all this."

"Uh, I guess?" My stomach twisted. "What are you going to say?"

"I'm thinking I might ask you a question and you can answer while recording. So you don't have to be on the video, but it emphasizes how this isn't only about one person."

"I guess I could do that." I didn't feel sure of this at all, but I reminded myself I wanted to be the friend he needed. "But if I don't like it, you either have to rerecord it or we cut it out."

"Definitely. Okay, let's go. My friend and I—say hi, friend."

"Hi," I squeaked out.

"We go to a math and science boarding school in Oklahoma. My friend is agender and I am transmasc. Neither of us is a girl. We each had our own rooms in the dorm until two days ago, when they suddenly kicked us out of our rooms and made us move into a shared room on the girls' side of the dorm. We don't want to share a bathroom with girls. Girls don't want to share a bathroom with us. But somehow the Board of Trustees, flush with power and privilege, decided we should be punished for daring to be who we are."

He talked a little more about the impact the move had on us, and then his voice faltered and he paused, so I stopped filming

"Is this sounding okay?" he asked me, grimacing slightly from nerves.

"Definitely," I said.

Mack nodded and tapped his upper lip. "Okay, let's finish it up, then."

I pressed record.

"These people making laws in red states do not have medical knowledge. They don't have an understanding of health and medicine, yet they're making decisions about people's bodies and medical care. It's bad enough in this country that for-profit insurance companies get to decide what medical care people get, but now we have a bunch of red state halfwits taking away our rights to control what decisions we can make about our own bodies."

He turned his head to the side slightly, still looking at the camera.

"And you know it's not just LGBTQ people who are affected by this hunt, right? Even if you're a white, cis, straight man and think you're safe, give them a minute—

they'll find something they don't like about you eventually. This is a huge moment—it's probably the beginning of the decline of what was formerly a pretty decent country. Historians will write about this period, always wondering how such privileged people could have voted in fascism, crying freedom the whole time, while actual freedom was being stripped away one law at a time. If you are old enough to vote, *please* look at what your legislators are doing. We need your help. *You* need your help."

He stopped and stared at the camera, still looking intense, his lips pursed.

I stopped filming. "Wow," I said.

"I've been thinking about that stuff, and it all just came together in my head now." Then he jumped up. "What time is it? It must be almost lights-out."

"Ten forty-seven," I said, reading it off my phone.

I loved that he had his energy back again, even if I knew it wouldn't last through his trip to the bathroom.

"Let's edit that bad boy tomorrow," he said. He went to his closet and grabbed his pajamas.

I made sure to properly save the video to drafts and closed the app.

Mack left the room for the bathroom. We had devised a plan regarding changing clothes. It was always done in the bathroom stall, or the shower if we'd just taken one. Nothing even close to semi-nudity would be happening in this room.

I wanted to watch the video again, but Mack was right— we had ten minutes before lights-out, and I needed to get ready, too.

Tomorrow we'd clean it up and share it with Jenna and Jacob, and then the world.

Saturday I was in the studio with all the other mentees, and we were working on our individual projects. Lily and I sat diagonally opposite each other, and Devin and Briana were working at one table, although Briana was with Clee at the moment. Addison had practically filled her table with butcher paper for her thumbnails. She'd embraced the idea of thumbnailing, except for the size—she liked to work big. I couldn't see what Devin or Briana were working on.

I was putting the finishing touches on the watercolor peach I'd started last night, and then, after meeting with Clee, I was going to work on the group project with Addison. She was doing the backgrounds for the dragon panels. It was going to be interesting to work from right to left.

She and I hadn't worked out exactly how to split the work up, but we were deciding today. Devin and Briana were handling the knight panels, with Briana doing the background and Devin doing the knight. We'd decided that Lily would do her creature first—she was still trying to figure out what it was going to be—and we'd add the backgrounds later. It was going to be really interesting. I was looking forward to seeing what we'd decide to do with the fight panels.

But for now, it was all about the peach. It didn't look terrible, but I didn't really like it. I'd gotten close with the color, but it was a little too yellow. Still, I had done a decent job with shading by tweaking the colors slightly. I was actually working on the background right now, adding some light layers over the wall to get the shadows right. I'd considered it done last night, but changed my mind when I got here.

I really wanted to pull my phone out and check on how

Mack's new video was doing. We'd posted it late on Friday night. It had a decent number of views this morning, but nothing spectacular. When I had checked on the way here, it had three thousand views, which was more than we'd ever had before. I had a good feeling about this one.

I glanced at my phone face down on the table, then stared at the paint on my peach background, watching it slowly dry.

I gave up and picked the phone up. I opened TikTok and went to our account screen. Holy crap! We were past twenty thousand views now!

I fired a text off to the group and set the phone down again, heart beating really fast.

I had to wait for my hands to stop shaking before I could put down one more layer of paint on the wall behind the peach. Then I studied the painting. This was insane.

I needed to try to focus on my work, not TikTok. I looked at the painting again. It wasn't bad. But I clearly had a lot to learn about color. I'd struggled with color in the acrylics I'd done in class, too. So I was getting nervous about the Harriet drawing. I loved what I had so far, and I didn't want to ruin it with a bad color job. I was actually thinking of asking Ms. Mangal if I could save color for the next assignment.

My phone vibrated and I pulled it out.

—*1100 followers!*— Jenna texted. —*We're past 1000!*—

Whoa! That was crazy. I hadn't even checked the followers, just the views.

"What happened?" Lily asked from across the table.

"We have over eleven hundred followers on TikTok now," I said quietly. "We only started it this month."

"Oh, wow," Lily said, nodding appreciatively. "Did you have a video that went viral or something?"

"Um, yes." I showed Lily the screen that showed all our

videos and pointed to last night's video—the one with the huge view count.

"Can I watch it?" she asked.

"Uh, sure." I brought it up and started playing it, turning the volume down so it wasn't loud.

Lily watched the beginning, when Mack said that perfect hook.

"What's going on?" Devin asked from across the room.

I paused the video.

"Nic and their friends have a TikTok account that is blowing up," Lily said.

Devin slid off his stool and walked over, and Addison followed. This was getting embarrassing. My cheeks were hot from the attention.

Devin and Addison got on either side of Lily and then he leaned forward, elbows and forearms resting on the table.

I was blushing fiercely at this point.

"Start it again, Nic," Lily said.

I scrolled back and played it.

There was Mack. When he said the first thing, both Devin and Addison looked surprised. "That is so true!" Devin said.

Addison and Lily nodded.

"Who is this?" Devin asked. He looked very serious, and Addison also was watching intently.

"My friend Mack," I said.

Devin nodded and I got a good look at his piercing. The septum location had always seemed odd to me, but the smaller ones on either side seemed cool. On the video, Mack was explaining how we got kicked out of our rooms. He paused before saying that we'd been assigned to the same room.

I had to look away. I knew he wasn't going to mention the part about us dating last semester, and I wasn't going to say anything. But that was a missing piece of the story.

"I don't understand why these people hate us so much," Mack said on the video. "Why do these politicians and terrible parents want to punish us for not being born cisgender? Who do they think we're hurting? It just makes no sense, and this move has utterly destroyed me." This statement was driven home by the fact that his voice had slowed at this point, like it was an effort to say it.

He'd perked back up after that part, but I was still worried about him, because he was deflated again all day yesterday. And it didn't help that our parents had told us the school didn't seem open to giving us our rooms back.

Devin shook his head when the video finished. "That's so fucked up."

"It really is," Addison added.

Lily nodded and looked at me.

"How many views now?" Devin asked.

"Twenty-two thousand," I said. This was insane—that was in just the last fifteen minutes.

"Phew, that's a lot. Congratulations." He pushed off the table. "What is your user name?"

"Yeah, I'd love to see your stuff," Addison said.

I gave them the name and they both followed us in the app, then returned to their table.

"Are you okay?" Lily asked. She took off her jacket and piled it on the stool next to her.

I looked down and shrugged. "I'm okay. I'm really worried about Mack."

"Yeah, he sounded really depressed in some parts. He's usually pretty upbeat, isn't he?"

I nodded my head in agreement, and we were silent until she said, "Oh, your painting looks good."

I looked at it. "The peach is too yellow."

Lily smiled. "Ever the critic. Let me see it. Is it dry?"

I turned it around and pushed it across the table.

"Okay, it is a little on the yellow side, but it's otherwise so realistic that I'm liable to assume that it's just an unusually yellow peach. Is this really your first watercolor?"

I nodded, boosted by her compliment.

"You may have found your medium. Or another one." She laughed lightly.

"Beginner's luck," I muttered, which made her laugh again.

"I'm hoping for some of that myself," she said. "The piece I'm working on for Ms. Mangal is all grayscale. It's surprisingly hard to change how I work. I'm so used to color."

"I'm sure it will look great. I love your stuff."

"Thanks." She blushed slightly.

There was talking behind us and I turned to see Briana coming into the room, wearing a long yellow skirt.

"Who's next?" Clee asked.

I raised my hand like a dork because my mind was all over the place. I should have just said something.

"Come on, then," she said, motioning with her hand and then turning around and heading toward her office.

I slid off the stool, grabbed my painting and the other pen drawing I'd done for her earlier in the week, and followed her. I really wondered what she was going to think about both pieces.

∼

Jenna had brought a tote bag with her when we went to dinner the next Saturday. We'd posted a few more videos and had good views, definitely more than we were getting at first, but nothing went as viral as Mack's. But our follower count was still growing.

I'd assumed Jenna's tote had books at first, but it didn't look heavy enough. I was curious, but all through dinner she refused to tell any of us what was in there. She'd brought four empty bowls and four spoons from the cafeteria line, and they were just sitting on the table, piquing my curiosity.

Mack and Jacob looked bemused. Mack seemed to be feeling slightly better since his video had gone viral. There were a lot of horrible comments on there, of course, but there were also some supportive people. He said it was cool that so many people had seen it—it was up to a hundred and fifty thousand now—because it was so important to get the message out. It was the only way people would stop voting for these horrible politicians. We were too young to vote, so spreading the word was the only thing we could do.

Jacob pushed his plate to the side, the last of us to finish. That prompted Jenna to ask, "Okay, are you all ready for the surprise?"

Of course, we all said yes.

"Okay then." She put the tote on the table and extracted a canister of whipped cream, a jar of cherries, and both caramel and chocolate sauce. And then she put out a stack of party hats.

"We are celebrating a thousand followers in style," Jenna said. "Let's go get our ice cream."

Jacob cracked up, and I had a huge smile on my face. Even Mack looked amused. He was wearing a baseball cap with a Houston Astros insignia, something I'd never seen him do. I thought he was hiding under it.

We went up to the nearest ice cream station and Jacob and I asked for two scoops of vanilla while Mack and Jenna both got chocolate. We sat back down and Jenna passed out the bowls, which we dumped our ice cream into. And then we started improving it with all of the toppings she'd brought.

I covered one scoop with chocolate and the other with caramel and added four cherries and about a pint of whipped cream spread over it all, which had everyone cracking up.

"It's *good*," I said, pretending to be defensive.

"The cherry is supposed to go on top of the whipped cream," Jacob said.

"Oh yeah," I said. I spooned out two more and dropped them on top.

"Now it looks right, but there are delicious landmines inside," Jenna said, laughing. Her own sundae had a more normal amount of whipped cream.

Mack put about a gallon of chocolate syrup on his, so the scoops were swimming in it.

"Yours looks like a professional made it," I said to Jacob. "You're just missing a banana." The scoops were perfectly positioned in the center, and one had a delicate coating of chocolate, and the other caramel, with each topped with a perfectly shaped dollop of whipped cream and a single cherry.

"My mom takes sundaes very seriously," he explained. "We learned very young."

Jenna passed out the hats. They were those pointy hats, red with silver glitter in the shapes of stars.

"Do we have to?" I complained. This was going to make

me feel very self-conscious, which was funny given how many people heard me speak on TikTok. But they hadn't *seen* me, so it was different.

"Yes, you do." She put hers on and so did Jacob and Mack, so I sighed and followed suit. Jacob was smiling, but Mack's face had fallen to neutral again.

"Okay, everyone," Jenna said dramatically. "We are celebrating because we've really done something. I have our Linktree added to our profile, and now we can start really spreading the message that people need to stop all the anti-LGBTQ+ legislation popping up all over the country. I don't think we should focus only on books." She stopped dramatically and motioned to Mack. "And our new status is thanks to the indomitable Mack here."

We all looked at him and he blushed, but he was smiling.

"Now raise your bowls," Jenna said.

We all raised them and Jenna started clinking hers against everyone else's, so we did the same.

"This is not normal," Jacob said with a laugh.

"Who wants to be normal?" I was having a ridiculously good time, even with the dorky hat on my head.

"Not us," Jenna said in agreement.

"I wish you all were a year older," Mack said, sounding kind of sad. "It would have been so much better last year if you'd been here with me."

That made me feel bad. Obviously it wasn't our fault, but it made me sad that he spent his whole junior year alone, with Rachel harassing him.

Jacob patted Mack's back. "I would have loved to be here then, too."

"Yeah, same, seriously," Jenna said. "But we're all here now, so let's par-tay."

We all dug into our ice cream, and I thought about how much better my life was here, even with the awkwardness of having to share a room with Mack on the girls' side of the dorm.

We should fight that. It was wrong. That's what Mack needed—we needed to fight back, not just sit here and take it. I'd talk to him about it tonight. I'd never tell him, but I'd grown to kind of like having so much access to him, even though he still did disappear a lot on his walks.

Our parents had told us the school still wasn't budging, but they also still weren't done fighting. Maybe Mack and I needed to advocate for ourselves and speak to the Board of Trustees directly.

The next day, Mack slept in, but Jenna and I went to breakfast, something we rarely did. Jacob was already having breakfast with Tiana and a couple other kids. Apparently this was a regular Sunday morning thing for them, which just shows how rare it was for me to get up early on the weekend, since I had no idea.

On the walk over, we talked about TikTok, then split up when we got to the cafeteria. I beat her to the table, and when she got there with her plate of scrambled eggs, she had a big grin on her face.

I looked at her quizzically.

"You should get your hair chopped off," she announced, sitting down with a flourish.

"Uh." It was true that I'd toyed with the idea a few times, but never seriously. I'd just always had long hair. But it was totally unstyled, so it pretty much looked the way it did on men with long hair, which, admittedly, must have contributed to why I got called sir so often.

"I'm not going to pressure you, but it would be so cool," she said. "Also, it's really convenient because it dries fast, so you don't have to go through your first two classes of the day with wet hair."

I stared at the ceiling—and its many rust-colored metal rafters—to kind of think about it uninterrupted.

Jenna started on her eggs.

I didn't know why I still had long hair, honestly. Well, it was obviously because I'd always had long hair and had never acted to change that. When I was little, my mom never wanted to cut it because she thought it would be a sign of me growing up. And then I treated it like a security blanket to hide under.

Jenna was watching me when I dropped my head down and looked back at her.

"What are you thinking? How short?" I took a bite of my grits, full of honey.

"I see you with short and spiky hair."

I laughed. "Like you. And Mack before he lets it grow out? We could all be twinsies."

She pointed at me with her fork, a twinkle in her eye. "Exactly."

"But I already get mistaken for a boy so much—won't that make it worse?" Maybe it really wouldn't, due to the long-haired-guy look I already had. But it seemed like it might.

"This is Oklahoma," she said with a laugh. "Nobody's ever going to get your gender right. But it doesn't have to be a cute pixie—spiky is pretty gender neutral."

"True. I'm thinking about it." I was. My stomach had gotten involved now, filling with butterflies.

We ate in silence for a moment, Jenna smiling at me, and my brain whirring away.

My stomach was now doing flips at the mere idea of a change that dramatic. But the idea was also exciting. Maybe I should do it. A new look might be cool. A new look for a new me.

I tried to spread some butter on my toast, but I'd let it get cold, so I was just dragging this firm butter over it.

Jenna picked up the other butter packet on my tray and put it under her plate.

"What are you doing?" I asked.

"Give it a minute. So, do you want to do it?"

I felt like I was standing at the edge of a cliff, about to jump into the ocean. But I was a new me and knew how to handle change now. Doing things outside of my comfort zone hadn't been terrible so far. "Okay."

"Really? That's awesome!" She grinned and lifted up her plate, putting the butter packet next to my toast.

I opened it up and it was warm and soft, so it went onto the toast like it was supposed to. I spread the grape jelly on after, and just kind of ignored what I'd just said. I'd shocked myself a little. But my stomach was still roiling.

"Do you want to go now?" she asked after a bit.

"Where would we go? And I didn't bring any money." I didn't know if I even had enough. I'd never paid for a haircut myself.

"I can cover it. We'll just go to Supercuts."

This was getting very real.

Jenna looked up where the nearest Supercuts was as we finished breakfast. We took our trays back, made a quick call to the dorm to let them know we were going off campus, and began the walk.

As we hurried along—I thought Jenna didn't want me to

have time to chicken out—she told me about when she'd first cut hers off. She'd had long hair up to that point, too, but she dove in in seventh grade. It was a good twenty minutes' walk, plenty of time for me to change my mind, but I didn't. Instead, I kept imagining what I would look like with very little hair.

I reached for the door to the shop, but Jenna put her hand on the door to keep me from opening it.

"Picture first," she said when I looked at her, confused.

We posed for a quick selfie in front of the sign on the door. She had a big smile on and I looked rather ... uncertain.

But then we went in, and the process truly began. There were three hairstylists in there, each with a client, so Jenna and I sat down. I looked at the stylists, and they were all young and white. One had blue streaks in her blonde hair, but otherwise they all seemed fairly conventional, a typical amount of makeup, even though the one with blue hair had a bit of a goth look.

Jenna started going through hairstyles on Google Images, showing me the ones she liked. They were all fine. I didn't think I was in a good position to know what to pick. I was focusing on tamping down the queasiness that had set in. Plus, the transition from long hair to super short was going to be such a huge change that the small differences between the different short haircuts didn't seem to matter.

I watched the stylists. One was working on a young woman with long straight hair. She also looked conventional, with the right amount of hair that men expected to see on women, and she was apparently just getting it trimmed.

It occurred to me that it was weird that I'd never cut off my hair before. I'd always defied the gender norms around makeup, but had still kept my hair long like I was "supposed to."

The other stylists were working on two frat-boy types, both with boring short hair.

Should I change my mind and just get a trim? My phone dinged with a text.

"I sent you some examples," Jenna said.

My stomach tweaked with excitement at the idea of short hair. I would not be backing out.

Eventually, it was my turn. The hairstylist who came up was the one with blue in her hair, so I took that as a good sign.

Jenna gleefully wished me luck and I followed the stylist to her chair and sat down.

As she put the cape over my front, she asked, "What are we doing?" She sounded bored.

"I want it chopped off." I tried to sound confident, though I don't think I managed it. This was rather terrifying, even though I definitely wanted it. I needed to stop following a gender norm that should never have applied to me. It was time to rid myself of this long hair once and for all.

"All of it?" Her eyebrows shot up and her voice was higher—definitely no longer bored.

"Well, I don't want it shaved. I want it like hers." I pointed to Jenna, who smiled and waved. "But not so girly."

"I'm not girly," Jenna said, sounding offended.

The stylist looked at me in the mirror. "So you want it that short, but you want a boy's cut?"

"No, I just don't want it to be feminine." I felt the others in the salon looking at me, so I looked down. I remembered my phone and pulled it out, opening up Jenna's links. "Here are some other examples."

She looked at them as I swiped through the pictures.

"Okay, so, gender neutral, then." She sounded like she knew what she was talking about.

I hoped for the best and said, "Yeah. I do want it to be spiky."

She nodded and pulled her scissors out of a drawer and grabbed a spray bottle. "Are you sure about this? Do you want me to just cut a bit off at a time, or do you want it done fast?"

"I'm not going to change my mind," I said, sounding more confident than I was feeling.

"Got it." She had a smile on her face. "Have you heard of Locks of Love?"

"I don't think so."

"Your hair is long enough to donate." She picked it up in the back. "They take it and make hairpieces for disadvantaged kids who've lost their hair to chemo and stuff."

"Oh, that sounds really cool." I didn't even know things like that were possible. "Do I have to do something?"

"I just put it in a ponytail and cut it up above the rubber band, and then we mail it in."

"Okay, let's do that." This made me feel even more confident. I would be doing something good for me, and for someone else, too.

My stylist smiled again and dropped my hair in the back. She aimed the spray bottle and started spritzing my hair with the water. Then she put a rubber band around it, and I felt the tightness pulling back on my face.

"Ready?" She was holding the pony tail in her fingers, scissors positioned to chop it off.

I paused for a second to make sure I hadn't just changed my mind, and then said, "Yep." My stomach flipped.

Snip. I couldn't see it fall, but I knew it was gone. There was no going back now.

And now my stomach was really roiling again. There was only one way forward.

"This is going to look great on you, kiddo," the stylist said. "I love being part of dramatic changes."

I didn't watch most of it, but once she had the majority cut off, I did look in the mirror, and my eyes widened in shock. It was all flat because it was wet, but it was very, very short. My heart sped up. I would really be going around with short, spiky hair from now on.

The stylist wasn't looking at me, and instead started cutting in the back, and I just let her have at it. I was still hoping she didn't do something terrible, but this was a moment I just had to trust someone.

After a bit more snip, snip, snipping, she asked, "How's that?"

I looked up and saw myself with really short hair. It was the same light brown I was used to, but it looked completely different. My stomach was roiling with both excitement and shock at the change.

"I need to do a little cleanup, and it won't be spiky without some product," the stylist explained. "Do you want me to put some in? Or do you have any interest in color? We could always turn you blue."

My eyes widened at the idea of having hair in a primary color. As fun as it sounded, I didn't know if I was brave enough. Let me adjust to this first. Plus, Jenna was paying for the haircut. I finally said, "I don't think I can do a color now. But yes to the product."

She did a little more cutting on top and then reached into the cabinet next to her station and pulled out a canister and squirted some stuff in her hands. I assumed it was mousse, though I wasn't sure why I knew that. I had never learned anything about styling hair.

She ran her fingers through the front of my hair and worked toward the back. I watched her make my hair genuinely spiky.

I stared at myself in the mirror. I had short spiky hair. I looked totally different. I turned my head to the side a bit while she grabbed a mirror. She turned me around so I could see the back, which looked fine. From the back, you could also see that it was spiky.

I had short spiky hair.

She took the mirror and turned me back toward the front and popped off the cape.

"Um, thank you," I said as I got up.

"It looks good. It really suits you."

She was right—she'd done a good job, as it didn't look feminine or masculine. Of course, because I was in Oklahoma and it wasn't feminine, it would be presumed masculine.

As per usual.

I finally noticed Jenna, who was grinning and standing by the cash register. "It looks so good, Nic!"

I nodded. It did actually look good, but it was so different. It would take some getting used to. It felt a little like my head was floating, without the weight of the hair holding it down. I'd never realized how heavy hair was.

Jenna paid for the cut and picked up a canister of mousse for me, and we left.

As soon as we were outside, she insisted on the After photo, so we took that and started back to the dorm.

I was speechless. It was chilly out and I was feeling the air on the back of my neck, which was totally new.

And then I wondered what other people would say. This

was a dramatic enough change that a lot of people probably would comment.

But the truth was, that didn't really concern me. I wondered what Mom and Isabella would think when I called them for our weekly FaceTime later today. They'd surely be shocked. And of course Rachel would have something mean to say, but most people here weren't like that. I would just have to see.

PART IV

TEN THOUSAND

I spent the next week staring at myself in the mirror and obsessively touching my hair. Some people were surprised, and I did of course get some insults thrown in the lunch room, but mostly people ignored it and me, like normal.

So by the time we got to Friday and the first group critique of the semester in art class, it was old news. The critique, however, was not. Jacob was on the spot, standing at the front of the room while we gave him feedback one at a time. He had on a light blue Marvel shirt—I think half his shirts were Marvel. I'd already said my reactions, so my mind was wandering, even though my turn in the hot seat was coming up.

After our celebration about TikTok Saturday night, we'd carried on, filming a few new videos and getting more views than we used to, although the number of followers leveled off at about twenty-five hundred. We were still getting new ones every day, but slowly. It was weird. I sort of felt ... famous, I guess. Even though I obviously wasn't. I was so used to being completely invisible that it was weird being out in the world for anyone to see. But Mack's video had topped fifty thousand views, which was just insane.

Jacob's critique wrapped up. I no longer dreaded these like I used to, but I'd be lying if I said I wasn't nervous as he picked up his piece. I was the last one to go.

He gave me an encouraging smile when I passed him on the way to the front of the room, Harriet Tubman drawing in hand. I'd stuck with black ink only on this one. I put it on the easel and did my intro talk about it.

After explaining the assignment—a historical figure doing something in a time period other than their own—I added, "I think she's the biggest American hero. She never stopped fighting for the right thing, no matter what obstacles were thrown at her."

People came up to look at the drawing and take notes, so I stepped aside and thought about what Harriet would have been like today. What would she have thought about the hunting of LGBTQ people? There were plenty of issues related to Black people's rights and lives to keep her busy.

Lily was looking closely at one part of the drawing, and it made me nervous, even though it shouldn't. She was always nice, and even if she did find something to criticize, she would be right. I still couldn't believe I'd let Rachel convince me that Lily didn't like me and even mocked me last semester. When I'd finally stood up to Rachel when she'd said something really mean, Lily came over and put her arm around my shoulders, and she and other people told Rachel she'd gone too far. Of course I'd still started crying and had to leave the room.

One thing about Harriet that I couldn't forget was how she was quiet about everything she did. She faced far worse than a bully like Rachel, and said very little. She wasn't a speechmaker from what I knew. I stuck with that in the drawing, as she was the same—working behind the scenes, drawing no attention to herself, seeking no glory.

I wanted to be like that. Good for the sake of being good, not for people's admiration.

But I wondered about what we were doing. It wasn't really quiet, was it? Could quiet activism even accomplish anything now? I mean, maybe we were still relatively "quiet" in the way I was thinking about it. We weren't trying to get people to buy stuff from us. We just wanted to get the message out to as many people as possible.

I was jarred out of these thoughts when Ms. Mangal said, "Okay, everyone, have a seat and we'll get started."

Everyone sat down, and I tried to clear my mind and calm the nerves that had started flickering.

We went around the room and everyone gave me their feedback. It was mostly positive, and Lily said she loved the detail I'd done on Harriet's dress. I was so glad we were friends.

Were we friends? I thought we were, kind of like I'd become friends with a girl in my art class in Emerson even though we were so different. It seemed like shared interests really could bring people together. I was finally starting to see that there were lots of ways to connect with people. You didn't have to be almost the same to get along, like it had been with Sam.

I put the drawing away and met Jacob at the table.

"That drawing really did turn out great," Jacob said. "It worked perfectly because it's exactly the kind of thing she would have done. But I did think of something that we didn't think of before."

I stopped in my tracks, alarmed. "What?"

"She was Black and Hitler was obviously hugely racist. I

mean, we talked all about Jesse Owens and the Olympics and all that, and it still didn't click. Harriet never could have gone under the radar there." Jacob stepped into the hall.

My mouth fell open and I followed him. "Oh, my God, you're right. It ruins the whole thing!"

"No it doesn't," he said. "The drawing was about who she was, the kind of person she was. That still applies. But it is funny that we didn't think of it, because it's so obvious."

It was loud with everyone in the hall, and we had to dodge to the right to avoid a guy rushing toward us.

"Your drawing was largely about how she handled things."

"I guess—I was thinking about that earlier, the way she just did things with no expectation of reward or fame." I was still stressed over his point, but he could be right that it wasn't totally ruined.

"Yeah," he said. "I can't stand show-offs."

"Same. What do you think she'd have thought about all the anti-LGBTQ+ laws?" I had to say it louder than I was really comfortable with. Fortunately, no one looked.

"I don't know. Obviously if she was transported here from her time, she'd probably find the whole concept really weird. But if she'd grown up in modern times, I am sure she would know what is right and what isn't. And what red states are doing is not right."

I nodded as we navigated past a group of kids standing near one of the bathrooms. "Is it weird that I think of her as inspiration for what we're doing on TikTok?"

He looked at me. "Definitely not. We're trying to stand up for what's right, and that's what she did."

"I still can't believe we have so many followers now."

Jacob smiled. "It's crazy, but cool. See you later." He gave me a wave as he headed into his classroom while I continued on to mine.

I was so curious to see where our TikTok would go, and now I was already thinking about my next drawing for class, and also my watercolor for Clee, which I needed to work on tonight, along with the other drawing for her. And physics, oh, my God.

It was a lot. But everything was important to me and I wanted to make it work. Could I keep everything going? I honestly didn't know.

Sunday afternoon, we met for our book group and filmed a video in the OIT library room we'd reserved. We'd spent several Sunday afternoons here with our book club last semester. But instead of talking about the book this time, we ended up talking about more videos. Mack wanted to record one about something one of the state legislatures had done. He hadn't told us what it was. But Jenna also had her laptop, so we were brainstorming and putting things in the spreadsheet.

But then Mack looked at me pointedly and said, "You should do a video about your own journey to coming out as agender."

At first I panicked, as per usual when I thought about being on camera. But surprisingly, that faded quickly. So what if people saw me? I spun my phone on the table. Maybe there were other kids like me out there who would feel better knowing they weren't alone. I actually knew there were. I'd kept myself locked in my room in Emerson, convinced I was a one-of-a-kind freak of the world. But I wasn't. I would love it if I actually helped someone—even just one person. "Maybe," I said, uncertainty still lacing my voice.

Jenna's eyebrows shot up. "Really?" she said.

"Maybe." I stretched the first vowel out, confidence growing as I said it.

Mack and Jacob looked equally surprised.

Mack leaned forward and fiddled with his right earring. "You should do it. It's an important story."

Jacob nodded in support.

But anxiety flared again. My phone slipped out of my hand as I tried to set it on the table. "I don't think I can do it. Not yet."

"That's okay," Jenna said. "You'll be ready one day."

That was a relief. This wasn't going to be a moment of peer pressure. My friends were good people.

It still struck me every time I thought about it—I had a group of friends who were all genuinely nice and liked me. Nobody made me try to feel bad about myself. Nobody was going to take a video of me in an unflattering position and post it online without telling me.

They were all looking at me, so I said, "Yeah. I will."

"Today?" Jenna asked.

"No. No, I mean, maybe." I nodded, all tension, but still certain I wanted to.

"That's awesome!" Jenna said with a huge smile. "Mack's, then yours."

I grimaced, the fear returning.

"We can convert this book club meeting into a TikTok meeting," Mack said. "I think we're all off when it comes to the book."

"I actually didn't finish it," Jacob admitted sheepishly.

"Jacob!" Jenna admonished. "Where are your priorities?"

We all laughed. Even Mack laughed—he seemed to be doing much better.

"I didn't finish it either," I admitted. "It's hard to get everything done." Physics had me so stressed, and it wasn't the only class I had to worry about.

"Maybe we should pause the book club," Jenna said. "We're all so busy. I had to stay up too late to finish last night."

We all nodded, though I felt sad about the book club ending.

"What do you all think of more officially switching to be an LGBTQ+ advocacy account rather than trying to be about BookTok?" Jenna asked.

"I was kind of wondering about that," Jacob said. "I think we need to be kind of focused, right?"

Jenna nodded.

"Yeah," Mack agreed. "I like doing the book stuff, but I care much more about LGBTQ+ rights in general. There's so much happening all the time, we'll never run out of content."

"I'm fine with it," I said. "We can still always talk about specific bills or whatever."

"Yeah, this sounds really good," Jacob said. "Let's work it out on the spreadsheet."

Jenna closed her laptop. "I want to film Mack's video first, and then, Nic, if you definitely want to do yours, we should do that. Then let's start assigning away."

Jenna had a mini-tripod she'd apparently started keeping in her backpack, and she set that up. "Ready?"

Mack nodded and she pointed at him to start.

"Does your school have a litter box for students who identify as cats?" He turned his face slightly to give the camera side-eye. "Mine doesn't either, because *no one's does.*

Some do keep cat litter on hand for use in school shootings, which is a good reminder of where the priorities of far-right politicians are. But last month, a North Dakota state legislator actually spent time—time that North Dakotans are paying for, I should add—trying to make a law that would address problems described in a right-wing urban legend.

"The urban legend holds that schools all over the country have litter boxes out for students who identify as cats. This is not something that has happened anywhere, but they believe it."

I was smiling despite my nerves. This was so dumb.

Mack paused for a moment. "I want people to think about this. A man wasted taxpayers' money to write and introduce a bill outlining punishment for schools that accommodate kids who identify as animals. Or let me break it down even further. A man wasted taxpayers' money to write and introduce a bill outlining punishment for schools that do something that no school has ever done or has any intention of ever doing. This is crazytown."

He kept going. "The litter box bill is tacked onto a bill that requires kids to use the bathroom matching the gender on their birth certificate. Just to be more hateful, it specifically bans kids from using gender-neutral bathrooms if they are available. It's about punishment, not anything else."

I was watching him and fretting about my video, and I suddenly had a feeling of despair wash over me. Things were so bad right now, and it seemed hopeless. It seemed impossible to stop these hateful people.

Mack continued. "There are way better ways legislators could be spending their time. How about working on helping people support all these extra babies they're forcing them to have? Or improving funding for schools? Making sure hungry kids at least get meals at school? Or securing funding to process all those rape kits sitting in storage?"

He was pretty much on fire, and you could see and hear his passion, in such contrast to how he was most of the time now. He must have done a lot of research on this stuff. Would anything I recorded be as good as this? I could be so flat when I was uncomfortable.

I glanced over at Jacob and Jenna, and they were intently watching him, too.

Mack kept going. "If you are eighteen or older, please vote for the good guys. Make sure to register far enough in advance! And if you aren't old enough, please talk to people in your families about voting, and why it matters so much. As long as it's safe for you. I know it isn't safe for everyone."

He looked off to the side, before concluding, "Don't stand by and let these people turn red states into real dystopias."

Jenna stopped filming. "Wow, Mack. I had no idea."

He shrugged. "I thought talking about money might motivate some people. I don't know."

"You sound all politically adult now," I said. I might have been stalling because I was getting really scared. My hands were shaking.

"You do," Jacob said. "How much research did you do?"

"Most of that was from one article, but I fact-checked it all," Mack said while Jenna was fiddling with the recording.

It was almost the now-or-never moment for me. Even though it was so intimidating, I was really thinking I would do it. Maybe even today. Mack didn't feel good, but he was still willing to step up. I should try it out and see if I could speak without being a nervous wreck or going all over the place. See if I could get some passion in there. We could always delete it if it wasn't good.

I could feel my palms getting sweaty. But I needed to be braver in life. "So," I started, my stomach doing a flip.

I looked up and they were all staring at me, which made my face flush. I guessed that had been a loaded "So."

"I think I'm going to try it." My heart swelled with another burst of confidence. I didn't know where it was coming from, but it felt good.

"That's awesome!" Jenna said. "Do you want to do it now?"

I bit my upper lip and stared into the distance. Processing options and consequences. Like lots of people seeing me versus helping someone like me who's stuck alone and uncertain. The benefits outweighed the scary stuff. I nodded.

This felt huge.

Jenna started prepping her phone. "I'm really excited, Nic. But I don't want you to be nervous. We can always re-film parts and edit the crap out of it."

"Okay," I said. I was trying to ignore my doubts and figure out where to start. Then the perfect opening came to me like a lightning strike. It was gold. "Okay. I'm ready."

Jenna nodded. "Go."

I took a breath. "Most people don't know what it's like to feel like you have no gender, so they think it's weird. I get that. Understanding something that's completely out of your experience is hard. But you can learn to understand."

I stopped for a second and took a breath. "Here's the story of how I figured out I'm agender. When I was in fifth grade, the girls in my class formed a girls' club and everyone except me was in it. At the time, it was painful because I had always been told that I was a girl, and I'd never known to question it, but I couldn't pass the real test. Of course, they weren't satisfied with just excluding me—no, they had to mock me at every turn. I started avoiding the bathroom because there would always be someone in there taunting me. There was also a vague sense of physical threat, although nothing ever happened. There was even a bitch teacher named Mrs. Black who said mean shit to me when no other teachers were around. She especially loved to do it when other girls *were* around."

I glanced over at Mack, whose face was pretty neutral, but he gave me a tiny nod, so I kept going. "Over the years, I've been told over and over that I wasn't doing *girl* right. I always felt like a failure, like this one thing that seemed so easy for everyone else I simply couldn't do—you know, just *existing* in the right way. I tried conforming, even though it made me so uncomfortable, because all the adults told me it was my fault I was being bullied—for not trying, not conforming."

I looked up, remembering this one stupid day. I closed my eyes for a second, remembering the humiliation. "I wore a skirt once in middle school, but people mocked me for it and I spent the whole day wishing I had something else— anything—to change into. I'd felt so wrong all day in the skirt that there was no way I could wear it again, especially not when it drew even more attention to the way I was failing at being a girl. Which felt like I was failing at being a human, because I obviously wasn't a boy, so that meant I had to be a girl. Just a defective one."

I looked at Jenna. "Can we stop for a second?"

"Definitely," she said with an encouraging smile. "Nic, you're doing great. If you're nervous, I can't really tell."

"Really?" I asked.

Mack and Jacob nodded, and Jacob said, "It's true. It's flowing well."

"Okay." I looked at Jenna and when she nodded, I

started again. "One other thing that started happening in middle school was that people started calling me a lesbian. This added to my confusion, because I actually liked boys and not girls." I blushed and looked away for a second. "But it also pissed me off, because if I was a lesbian, why would that be a problem? Oh, because we're in small-town Oklahoma, that's why. But it was confusing."

I paused, looking at the ceiling and gathering my thoughts. "Some girls I knew through my parents somehow convinced me I needed a makeover—they promised it would be natural. Let's just say, it wasn't natural, and I completely freaked out because it was so wrong on me. I *hated* it. Like, I don't think I've ever hated anything as much as I hated that feeling of all this makeup all over my face—but that didn't stop them from posting pictures, and me getting mocked at school again for it. It was final proof that, even though everyone told me it was my fault I was an outcast, and my life would be better if I would just conform, they were wrong. Even when I conformed to a female look, I was laughed at, because everybody knew it was wrong. I wasn't a girl so I couldn't do *girl*, no matter how hard I tried."

I glanced around the room and took a short breather.

"Do you want me to stop for a sec?" Jenna asked.

"Sure."

"You're still doing great," Mack said.

I nodded. "Thanks." People were walking by the room, visible through the glass. There was a whole ugly world out there that we were currently safe from. I told Jenna I was ready and started again.

"After that incident, I spent some time googling, and this is when I learned that the gender binary is a myth. I don't know how I missed this message before, but I did, so my mind was blown. But I still wasn't sure what to do. I glommed on to the term gender nonconforming, but I didn't tell anyone, because I knew if I did, I'd be bullied even more. Obviously, using they/them pronouns was out of the question."

Mack nodded in understanding.

I kept going, feeling both emboldened and surprised at how much I was telling the world. "But then I came to this boarding school, and everything changed. It's in the suburbs of Oklahoma City, which isn't quite as red as my small town was. And even though it was scary, I finally admitted that I was agender and asked my friends and family to start using they/them pronouns for me. It was so weird how much better I felt after this. For the first time in my life, I felt like my body was mine, like I wasn't just inherently wrong or a big mistake by the universe. I'd always known I didn't match with my body, but I'd assumed it was because there was something wrong with *me*. But recognizing I was agender meant I realized that there was something wrong with my *body*, not me. It was a huge weight off, and a lot of the constant negative intrusive thoughts stopped coming."

Mack frowned at that, and Jenna's lips were pursed. They and Jacob all knew what it was like to be different. It was so nice to have people around me who understood.

"It's not been perfect," I continued. "There are still some people who won't respect my pronouns, and the school has been pretty horrible, but how I feel inside is like a real human now. At the beginning of the semester, I got permission to move out of the girls' side of the dorm and got a room in the neutral downstairs. It was such a relief. For the first time in my life, I actually felt *good*. I didn't dread every day, because I was no longer being made to feel wrong constantly."

I gave a bitter laugh and saw Jacob shake his head

slightly. "At least until they took my room away and made me and my friend, who's a trans boy, move into a room on the girls' side of the dorm. This is a nightmare because we don't belong there and a lot of the girls are shitty to us whenever we're in the bathroom. We both avoid it as much as possible. I'm dehydrated half the time because I never drink water so I won't have to use the bathroom. I'm back to dreading things every day again, and for what? So some bigoted assholes on the school's Board of Trustees can get off on their sadistic desires to hurt people who aren't cis? It's stupid. This situation is not right for anybody."

It was time to wrap this up, as I was running out of steam. "Can we stop for a second. I don't know how to end it."

Jenna set her phone down. "I think the story is good. But you need to ask people to share this message."

Mack nodded. "And to stop enabling these hateful people, whether they're politicians or in other positions of power."

"Okay," I said. "Let me think for a second."

Jacob gave me another encouraging smile.

"I'm ready."

Jenna started filming again.

"So I'm asking everyone, whether you're old enough to vote or not, please share my story so more people can understand that we are people too, and it's not just a phase. We're not doing this for attention, or to embarrass you, or anything like that. We're doing it because it's the right thing to do. And stop letting people abuse their positions of power to hunt down trans kids instead of doing what they're supposed to do, as in help citizens." I gave what was intended to be a sign-off nod.

"That was great!" Jenna said. "I'm so proud of you. I'll get it edited."

"Yeah, Nic, that was good," Jacob said. "Does it feel good to tell your story?"

I was blushing from the praise. "It's okay. I guess it will be a bigger deal once it's actually posted."

"Good job, Nic," Mack said, pulling his black fleece off the back of his chair. "Are you all ready for dinner?"

That was a rather abrupt topic change. I wondered if my story had triggered him.

"Definitely," Jenna answered. She laughed. "You and your light jackets, Mack."

"There is a reason I don't ever wear a heavy jacket," he said, sounding a tad annoyed.

We all looked at him, curious.

"It's because I bind. It gets hot." He stood up and slipped his arms into the sleeves.

"Oh, I never would have thought of that," Jenna said.

Now I felt bad about teasing him for it. I should have realized.

It was an awkward moment until Jacob did a dramatic clap, said, "Ready?!" and gave me smirky glance. "Let's go."

I laughed and Jenna looked at us, curious.

"Ms. Mangal claps a lot in class, to punctuate points and stuff," I said.

"Ah," Jenna said. "She seems great."

"She is. She's the best." She really was. Not only did I have great friends, but I had a supportive teacher to counter the physics teacher who didn't like me.

We packed up our stuff. I watched Mack. He was waiting impatiently by the door. I wondered which thing had him stressed—my story, or getting teased about his jacket.

My own sense of accomplishment was already fading.

I was guessing that telling your story only feels good for a while, and then you have to get back to shitty reality. We were still sharing a room, after all.

Wednesday morning I rolled into physics class, a bundle of nerves because we had our first test. Dr. Jones glanced at me as I walked through the door but then looked away. No encouragement from her. Just straight-up disapproval.

Apparently I was early, because no one was here yet. I checked the time on my phone. Yep. Five more minutes, and I was stuck in the room with a woman who hated me. I really didn't know what her problem was. Why did she care what I looked like or what nickname I used? I took my customary seat.

One of the other students came in and sat in the front, receiving a smile from Dr. Jones. He was wearing shorts because it was supposed to be unusually warm today. I'd seen several kids in the hall wearing them. Then I heard voices and looked up to see Tiana and Jacob walk in together—and of course he had on jeans. I really wondered if I'd ever see him in shorts.

But while all that random stuff was going through my head, I saw Dr. Jones look at them too, and this dark expression passed over her face, just like it had with me.

Wait a minute. How could she not love Tiana? I thought back and realized she'd never really engaged much with Tiana. Normally, when a student was so obviously great, the teacher would talk to them more. Like a teacher's pet, but not necessarily with the negative connotation. I'd seen this both here in other classes and back at Emerson High. So what was up with this?

Oh, my God—was Dr. Jones a racist, too? Was that what it was?

Tiana went to sit in her regular seat while Jacob came back and sat next to me.

I was sure my face revealed my shock because he gave me a funny look.

In the corner of a notebook page, I wrote, *Is she a racist?* and showed it to him.

Now it was his turn to look surprised. *How did you know?* he wrote under mine.

She gave you two the same look she always gives me, I wrote.

He nodded and looked back at his stack of notebooks, obviously not interested in talking about it.

This sucked. Tiana should get to bask in the glory of being a physics superstar, and instead she was judged not for her abilities, but the body she'd been born into.

I'd actually found out more about her during our tutoring sessions, and she was really interesting. Apparently she'd been good enough at basketball at her old school that she was on the college scholarship track. She'd given that up to come here, where there was no basketball team. Her dad had been pushing her to stick with basketball, but she had an older sister at MIT who'd supported her in choosing physics over basketball. Their mom had actually been a college professor, but she'd died a few years ago. Tiana said she'd really fought her dad, but he'd eventually relented.

Just as I finished that thought, the superstar in question turned around and gave me a big smile and mouthed, *Good luck.*

I smiled and mouthed, *You too*, even though she obviously didn't need it.

Dr. Jones cleared her throat and said, "Everyone face forward. We're going to start."

Tiana's smile dropped and she turned around.

I didn't know how she could maintain such a positive attitude in the face of this hate. The bullying back at Emerson High had had me completely beat down to almost nothing.

But I was so sick of this bullshit. Why was the far right—pure hate—winning?

Dr. Jones passed out the test and we shifted our belongings to make room for it, our calculators, and our elbows.

I closed my eyes and took a deep breath before really looking at the test. Okay, the first question was one I could do. I looked through each of the six pages and they all seemed like things that I had studied, and I knew I should be able to do fine on this test. Six problems, eight minutes each with about five minutes to look back over everything.

I got to work, hoping my initial assessment was right and I wouldn't suddenly forget something in the middle of the test. I felt good about it, but time would tell.

The next day, we were outside on the lawn again, about to film another video. I was obsessing about my video, however, because Jenna was posting it tonight. Just thinking about it made my whole body jittery.

Also, I was going into the world with short spiky hair, and I still wasn't totally used to that. I'd sent Sam a picture of it and she thought it was very cool, but I kept shocking myself by looking in the mirror.

But honestly, I liked it, and I was getting used to it.

I was also frazzled because I'd had another counseling session today, and the guy pissed me off as always, trying to get me to explain why I mistakenly thought I was not a girl. Which was obviously unanswerable, since I wasn't mistaken about it.

We didn't have Sophia's tripod tonight, and Jenna was going to be the one on video, so she handed me her phone.

"Thanks," she said. "I'm going to talk about the hypocrisy over breast enlargement versus care for trans kids."

"Great." I opened up TikTok on her phone and clicked to start a new video and aimed the camera at Jenna. This would be good. "Ready."

She started by talking about how all these red politicians were pretending like they cared about the welfare of kids and claimed they were "protecting" trans kids from evil medical professionals and their own "bad decisions," when it had nothing to do with actual medical reasons, and they disregarded the actual medical facts.

She turned her head for an angled look and the sun glinted off her nose ring. "Trans kids who have gender-affirming care almost never regret their decisions. More people regret having knee or hip replacements than regret gender-affirming care."

Mack nodded in agreement.

That fact was interesting. I know she would have gotten that from a reputable source, but I'd never come across it. It was actually comforting. I had a burst of confidence. My video being out there would be fine.

"But here's the real kicker," Jenna said. "These same very concerned politicians have no qualms whatsoever for teen girls getting breast enhancements. None of them care if the girly-girls go under the knife to get boobier—"

Jacob and I both barked a laugh at the same time, and I jerked forward so I messed up the filming, getting a nice view of the grass.

I stopped recording so we could all finish laughing, as Jenna was cracking up, too. Jacob had his head hanging down, and even Mack was smiling.

"Okay, I'll say that sentence again, so be prepared," Jenna said.

We all nodded, and I got the camera in position and started recording again.

"None of them care if the girly-girls go under the knife to get boobier."

Jacob snorted but Jenna kept going. "But somehow a kid going on a hormone to feel more like they belong in their body is abuse. You cannot seriously argue that breast enlargement is not gender-affirming care, but it's allowed because it's affirming the gender these judgmental chauvinists approve of. Also, the only reason anyone gets breast enlargement is to be more attractive to men, so it's inherently sexual. And it means they might never be able to breastfeed a baby—which you'd think these dinosaur men would dislike, but they're all cool with it because it will make the women hotter. The gender-affirming care that trans and nonbinary minors get has nothing to do with sex."

Who were all these people, trying to tell us how to feel and how to be? I hated them. Maybe my story would help some kid out there stuck in a conservative hellhole. It would have been great for me to know I wasn't crazy when I first started looking into things last year in Emerson.

But thinking about it had my nerves jumping all over the

place again. It would be up tonight, where anybody could see it.

Jenna narrowed her eyes. "Just remember—everything these people say is at best a twist of the truth, and at worst an outright, bald-faced lie. And if you think what I'm saying isn't true, a couple weeks ago, Utah specifically excluded cis breast implants from their trans care ban for youth. They don't mind if cis girls make their boobs bigger—i.e., assert their feminine gender identity.

"It's real. We need to hold them accountable and stop voting for them when they aren't doing work that the people they represent really need, but instead do things for their own hate-filled purposes."

Jenna was right about the importance of what we were doing. I was not going to let myself chicken out.

Jenna continued. "This whole idea that these politicians represent anybody is a joke. Get rid of them and bring someone in who's going to do things that will help people. Go forth and do the right thing."

She was holding a serious face but was done, so I stopped the recording.

"That was really good," Jacob said.

"It was," Mack echoed, but he sounded flat again.

"Do we have more?" Jenna asked.

"Not me," Jacob said.

"Dinner?" Jenna asked.

"Sure," I said. We started heading to the cafeteria and Mack and I felt into step.

"How are you feeling, Mack?" I asked him. "Don't get too caught up in the negativity. I'm not sure it's good for our mental health."

I wasn't going to mention how fretting about my own video wasn't good for my mental health, either.

"I know." He ran his hand through his hair. "It does stress me out. It just seems so important, and we can't wait. I mean, what if Trump gets reelected? I know we don't even know if he's definitely running yet, but I'm not holding out much hope. We've got to have as few as possible of these extreme-right nutcases in office everywhere, or it will be a dystopia overnight."

"Yeah. Then all these idiots who vote for these people will be like, 'Wait, you mean I can't do what I want to do anymore?'"

I was going to be stressing about my video going up for a while. Jenna might post while we were in the cafeteria. My stomach was doing acrobatics now. What would it be doing after Jenna pressed Post?

Friday morning I woke up before my alarm, and then checked my video. We'd posted it at about eight and I'd watched it several times last night with the sound off so I could stare at my hair. Which I definitely liked. But there were already ten thousand views by the time I went to bed at eleven, which was insane.

Now it was sixty thousand. *Eighty thousand*. My stomach dropped and my pulse immediately quickened. Who were all these people looking in the middle of the night?

Well, obviously most of them were not in America. We weren't the only country with problems for LGBTQ people. Some places it was even way worse than here.

"You awake?" Mack asked.

"Yeah." I realized I had a text and saw it was from Sam.

—*OMG, Nic! I'm so proud of you but also just OMG!*— Her text made me smile.

"Did you look?" Mack asked.

"Yep. Crazy." This really was insane.

"You're a superstar." His voice was flat, but there was something in it that told me he was trying to be enthusiastic.

"That's quite an exaggeration." I turned off my alarm.

"I know, I'm kidding. But that's a lot of views. And likes. And new followers. And comments."

I clicked into the video to see the likes—over a thousand. New followers—six thousand! Holy shit. "Mack, I can't believe it."

"Don't look at the comments," he said. "Some of them are really mean. But there are a lot of good ones, too. A lot of people are saying it was also like that for them, and they're struggling in unsupportive places. People are thanking you for sharing, and saying you helped them understand someone in their life."

"If there are bad comments in there, maybe you shouldn't be reading them, either." I was still worried about him.

He laughed, but it was weak. "You're right. I'm just impressed you went through with it. Do you think you'll do more on camera?"

"Maybe? Why not? It wasn't so bad." I sounded a lot braver than I was feeling, but wasn't what I was saying true? Nothing bad had happened so far with our other videos.

Mack's alarm went off.

"Oh, shit. We have to actually get up now." He sounded so tired. "My aunt's going to be here in thirty minutes."

He had his T-shot appointment today. His aunt was picking him up at eleven.

We both got out of bed and started getting our clothes together. After stressful trips to the bathroom, we were both ready for the day.

Mack sighed. "I'm glad it's Friday, but weekends here aren't nearly as chill as they were at home."

Jenna and Jacob had been texting us, and we were all freaking out about the video. But Mack and I got our backpacks ready and walked over to the classroom, splitting up when we got inside.

When I got to physics, Jacob said my name excitedly. "You're famous!"

I flushed. "Famous is an exaggeration."

He laughed. The two other students in there were looking at us, but then more people came in so we talked quietly about it until class got started.

By lunchtime, kids were looking at me in the hall with something like interest. I'd been checking the video all morning, and everything was going up and up. By the time I was in line for today's chicken enchiladas, we had over a quarter of a million views. I was vibrating with energy. I couldn't tell if it was nerves or excitement—probably both.

I got to the table before Jenna, but she was grinning when she sat down across from me. "It's amazing, Nic. You're like our breakthrough star."

"I don't think it's that big a deal." I knew I was blushing again. But holy crap. I wanted to talk to Sam about it. Maybe I could talk to her right after school.

"Now I'm wondering if I should go ahead and post the bush incident video for all of your fans." Jenna winked at me, which made me laugh. I knew she was kidding.

A group of seniors walked by and one of them coughsaid, "Faggot."

I flushed again, assuming it was directed at me, even though it made no sense. They were gone before we could react, but then Jenna actually laughed. "It seems that a lot of them don't know the meaning of the slurs they're tossing around."

Why did everyone think gender and sexuality were the same thing?

Another couple of girls walked by and stared at me, curious.

"So apparently people know about it," I said sardonically as they walked away.

Jenna smiled. "You really are famous, just on the small scale."

I wondered who else knew—did the teachers? What about the administration? I had complained about the school in the video, even though I didn't name it. But it wouldn't be hard to figure out what it was based on the info I shared. Who would the next person to comment be, and would it be good or bad?

Addison and I were sitting together on Saturday, working on the design of our panels. We'd all decided to leave the middle panel—where the knight, dragon, and possibly Lily's energy creature meet—till later. So we were all focusing on the journey at this point.

But I could not focus at all. When Lily and I had walked in this morning, Devin and Addison were both like, "Oh, my God! Your video! And your hair!" Not word for word, but that was the sentiment. They apparently liked both.

The video was up to over eight hundred thousand views and three thousand likes, with almost seven thousand followers.

I was in utter shock.

Lily laughed. "Nic is totally speechless."

I nodded, flushing. This was so weird, and it made me queasy. Theoretically, anyone in the whole world could watch it and know all about me. It was nerve-racking.

But Devin and Addison were very cool about it and didn't hound me, and we all got to work. Briana came in a few minutes late.

Addison and I had one panel fleshed out really well. But we were stuck on the background for the second.

"I like the idea of showing different terrain," Addison said.

"Me too," I started, "but I don't know what. And should we consider what they're doing for the knight?"

"Yeah, I don't know."

We were silent for a while, until her eyes lit up and she said, "What about showing the struggle of the journey, even for a big, strong dragon? Like maybe it has to find shelter in the rain or something."

"Oh, I like that. Like it can't find a cave."

We laughed, but then we were off, brainstorming different obstacles a dragon could face on a long journey.

After a while, and a good but short list, it was my turn to talk to Clee. Addison was going to work on thumbnailing the backgrounds.

I grabbed my ink drawing and watercolor for the week, and headed back. Stopping for just a second to check TikTok.

It had close to nine hundred thousand views right now. I carefully avoided the comments. But holy crap. I felt weirdly giddy and nervous at the same time, but giddy was what was winning on my face because I had a huge grin when I walked into Clee's space.

"What's so amazing?" she asked, smiling.

"Oh, um." I scratched the back of my neck. "Uh, so my

friends and I have a TikTok, and a video I did has a lot of views."

"That's really nice. What's it about?"

I looked down. "My, uh, trouble with my body, I guess. My gender. And how my friend, a trans boy, and I originally had our own rooms downstairs, but they made us move into a room together on the girls' side of the dorm, when neither of us is a girl. I talked about that some."

"That's rough. That's a great story to get out there, to help people understand. And you've gone viral?"

"I'm not sure what counts as viral," I said with uncertainty. But a million views probably did count, and we weren't far off.

She motioned to the chair next to her and I sat down, setting my work on the table.

"Yeah, I don't know, either. I've just started on Instagram, because I have to be. It's one of the best platforms for artists. But I'm lucky if I get a hundred likes." She laughed.

"Yeah, I'm not sure what happened with us. Something."

"Well, congratulations. But let's get started." She picked up the watercolor, which was on top. This was a small bowl of fruit, with a banana, green apple, and a slice of watermelon.

She studied it, nodding.

The yellow of the banana looked pretty good, although the spots were too black, not brown enough.

"The apple looks really good," she said. I love how you captured the lighter color underneath the brightness of the darker green. It's really nice." She had some other comments, and funnily enough she had the exact same assessment of the banana as I did.

It was probably a good sign when I could recognize my mistakes, because then I wouldn't make them again. The brown spots on any banana I might paint in the future would be suitably brown.

Not that I would ever paint another banana. They weren't the food of dragons.

"I love the sense of pending action in this piece," Clee said about the ink drawing. It showed the first hatchling in a nest trying to figure out what was going on amongst all the other, unhatched eggs. The tiny dragon looked confused, but one of the eggs in the front of the drawing had a crack with some small talons poking out and an eye visible, and some of the other eggs had cracks running along their sides.

She continued, "It makes me think that any second now, the front egg is going to crack open, and then all the rest are going to burst open at once and the baby is not going to be alone anymore."

I smiled. "That's what I was thinking when I was drawing it."

"Great. Do you have any questions about either of these pieces or techniques?"

I shook my head. "Nothing specific right now."

"Okay, then. I have some things I wanted to talk about for both your ink work and your watercolor." She delved into some new techniques, and I spent the rest of the time with her absorbing all this amazing information.

Afterward, I checked TikTok on the way back to the back room. We were less than two hundred thousand away from a million. It seemed like there was no way we wouldn't hit a million.

How had I been part of this? It was unreal.

Briana and Devin were talking quietly at their table, and the other two were working away. I couldn't believe I'd been lucky enough to get accepted to this mentorship. They were all better than I was, but I was starting to feel like I was good enough to mix with them.

I sat down across from Addison and she looked up and smiled, which reminded me of how judgmental I used to be. Last year, I would have dismissed her as too normal, like that was automatically a bad thing. It was no wonder Mom used to call me Negative Nic a couple years ago. She stopped when she saw how upset it made me, but she wasn't totally wrong.

Even with the room-sharing situation being pretty bad, overall my life was so much better here. Could it stay this way?

My friends and I were all coming back to the dorm after dinner at the cafeteria Sunday night, with Sophia in tow. We'd passed a million views last night, but it had definitely slowed down. But Jenna had also posted Mack's newest video last night, and it now had over three hundred thousand views. Sophia was excited for us.

Mack and Jacob were up ahead while Sophia, Jenna, and I were talking about physics—I was still waiting for my test grade. Still nervous.

"When I first got here, I thought I wouldn't care about physics since I'm all about biology," Sophia said. "But now I've learned there are all these different fields that combine different major fields, like biophysics, and now I figure I should learn everything because you never know what might be interesting."

"I think it's a matter of trying to get everything you can out of opportunities," I said, feeling strangely wise. "I never thought I'd come to a math and science school and have art

teachers who would help me develop skills that will supposedly make going to art school an easy transition."

"You're lucky," Jenna said as we passed a row of cars. "I
haven't really found anything particularly revolutionary
here."

"That's because you're from Oklahoma City," I
explained. "We're both from Podunk towns. Things are
completely different there."

"Yeah, I totally didn't appreciate that," Sophia said,
sounding sheepish. "I had no idea how limited the view
from home was. I really debated coming here because I
didn't want to leave my boyfriend, but I'm so glad I came.
I've largely outgrown him, anyway."

"I wondered why you haven't been going home every
weekend," I said. I'd seen her on two different weekends
lately, whereas before she would cut out after classes Friday
and come back right before study time on Sunday night.

We stepped onto the curb near the dorm.

"That's why," she said, cocking her head. "He's just ...
ignorant. He makes jokes about gay people all the time, even
though he doesn't actually have a problem with them. His
cousin is gay and they get along really well, and he's never
said anything specific about his cousin. But he says stuff like
his friends say. It just ... makes me think less of him."

Jenna nodded as we crossed the lawn. "My mom's new
boyfriend is very vocal about what he doesn't like about gay
people. Which is apparently everything. I'm glad I'm not out
with her. But I hate hearing it so much." She paused for a
second, sighing big. "I don't know why she puts up with it.
She doesn't think like that, either. Or she didn't. But I'm
afraid she's going to turn the same way as him. I never
thought my mom and I wouldn't be close, but now I'm not
sure."

"I'm sorry, Jenna," Sophia said. "I went through something similar with my mom. She used to be pretty ... I don't know ... kind, I guess? Like she didn't say horrible things about poor people, or you know, other races. But then she got with her current boyfriend. She totally changed. It's another reason for me to not go home. He's always given me the creeps, anyway."

I guessed I was really lucky. "That sucks."

They both said, "Yeah," and we went quiet.

Mack and Jacob were waiting for us in front of the dorm door, still going on about their comics. Mack opened the door and held it for us, but he was staring inside, eyes narrowed.

There was a man standing at the front desk, talking to Ms. Patton. His back was to us, but he was saying something about making sure she got it taken care of immediately. She spotted us and quickly looked away, which was odd.

After we were all through the foyer, Mack made a beeline for the stairs without saying anything to us, and disappeared up them.

"What happened?" Jenna asked, looking after him. Sophia and Jacob looked equally confused.

"I don't know," I said, but I looked at the man's back. He had on a bomber jacket but there was nothing else really notable about him, except that he was obviously an asshole because he was still going on to Ms. Patton about her responsibility.

Something bad was happening, or was about to happen. My heart was racing and my mind was buzzing. We all looked at each other with grim faces, and Jacob whispered, "Text me if you figure anything out," and headed off to the boys' side of the dorm, and Jenna, Sophia, and I quickly retreated up the stairs.

Without saying anything, we all just headed to my room.

When I opened the door, Mack was sitting in his desk chair, computer on his lap, and said, "Oh, my God! That's Rachel's dad! He's on the Board of Trustees—he's the reason we got thrown in here, Nic, and what's he trying to do now?"

"Are you serious?" I asked. My heart hadn't slowed down and now I was feeling really queasy.

Sophia and Jenna stepped in and shut the door.

"I looked up the board after we got kicked out, but it still had last year's board members listed," Mack explained, more animated than I'd seen him in a while. "But when I checked it just now, they've updated it since then, and he's on there now."

"Um, what's up with Rachel's dad?" Sophia asked.

Mack fell back into his chair, his hand on his forehead.

I looked at Sophia. "It's a long story that starts long before OAMS, but he has it out for Mack because he doesn't approve of him being who he is."

Sophia nodded, at least understanding enough to know that this was all very bad.

"Do you think it's about us?" Mack asked, all nervous energy.

"Ms. Patton gave me a look when we were downstairs that was ... not positive," Jenna said. "I have a bad feeling."

I felt queasy, right in line with Jenna's bad feeling. I was wondering if it had to do with our TikToks. I glanced around and everyone was looking down, faces all serious. I guessed that they were thinking the same thing.

"I'm going to go back to my room," Jenna said. "I'll text Jacob."

"Yeah, I'm going to go, too," Sophia said. She followed Jenna out the door.

I didn't blame them for wanting to get out of there. This

was bad in some way, but we didn't know how yet. My pulse was still up and my stomach was still roiling.

Once they were gone, Mack and I looked at each other. He had that haunted look back. Just then, his phone rang.

"Hello?" he answered.

"Fine," he said, not sounding fine at all. "Did you hear something?"

I knew I shouldn't stare at him, so I went to my desk, but couldn't help but listen. It wasn't any of my business, but I was curious and it was distracting me from all the nervous crap my body was doing.

"Mom, no. It can't be. Why?"

He was quiet for a while, but my heart was still going hard. I was so nervous. I stared at the portfolio at the back of my desk, propped up against the wall.

"Okay," he finally said. "I'll tell them. I love you."

Was I the "them" there? What was this about?

"Nic, they said we're not getting our rooms back."

Shocked, I turned around to face him. I couldn't say anything, but he looked like he might cry, even though he wasn't looking at me.

He shook his head, looking beat down, with a frown and downcast eyes. "You know how your mom has been working with mine? There's basically nothing else they can try."

I knew they'd been talking to the school regularly, but I thought it would work. I also wanted to cry, but it was partially because he was so upset by this.

"Why, Nic? Why are these people out for blood?"

I shook my head. I had no idea.

My phone dinged with a text.

"Your mom?" Mack asked.

I nodded. She was telling me the same thing, and how sorry she was. She asked if I wanted to talk, but I said no.

Mack ran his hand through his hair. We were both hunched over.

"I guess we just have to wait now to see if there is more bad shit to happen to us," Mack said.

He wasn't wrong. Bitter dread filled my stomach. What else would the hateful world throw at us?

The four of us stood outside Ms. Patton's room after school the next day. We'd all dropped our backpacks off in our rooms and gone straight down there. We'd all been ordered to come here.

"I don't want to go in there," Jenna mouthed while we all looked at each other. Then I looked down. That stupid industrial gray carpet.

"But one of our videos hit a million views, you all," she whispered. I shook my head. We still had no idea how this was really happening.

The day had started off good, because I got my physics test back and I'd made an 87. For the first few seconds after that I'd felt happy, but then the dread from Rachel's dad's appearance last night rolled back in.

The rest of the morning had dragged on, and then Ms. Patton found Jenna and me in the cafeteria at lunch and told us to see her directly after school. We spent the rest of lunch trying to guess what it was about, and I continued down that road for the rest of the day. I got some smirky looks from Rachel in art, and I kept coming back to TikTok, but I didn't know what about it would come up.

So we were still standing in the hall in front of her door. Before any of us could actually do anything, her door swung open and she seemed unsurprised to see us. Her face was grim. She had her hair back in a ponytail and didn't have much makeup on, unlike normal.

Ms. Patton stood to the side. Jenna went in first, then Jacob, and then Mack and I almost ran into each other in the doorway. Neither of us cracked a smile, and he motioned for me to go first.

Ms. Patton shut the door and went to stand in front of the TV, facing the couch. "Have a seat."

We awkwardly moved toward the couch and shuffled around. I ended up in an armchair and the others filled the couch. This was definitely a déjà vu moment, and I glanced at Mack, who met my gaze. This was already horrible.

"I'll just cut to the chase, guys," Ms. Patton said. "You need to stop posting your TikTok videos."

She looked tired and sighed, her gaze on the wall over our heads.

"Is this coming from the Board of Trustees again?" Mack asked, not hiding the disgust in his voice.

"Yes, it is. But you aren't supposed to be using TikTok at all." She looked at him.

"The Oklahoma government does not own the cellular networks," Jenna cut in, her voice sharp. "And freedom of speech still applies to students, since we're American citizens, too."

I'd never seen Jenna like this. She was so pissed.

I looked over at Jacob, who was as quiet as me. His hands were clasped in his lap and he was staring at them. Shy people did not generally shine in moments of interpersonal conflict.

But I didn't want to be that way anymore.

"What happens if we don't stop?" I asked, my voice shaking, but I got all the words out.

Ms. Patton looked at me. "Nic, you know there will be consequences. Don't fight this."

Mack pushed back. "What are those consequences?"

Ms. Patton tented her hands in front of her face. "It would be in all of your interests to follow these rules. You don't want to jeopardize your education. It's simply not worth it."

"This is utter B.S.," Jenna said, abruptly getting up and walking out of the room. The rest of us stared at the door after she left, even Ms. Patton.

"That's really all I have to tell you," she said, sounding resigned. "You can get on with your day."

There was nothing else to say. We got up and left. Jenna was nowhere to be seen in the hall.

"I'm going for a walk," Mack said.

Jacob put his fingers to his forehead. "I'm going to ... do something."

That made me laugh inside, but nobody smiled.

Then the two of them took off in different directions, and I decided to go check Jenna's room to see if she was okay.

The whole walk up the stairs and down the hall to her room, I got increasingly queasy. I didn't know what to feel. I was pissed, and I was scared, but mostly I just felt beat down. Why were the bad guys always winning here?

When I knocked on her door, she said, "Come in," so I did.

She was lying on her bed, knees bent and arms above her head.

Jenna barely glanced at me. "I have never been this angry, Nic. I don't know why. Lots of horrible things have happened, but this is just not okay. I'm not going to stop. The rest of you can, but I'm keeping it going."

I was standing awkwardly in the middle of her room. I felt what she was saying, but the fear was prominent, too.

"Do you think they would kick us out?" I asked.

"I don't know. But I really do think this is an issue of freedom of speech. Students still have rights. They could probably forbid us from recording in the dorm or classroom building, but can they forbid it across the whole OIT campus?"

I really didn't know. Our school was kind of odd, being on the corner of a college even though it was a separate entity. But OIT was a public school so the ban on TikTok was in effect on its Wi-Fi network, too. They couldn't stop people from getting on the cell networks, though, so people everywhere still used it.

But really, the TikTok ban had nothing to do with our situation.

"Are you with me?" Jenna asked, all intense. "You can sit down."

"I don't know, Jenna." I got her desk chair and pulled it closer to her bed, then sat. "I have to admit, I'm scared. I'm not normally someone who gets in trouble or fights authority."

"But you *are*," she said, turning her head to face me. "You are fighting a much bigger authority than some high school's Board of Trustees."

I nodded. She was right, but the stakes were different.

She closed her eyes and sighed. "It's not *right*, Nic."

"I know. But I can't go back to Emerson. My life was terrible there. It's good here." Here I was, on the verge of tears, though Jenna didn't know since her eyes were still closed.

It was a little odd that I was talking about how much better my life was here than in Emerson, yet it wasn't the first time I'd cried over the way I'd been treated here. I still preferred OAMS to Emerson.

"I think I need to be alone, Nic," she said. "I'm sorry. I'm not mad at you, just the world."

"It's okay." I stood up and dragged her chair back to her desk. "This is really fucked up."

"Yeah." She wasn't looking at me. "I'm going to skip dinner."

"Okay." I left and walked slowly down the hall and stairs. I really was in shock. I wanted to be brave, but I didn't want to ruin my life. But I also didn't want to roll over and let the biggest bullies I'd ever encountered win.

As I opened the door to my floor, I remembered something I'd done back at Emerson. I was just constantly teased and mocked there. People were forever doing their level best to make me feel like a loser.

One day I was minding my own business, reading in a restaurant while I was eating my sandwich, and these two assholes from school came in and started making a big scene, saying "Is it a girl or a boy?" They asked each other and the only other person in there, the woman making sandwiches. And then one of the guys said, "I'll find out," and put his tray on the table right next to me, even though the place was otherwise empty. He went to fill his cup at the Coke machine behind me, then intentionally spilled some of it right next to me, and it was *so obvious* that he was trying to get me to look up so he could see my chest, and I just lost my mind.

I stood up and threw my drink in his face and said, "Did you figure it out, you stupid fuck?" And then I ran out of there as fast as I could.

When I'd gotten home, I sat there going, uhhh. But it had felt so good to have fought back. I hadn't rolled over and taken it. That stupid kid's shocked face was permanently etched in my mind as a life win. He hadn't been used to the "losers" responding instead of shrinking to nothing.

I got to the end of the hall in the dorm and unlocked the door, wondering if Mack would be in there. Nope. The room was empty.

He was probably going to be on his walk for a while. It was a coping mechanism for him.

I fell onto my bunk, finding myself in the same position Jenna was in. It seemed a good thinking position.

With the Coke incident, I think my therapist thought it was funny, though she did try to stay professional. But she also thought it was good that I stood up for myself, even though we both knew that doing something physical was not the best thing.

I closed my eyes and tried to think about the current situation. If I didn't fight back, I would always feel like that wimpy loser who let people walk all over them.

But there were real consequences.

I needed to find out what rights we really did have. People were always throwing around the phrase "freedom of speech," but I really had no idea what that truly meant. Even the word freedom on its own had somewhat lost its meaning with the way the far right used it. *We will fight for the freedom to take away all your personal freedom!*

But freedom of speech was in the Constitution. Or an amendment. I couldn't remember. But it really did have legal meaning. And even though we were minors and students at a public school, we still had rights. Just like Jenna had said.

I would start fighting back by understanding the situation, options, and possible consequences first. Google, here I come.

My group and I got to the cafeteria the next day for dinner and split up to get food, then meet back at our regular spot. I headed off to the stir-fry station. I grabbed a plate and started working my way down the line, piling on vegetables and some chicken.

We were all still reeling from yesterday's mandate, but we also were planning to have a serious talk once we were at the table. We'd all done research and were going to come up with a plan.

I stirred the onions in the wok and dropped in the chicken, spreading that around.

I guessed we'd all looked up the same thing, trying to figure out if we did have freedom of speech in this case. And it seemed we did. But of course the school wouldn't honor that, so it might be a fight. I dropped the rest of the veggies into the wok.

Tonight was about figuring out if posting more videos was worth the risk, and how to go about doing it.

I poured some hoisin sauce into the wok to finish up, breathing in the delicious smell as I got everything onto my plate.

The only good thing happening right now.

I was the last to arrive at the table.

"Okay, good, you're here," Jenna said.

I nodded and sat down.

"So, as you all know, I am super pissed." Jenna's voice was strong and bold. "The First Amendment absolutely gives us the right to make TikToks, even though we're students. We just can't do anything that would disrupt school, bully or harass, or interfere with other students' rights. They really can't do anything if we are off campus."

"Do you think 'campus' refers only to the OAMS buildings, or all of OIT?" Jacob asked.

I took a bite of my stir-fry. It was really good.

"If it includes all of OIT, we can go to the public library," Jenna said.

"If they still let us off campus," Mack pointed out.

Jenna exhaled heavily. "Yeah."

"It would be obvious discrimination if they didn't let us off campus," Jacob said.

"Yep, which won't necessarily stop them," Jenna pointed out.

I didn't have much to add here. I'd found the same info Jenna had. So I kept eating while they discussed things. But the tension was still building in my chest.

"You've been awfully quiet, Nic," Jenna said.

I put my fork down. "No, I agree with you. And you obviously have a handle on everything. I think we read the same websites."

"Okay," she answered. "So I guess what it comes down to is whether or not we are willing to take the risk of continuing."

"The elephant in the room is what the risk actually is," Mack said matter-of-factly. "Which I think we all can agree is probably getting kicked out."

We were all quiet. I didn't want to have to go back to Emerson. But I also didn't want to be a person who wouldn't fight for what's right.

"I'm in," I said, surprising everyone by going first, including myself.

"Me, too," Jenna said

Now I felt queasy. I was risking everything. And it wasn't just having to go back to Emerson. It was also my mentorship.

"But what if we really lose?" Jacob asked. "You already lost your rooms, even though you were right and they were wrong. They took away your access to the staff bathrooms. Right doesn't always win. I really don't want to go back to my old school."

"It's a real risk," Jenna said gravely. "I think if we pushed back, the bad publicity might make them back off. But I don't know for sure."

"And we might miss school while it was being sorted out," Mack said.

We all nodded, and I wondered if me being in was a mistake.

"You guys don't have to do it," Jenna said. "I won't be mad at you, or lose respect, or anything. It's up to you."

Jacob nodded and took a bite of his salad while Mack stared at an empty plate. He must not have gotten much food, because I didn't even really see him eating.

Jenna looked at Mack. "I think in some ways, you have the most to lose, because it's your senior year."

"Yeah, I was thinking of that." He frowned. "But we always let the bullies win. I don't want to do that."

Jacob nodded, still working on his salad.

"So I think I'm in," Mack said.

We all looked at Jacob. It was stressful looking at him, knowing how stressed he was about this decision.

"Hey, we shouldn't all stare at him," Jenna said. "This shouldn't be a peer pressure thing. It's okay to not join us, Jacob."

Jacob closed his eyes and swallowed. "Okay. I'm in. If you all are going to do it, then I want to be with you."

I'd thought Jenna might smile, but she didn't. She looked serious and said, "I'm thinking maybe we should only film off campus. That is one part of the law—schools have even less right to punish students for things done outside of school grounds and time."

"That makes sense, and makes me feel better," Jacob said.

"We need to make it obvious where we're filming," Mack said. "And we have to be really careful to let the front desk know when we're going off campus. No more just going."

We all nodded. We had to be really careful about everything.

"When should we start back up?" I asked.

"Let's give it a few days so they think we've complied," Jenna said. "I say Saturday."

"I agree," Mack said.

Jenna looked at Jacob and me and we both nodded in response.

"It's a plan," she said. "I was also thinking, and this affects you too, Jacob, that going high-profile like this kind of makes it obvious that I'm not straight and cis. Well, I am cis, but I'm not straight. I think I have to be out. Does it seem that way to you, Jacob?"

He nodded. "It's kind of like, we were the odd ones out. I think I'm okay with coming out as part of a good cause."

"I'm not sure you two really have to be out," Mack said. "You could just be allies."

"I don't think we necessarily have to explicitly come out," Jenna said. "But I think by being on these videos, it's kind of … implied."

"I think her point is that we risk being assumed to be queer," Jacob said. "So we need to be comfortable with that, even if we never say what makes us queer."

"Exactly. And I'm willing to do it." She put her fist out toward Jacob, and he fist-bumped it. "Should the return video be about them trying to ban us?"

Jacob laughed. "That will piss them off."

"True," Jenna said. "But we can address the fact that they can't legally stop us in the video."

"I think it makes sense," I said. Even though it was terrifying. This whole thing was so far out of my comfort zone, but it was also exciting because I was doing something important. If you didn't fight back, the bad guys would always win.

"Okay, we'll wait until Saturday," Jenna said. "And then we're back. We'll see what they do next."

Yes, we would have to wait and see.

I was working in the art studio again Friday night. I had to get both my watercolor and ink drawings done for the mentorship tomorrow, and I wanted to work on the one for class, too, but I didn't think I'd have time.

Jenna had been sending her funny memes like she was prone to do Friday nights, so I'd muted my phone so I could focus.

I'd applied some paint to the flower piece and was waiting for it to dry, so meanwhile I was inking the drawing, which was actually an ocean scene, and it didn't look great. Clee wanted me to try water, and I clearly had a lot to learn. But it wasn't all bad, and I had some specific questions for her tomorrow, so she could help me figure out why some parts worked, and how to fix the others. I was going to ask her if I could redo this scene as my ink piece for next week. Next week was going to be busy because I had to write a paper for English.

But this one had been a long week. We were approaching a million and a half views on my video yesterday, and Mack's views were going up, too. Several of our others were getting a lot of views. We were really confused. Our content was fine, but to get these kinds of numbers was actually weird. Not that we were complaining.

We'd also realized it was weird that Ms. Patton hadn't told us to shut the account down, so we'd made the account private for the time being.

But we hadn't made any videos, like we'd agreed. We'd decided to do some on Sunday because that was the next time we could get a room at the public library reserved. We were going to be talking about them banning us, and how we actually still had the right to make the videos and they couldn't stop or punish us. Even though the account was private now, we had a lot of followers—eight thousand at this point. But if we wanted real views, we'd have to take the account off private.

I looked back at my drawing, which had a small boat on the right side. I was working on that, trying to get the right lines on the paper. So much of art was suggesting things with carefully placed lines rather than actually putting ink down everywhere.

TikTok was completely different from that, at least for us. We couldn't hint at things—we had to come out and say the bad parts out loud, because most people weren't paying any attention as this whole country descended into hell. We had to make things completely clear.

I checked the flower painting, and it looked dry. I was having to put a lot of different layers down on the petals to get the subtle changes in light, but it needed to dry in between layers. I put down some more soft gray on the white petals, which were starting to actually look good. I'd never done a flower before, so I was surprised at how decent it looked.

Life was so weird right now. My friends and I were famous in a small way, I was learning so much about art, getting better every week, and I was doing decent in physics and all my other classes. Chemistry was getting harder, but I was staying on top of it. So much was going on. I honestly didn't know what to think. Could things stay like this?

I'd just have to wait and see.

Tuesday evening we were at dinner. We were fairly quiet because we were all thinking about what to do next after Jenna asked us what we wanted to do about TikTok.

Sunday afternoon, we'd trekked to the public library and recorded two videos.

The first video was all four of us talking about being told to stop posting to TikTok. It wasn't very interesting, just matter-of-fact information about what had happened. We did also talk about why we decided to continue posting, after looking up the laws on it.

After that, we recorded Mack talking about the state of anti-trans legislation across the country right now. The Substack he followed periodically published a color-coded map that showed which were the worst and best states for LGBTQ people. One had come out last week, so he was working off that, going through activity in the worst states— Oklahoma was one of the states in the darkest red, like always.

We had posted those videos, the first Sunday and the second on Monday. But we'd cheated by putting the account on private.

At dinner, Jenna asked. "What do you think we should do now?"

I wadded up my napkin and dropped it on my plate. "Everything is terrible." I sighed. It really was. I didn't want to do nothing. "I think we should take our account off private."

Everybody stared at the table. Basically, we'd wimped out, despite the big deal we'd all made last week about keeping going.

Even Jenna had chickened out, and she wasn't the first one speaking up this time.

"You know," Jacob started, "we're telling people they need to get out and fight. I mean, that doesn't necessarily mean risking something. Voting the right way isn't dangerous, at least not for most people nowadays. But maybe we should lead by example."

I was impressed that that sentiment was coming from Jacob since he'd been the most cautious one so far, and it filled my heart with positive energy. It was like it was charging up.

Jenna nodded. Mack was still looking down.

"I agreed with Jacob," I said. "I think if they do punish us, we can still win. I'm sure it will take a fight. I think my parents will support us."

Jenna nodded again, more emphatically. "I've gotten scared since my burst of anger last week. I'm like you all—I don't want to get kicked out, either. But I also think we can win if we really fight hard. I think my dad will support us. My mom's distracted by her new boyfriend, but she still might come through if necessary."

"My parents would support us," Jacob said. "Although it would stress them out."

"My parents, too," Mack said. "So I'm in."

"Let's do it," Jacob said.

Jenna opened up TikTok and clicked through to our

settings, her finger poised to switch our account to public again. "Ready?"

"Yes," the rest of us said together, like we'd planned it.

She swiped. "It's done." She locked her screen and put the phone on the table.

We all looked at the phone and then at each other across and around the table, and I instinctively knew this was a moment I'd never forget. It would forever be in my mind as the point everything really began.

Thursday I arrived at the counselor's office and was told my session was canceled for today. That was weird, but I didn't think much about it because it meant I could go to art class.

I found Jacob sitting at our table, grinning.

"Did you check recently?" he asked.

"TikTok?" I asked, dropping my bag on the floor and sliding onto my stool.

He nodded, his eyes twinkling from his grin.

I pulled out my phone. Over five hundred thousand views already. "Wow."

The views on our video about the attempted ban were growing by the dozens every minute.

"Did you look at the followers?" he asked.

I quickly checked. Over ninety-six hundred. My eyes widened and I looked at him. "Holy crap. We're going to get there any minute now. Well, any hour."

He wrinkled his nose and emphatically said, "I know. It's crazy."

Lily came in and waved at me before sitting at her front table. I waved back and looked back at Jacob.

"What do you think we should do next?" Jacob asked.

"I have no idea." But then I had one. "Maybe we need to start going through every law that's out there, one at a time. Or a few at a time."

"Yeah." Jacob still looked happy. "We could do a state roundup video, one a day, or something like that."

"Having fun?"

We both turned to see Rachel standing across the table from us. Neither of us said anything, but my good-feeling bubble burst.

"You won't be smiling this time tomorrow," she continued.

We both just looked at her in silence. She hadn't been that horrible at the art club board meeting on Tuesday, but today she obviously had something on her mind.

"You're not going to get away with it." She smirked and went back to her table in the front.

Jacob and I looked at each other, my stomach now in turmoil.

"Okay, so now I'm scared," Jacob said. He wasn't being sarcastic.

"Me, too. Her dad is the root of all evil. She must know something. We should warn Jenna and Mack."

Jacob nodded gravely, typing out a message on our group text.

After he was done, he quietly said, "Doesn't she seem like a one-dimensional villain in a book, though?"

That made me smile, even if it was subdued. He was right. The truth was that after I'd told her off at the end of last semester, she'd become rather inconsequential—until her dad got involved.

Ms. Mangal came in, her colorful mug of tea in hand. She set it down on her desk and clapped her hands to start class. Jacob finished typing and I felt the vibration in my phone from the text coming in.

"Let's keep working on your projects," Ms. Mangal said. "I'll be coming around if you need help with anything."

Jacob and I went to get our projects from our cubbies, not speaking. Our good cheer was gone and all I felt in its place was dread. What was it going to be? And when?

Later that day, we went on to dinner, acting like everything was normal, even though we were all freaking out inside about Rachel's threat.

We'd been fairly quiet during dinner. Jenna finished first and pulled her phone out.

"Oh, my God, you guys! I mean, you all! We're at ninety-nine ninety-nine!"

She put the phone in the center of the table on the profile so we could all see the number of followers. We all stared, rapt.

And then every digit flipped. Ten thousand!

Jenna threw her hands up in the air and cried, "Woo!" while Jacob and I hooted, something I had literally never done before in my entire life. Mack looked happy. I think us deciding to continue on TikTok had really reduced his depression. Maybe because he felt there was purpose.

Then we were all laughing, and people at other tables were staring at us.

"This is incredible," Jenna said. "In less than two months, we went from being a bunch of total noobs to having ten thousand followers and multiple videos with more than a million views. I mean, obviously something really weird happened, but this is huge!"

"I think we can actually change things," Jacob said, eyes still glowing even though his smile had relaxed. "I think it might really work."

"One person at a time," I said.

"I think you all are right," Jenna said. "If we were trying to convert people, they'd say we were doing God's work. But we're not doing it to gain favor with some supernatural being. We're doing the most genuinely noble work there is."

"Fighting for basic human rights," I said.

"Exactly," Mack said.

Jenna had picked her phone up and was looking at the screen. "It's not done going up."

"A hundred thousand followers, here we come," Jacob said.

"Yep," Jenna said. "We just need to keep cranking out the content."

"Nic and I were talking about that today," Jacob said. "They said we should focus on the laws, and I agree." He explained his idea of doing a video for each state and talking about the current laws in those states. Jenna pointed out that we could even cover the states that are passing protective and safe haven laws.

"I think we should," Mack said. "I also saw this thing recently where the Texas attorney general demanded that a hospital in Washington State give them records of minor patients who had received gender-affirming care if they were from Texas—including people who had officially moved to Washington."

My stomach was roiling at this. But Mack wasn't done.

"This is insane for so many reasons," he said, "one of which is that there are federal laws that keep doctors from giving medical information to anyone. It's supposed to keep patients safe. But also, how can anyone not see that we're being hunted? You once lived in Texas so you can never do anything that fascist state doesn't want to let people do?"

"What did the hospital say?" Jenna asked.

"They said, 'Fuck off,'" Mack said.

"Thank God," Jacob said.

"Yeah," Jenna and I said at the same time.

Rachel walked by our table with her friends, loudly saying, "Losers."

And then this amazing thing happened—all four of us said, "Fuck off," at the exact same time.

It made her jerk her head back and look at us. But then she and her fake Christian entourage was gone.

Then Sophia came up behind me and was cracking up. "How did you do that? I was coming to congratulate you, just in time to see that whole thing. That was epic. Your group is like magic."

"I do think we're rather in sync," I said.

"Clearly," Sophia said, still smiling. "So, congratulations on your ten thousand. You all are doing great. And I wanted to also say, I'm sorry for disappearing."

She grimaced. "I feel bad, but I need to keep my distance from your recording. I just can't risk getting kicked out, and I don't know what they'd do here. I simply can't go back to BFE, Oklahoma." She put a hand to her forehead, obviously stressed at the thought.

"It's fine," I said. "You've already helped us a ton. We've all agreed to take the risk, and there's no reason for you to get in trouble." I did feel some disappointment that she wouldn't take a stand with us. She clearly had the option to walk away, whereas the rest of us really didn't.

"Ironically, the reason that I can't go back is partially from meeting you all," Sophia said. "I'd never realized how myopic small towns are. It's just not for me anymore. But seriously, how did you all say that at the same time?"

"The 'Fuck off'?" I asked.

"Yes." Her eyes were wide from curiosity.

I nodded. "Mack was just telling us about a children's hospital in Washington that told the Texas attorney general to fuck off when he asked for records of former Texas patients there, and that was the exact moment she came by."

"I think it's called priming," Jenna said. "That phrase was in all our minds at that exact second."

"Well, it was awesome. Congratulations on being amazing and successful people." She waved. "See you later."

We all said goodbye, and she left.

"That *was* pretty awesome," Jacob said. That got us all laughing.

So we dropped our trays off and left for the dorm, chattering about random stuff, all thoughts of impending badness gone.

But as we approached the last row of cars in the lot, the ones closest to the dorm, Jenna got quiet.

Then she stopped. "That's my mom's car." She pointed at a silver Camry.

That stopped all of us. My pulse started racing. We stared at the car, which was empty.

My phone vibrated in my pocket and I pulled it out. It was from Mom. —*What did you do?*—

"Oh, my God," Jacob said. He was also looking at his phone. "They texted five minutes ago but I didn't hear it."

Mack put his fingers to his forehead and closed his eyes. Then he looked at his phone. It rang in his hand. "Hello?" he answered.

We all stared at his grim face, desperate to know what was being said.

He frowned. "Okay. I will be ready. Bye."

"Yeah, they've suspended us," he said.

No one said anything and we stared at each other in horror.

"I've never gotten in trouble before," Jacob said in a small voice.

"I have," Jenna said. "But for much more legitimate reasons than this."

She was the only one who was local. It wouldn't have taken her mom more than a few minutes to get here. But the rest of our parents had a two-hour drive, and Mack's aunt even more.

"I don't want to go in," I said. The understatement of the year.

"Okay, everyone, look," Jenna said. We all faced her. Mack wiped his eyes. I had never felt heavier dread than what had amassed in my stomach. I was on the verge of throwing up.

Jenna continued. "Get ready to fight. I'm going to contact the ACLU tomorrow. I'll talk to my dad and see if he'd be willing to find us a lawyer. He knows a lot of people. We're going to be okay."

Mack wiped his eyes and looked back up. "We're in the right. At minimum, we are going down on the right side of history."

"It's not that bad," Jenna said. "We are going to win this right now. I'm sure of it. We don't have to wait for it to be history."

"I wish I shared your confidence," Jacob said, his voice shaky.

"We're not going to stop, right?" I asked. "I mean, we are going to fight. At least I am. I don't know how, but I will."

"I will, too," Jacob said. "I just ... Yeah."

"However this turns out, you'll be proud of yourself," I told him.

"I'm just glad we're all together," he said.

"This is so true," Jenna said. "We are *all* together. Strength in numbers."

Mack nodded and hugged Jenna, and then we all exchanged hugs. I even didn't mind them this time. These were my best friends in the world, and we were about to be split up geographically, but nothing would break our friendship or our purpose.

I didn't know what was going to happen, or how we were going to deal with it, but Mack was right—if we were going down, it would be fighting.

PART V

THE SKY'S THE LIMIT

Mom was quiet for the first few minutes in the car on the way back to Emerson. I was embarrassed so I didn't say anything either. I just felt the queasiness that had taken over my stomach and tried to remember the commitment we'd all made to fight. This depended on us getting our parents on board, but now was not the time to talk to her about this.

It was crazy that two hours ago, we were celebrating getting to ten thousand followers.

We'd gone into the dorm after seeing Jenna's car. That had been the heaviest walk I'd ever done.

As soon as we had the front door open, a woman shouted, "Jenna! What have you done?"

"Hi, Mom," Jenna had said, blushing red.

Things went from there. Ms. Patton told us what was going on—we were suspended pending a final decision by the Board of Trustees about expulsion, and our parents were all on their way to Burnside—or, in Mack's case, his aunt.

We were told to get our stuff and come back down to the lounge to wait.

So that's what we did. Jenna was gone when we got back, so the rest of us sat at a table down there, not really talking. But word had gotten around after some kids saw Jenna leaving with her mom, so we had to field some questions. It was nice to see that a lot of kids thought it was bullshit. Which of course it was.

Mom got there first, so I said an awkward bye to Jacob and Mack, and we left.

"Nic, I don't understand why you did this," Mom finally said, still gripping the steering wheel like she had been this whole drive. "You loved it there—why would you pull a stunt like this and ruin everything?"

I felt instant shame, but then I remembered why we'd done it, and that we were being unfairly targeted. "Mom, we didn't do anything wrong. They're discriminating against us because we're all LGBTQ. We investigated it, and even high school students have the right to say what we want, within certain rules." I explained some of the limitations and rules. "We were careful. Everything we did was above board. We did nothing that they are allowed to punish us for, much less a punishment as severe as this."

She didn't say anything, but her frown was deep.

"We knew this might happen." I tried to keep my voice calm, but wasn't totally successful. I was speaking fast, my pulse picking up. "We are going to fight it. Somebody needs to stand up for what is right in this country, especially in hellish backward states."

"Why are you talking like that?" she asked. "It's not that bad here. I know there are bullies, but most people here are good people."

"I don't think you're wrong about most people here being decent. The problem is that the people with political power are making laws that are incredibly dangerous for some people—people like, you know, *me*—and all these so-called 'good people' are still voting for them." I was getting completely worked up. "You know how Oklahoma is always trying to one-up Texas, like with our abortion law that's even worse than Texas's—and I know that one pissed you off—but did you know that the Oklahoma ACLU has issued a travel advisory for Texas because of all the anti-immigrant laws?" I was almost yelling, and it was probably scaring Mom, but I couldn't stop. "Basically, if you look at all Latino, it's too dangerous. It's not just LGBTQ, it's not just women, it's everybody they don't like, and they only like other horrible, evil people."

And then there were tears in my eyes. My voice got thick, but quieter. "It started with all the sports bans, but now trans people are banned from using the right bathrooms, and some places are criminalizing it. They claim it's to keep people safe—all but saying that trans women will attack other women in the women's restroom, when there has never been a single incident of that."

I had to wipe away more tears. "The incidents involving people being attacked in bathrooms involve cis men attacking trans women forced to use the men's bathroom. The laws rely entirely on lies. Bathrooms are a nightmare for trans people. I don't even drink anything so I can avoid them now."

"I can see that you are passionate about all this," Mom said, her voice desperate.

"It just matters so much, and nobody is doing *anything* to stop it." Then I really was crying.

"I don't know what to think, Nic," she said, voice

strained. "Why did you have to stir the pot? Why not stay under the radar?"

I sniffed. "You know I can't be under the radar. Just being me puts me in the radar's sights."

Mom reached over and squeezed my shoulder. "Can you tell me everything that happened?"

"Yeah. There's a lot." I wiped a couple tears from my eyes.

"If I'm going to help you, I need to understand everything that happened."

"Okay. So, we've been making TikToks since the beginning of January." I told her about shifting content from book reviews to LGBTQ+ advocacy, and telling our experiences. When I got to the part about them telling us to stop, and how we didn't post for a few days, she nodded and sighed.

"And this is where it goes bad," she said in understanding.

"Yeah. We had a serious talk with each other about whether it was worth the risk to start again. But we'd done the research and knew we were in the right, so we decided to start posting them again."

"Okay, honey. This is very upsetting, because I believe that you are right, but people like this have so much power and can basically do whatever they want."

"I know."

"Yeah, you do. You definitely do."

"Some of our videos went viral," I added. "I'm sure that's how they found out about it. We have two that have had over a million views."

Her eyes widened, and she was quiet for a moment before saying, "I need you to show me some of these videos."

"I can play them for you right now. You can just listen.

That's the main point, anyway. But the school is mad because we talked about what they did to us, taking our rooms away and denying our gender, and then trying to block our free speech. It's all so messed up."

So I went through the videos, starting at the beginning. Most of them weren't very long, so we actually listened to most of them. I watched Mom the whole time. She was obviously really trying to listen, but she looked tense, and she didn't really let up on her steering wheel grip.

After I finished the last one, Mom glanced at me. "So what is your plan? You know we can't afford a lawyer."

"Jenna is contacting the Oklahoma ACLU tomorrow. Maybe they'll help." I paused. "Otherwise we need you to advocate for us. I know you aren't used to this, but parents have power in these situations. Especially if you all work together."

I took a deep breath and realized we were almost home. Mom exited the interstate and got on the state highway that would take us into Emerson.

It wouldn't be long before I got to see my sister, the single good thing about all this. She would make me feel better.

Friday afternoon I was lying in my bed texting my friends. We were all still completely in shock.

—*I still can't believe I'm missing the mentorship*— I texted, truly heartbroken since I'd realized this a few minutes earlier. I'd stopped crying, but I was glad nobody could see me right now.

—*Hey, I asked my dad and he said you could stay with us Friday nights*— Jenna said.

—*You already asked?*— I texted. How had she thought of it before I did?

—*Yep. My mom thinks you're a bad influence, but my dad's okay. I'm not usually over there on the weekend anymore, but he said it was okay*—

—*That's awesome*— Jacob texted. —*I was stressing for you, too*—

At first I was excited, but then I realized the problem. — *I'd have to get someone to drive me. I'm not sure that can happen*—

—*Buses exist, Nic*— Mack texted, following with a laughing emoji.

—*I'm not sure my mom would let me take a bus by myself*— I said. Public buses were pretty sketch. But maybe if I begged, they'd go for it. Mom at least understood how important my art was. But she almost always had to work on Friday nights.

—*I could probably borrow my brother's car when he's at work and come get you, or I'm sure we could figure something out* — Jenna texted.

She was so great. How had I ended up with such a perfect friend?

For a second I felt bad, like I was being disloyal to Sam. But I wasn't. She had made new friends in Scotland, and that didn't mean she wasn't still my friend. The same was true for me.

—*Thanks*— I texted. —*You're awesome*—

She just sent a smiling and blushing emoji.

—*Okay, moving on from the love fest*— Mack texted, adding several hearts. —*We still need to figure out if we should post or not*—

—*Let's wait until after they talk tomorrow*— Jenna said.

Our parents were meeting Saturday afternoon to make a

plan. Jenna hadn't heard back from the ACLU, so they might not help. We'd have to see, but obviously we had to act as if they might not help at all.

—So I actually have an idea— Jenna said. *—I don't think we should post, but I think we should each record our own video about this whole thing. So we can capture how new and shocking it is, so we don't lose that authenticity. We can decide to post whenever—*

"Nic!" I heard through my bedroom door.

Isabella.

"Hey, come in."

She opened the door, all one big grin, ran in, and jumped on the bed to give me a big hug.

Isabella was the only person I'd always been completely comfortable hugging. It was all endorphins, none of the anxiety. After we finished, she pushed on my shoulder so I'd scoot over so she could lie there, which of course I did.

"Let me text my friends," I said. "We were just chatting."

"Okay," she said while I typed a message in.

Once I finished, she took my hand and we lay there for a while.

"I miss having you here, Nic," she said. "I'm so sick of Caleb. Why is he such a jerk?"

"I don't know. He used to be nice. But I think a lot of teenage boys turn into assholes. Maybe he'll outgrow it."

"I'll never forgive him, even if he turns nice later." She stuck her tongue out in a disgusted motion.

"So how was school?" I asked.

"There's always so much drama. Charlotte likes Abel, but he's really immature—I honestly don't know what she sees in him—and so he's all mean to her. She cried today, and all her friends were all sympathetic, but then one of them was talking to Abel later and he kissed her. She said it was just him, but now everybody is mad at her, even though I think what she said is true, so Charlotte was mad and crying more. What a mess." She shook her head.

I'd started laughing in the middle of her speech. She was only eleven and in fifth grade. "I can't imagine how bad it's going to be when you all are actually teenagers."

"I know. I'm never going to be like that, though. If a boy treats me bad, he's a jerk and I'm not going to like him."

"That's good." I squeezed her hand. "You should always have self-respect. Respecting yourself is far more important than having a boyfriend."

This was kind of hilarious coming from me. I'd never had self-respect. Or a boyfriend. Instead, I'd absorbed all the hate and disdain from my peers that I'd grown up with. It was only after I made some good friends and came out as agender that I started to gain more confidence.

"You should like yourself more, too, Nic," Isabella said.

"I'm getting there. It takes time to come out of the hole I was in." An understatement, but still truthful.

"I'm so glad you're home now. Even though I know the reason is bad."

"Yeah. Hopefully I'll be gone soon. In the meantime, do you want to work on some crafts?"

"I finished my last kit on Sunday."

"We can find something." Isabella got a monthly craft kit that usually had a couple projects in it. We used to always do them together, but when I left last August, she'd had to do them herself. Mom sometimes helped, but Isabella said she was often more trouble than help, which cracked me up. Nobody knew where my art ability came from, and Isabella also had an artistic streak, even though she wasn't as serious about it as I was.

"Should we go to my room?" she asked.

"Sure. But let me grab something." I went into the closet and got some markers and art paper. "I'm going to show you something you'll like."

"What?" she asked as we walked into the hall.

"One of my friends"—I loved that I could call someone like Lily a friend—"makes this really cool art. I'm going to show you what it looks like. You might like it."

"Do you have pictures?" she asked.

"So, actually I don't. I'm going to try to show you what she does."

I sat down in the middle of her floor, all the art supplies in my lap. Isabella went to her desk and started looking through a bin on one of her shelves.

I started telling her about Lily and how we were on the mentorship together, and then I ended up telling her about the group project we were doing, and we sat there while she made a bracelet from some beads she found and I tried to duplicate Lily's style in a drawing of Isabella working on the bracelet. It was nice to chat with my little sister and pretend —just for a few minutes—that everything was normal, right, and fair in the world.

When really what was happening was that my friends and our parents were preparing for war, with no idea how it was going to go.

The meeting with the parents Saturday afternoon was going well. We were all on Zoom so we could tell our parents exactly what had happened this semester, and they had all compared that to what the school had told each of them. Which wasn't the same.

It was weird to be meeting my friends' parents all at

once. I'd been nervous before the call since my other friends' parents hadn't always liked me—Sam's mom had thought I was a bad influence on her. I'd talked to Sam this morning, and she was as pissed off as I was and glad we were fighting it. She was also convinced we could win.

Despite past experience, my current friends' parents were all nice, and everyone said to call them by their first names. Mack's parents, Russ and Mariel, were on the screen, but Mack himself was at his aunt's in southeastern Oklahoma. Jacob was sitting between his parents, King and Jamie, and Jenna's mom wasn't helping, but her dad, Thomas, was. Jenna wasn't on screen because she was at her mom's and she didn't want her to know about the meeting, so she was just on her phone. Mariel, King, and my dad were quiet, but everyone else was highly invested in the conversation.

Apparently, the school had made it sound like Mack was the ringleader and Jacob probably had been coerced into participating, and Jenna and I had just followed along. Who knows where they got any of their ideas. My stomach twisted with jealousy—I'd been important, too, after all—but also with discomfort at being in such big trouble at all. Above all, I hated them.

"I contacted my lawyer yesterday," Russ said. Mack's face lightened, but then he looked uncertain again. I knew he was worried that his parents couldn't really afford this. They'd been going through some financial trouble. I didn't think it was as bad as my parents' situation, but it wasn't nothing. I really didn't think my parents could afford to help.

"I also contacted mine," Thomas said. "You're in Texas, right?"

Russ nodded. "My guy is looking for someone in Oklahoma to recommend. The challenge is mostly that he doesn't know a lot of people who deal with this kind of case."

"Yeah, that's the same with mine. He's also got an ear to the ground."

Jacob's parents and mine were quiet. I knew mine didn't have money to add to this, and they definitely didn't have a lawyer a phone call away.

"I'm glad Mack and Jenna will be supported that way," Mom said. "Unfortunately, we are unable to hire a lawyer right now. Should we start talking specifics for the Friday board meeting?"

"Yes, but I do want to say that my lawyer will not be helping only Mack," his dad said. "The kids are all in this together."

"Oh, thank you," Mom said, blushing.

"We really appreciate that, too," Jamie said, looking relieved.

I was so impressed. Some parents were rotten, and then there were good ones like Mack's. They'd supported him from the beginning of his journey and never wavered, and now they were going so far as to support his friends, too.

"It's no problem," Russ said. "I think we may have all the info we need from the kids, right? We can let them get back to their busy lives and talk about this on our own."

Everyone laughed, and my nerves pulsed.

"I think that's true," Jamie said. Jacob waved, stood up, and was gone before anyone else had moved. But the rest of us left too, and all the parents—and aunt—stayed on.

I almost tripped on Isabella when I turned into the hall because she was crouched around the corner, eavesdropping. "Oof!"

I caught myself against the window frame after half-running down the hall. Isabella giggled and followed me toward the stairs.

"Did you hear anything good?" I teased once we got upstairs.

"You guys are so cool," Isabella said, a big grin on her face. "I still never thought *you* would get in trouble. Especially really big trouble. I'm so proud of you for speaking out about something important, though."

I laughed as we went into my room. "You sound like a mom."

"I don't think Mom is happy about what you did." She sat on the side of my bed.

"No. But I'm kind of surprised how she's supporting me. She always seemed kind of a wimp." I sat in my desk chair and started spinning side to side.

"I know. Same with Dad."

I turned in the chair to see what was on my desk. I had a bunch of D&D figurines and the markers from yesterday. Isabella had kept the portrait I'd done of her Lily-style. It wasn't good, but it did look like Isabella, so I let her keep it.

"You know, Nic, I thought you were kind of a wimp, too. But I kind of understood why."

I laughed. "You know, I totally was. But I think it's because things are different at OAMS. If I'd fought back against the bullying here, I still would have lost overall. That's how this kind of bullying works."

"But why? I see people who stand up for themselves."

I thought of the kid whose face was decorated with my Coke. If he was somebody I saw day-to-day, he would have figured out a way to get back at me. I had no power here. I hated that feeling, but some situations were just unfixable in the short term. This was why leaving was the right thing for me to do.

"I'm not quite sure. Sometimes there aren't reasons for things, I think. Have you noticed how sometimes there really isn't anything special about the most popular kids? They're not really objectively better."

I looked at Isabella, so cute, and I knew she wasn't unpopular, but she also wasn't the most popular. I thought she was tier two, so she would know what I meant.

I continued, "And the most bullied kids aren't always the ones with the most problems—cheapest jeans or whatever stupid shit they care about. Sometimes it's based on something that happened a while back, but I think it can also be random. Like, when we're all really little, kids just decide this person is a loser, this person is cool, and so on, and it sticks for whatever reason."

Isabella frowned, thinking about it. We talked about the most popular kids at school and the least popular, and she came to agree with me.

"You should be nice to the unpopular kids," I told her.

She gave me a sheepish smile. "I talk to Maggie, but sometimes not when other people are around."

"Isabella!" Was she a bully? I couldn't believe it.

"No, Nic!" Her face was stricken. "I'm not mean to her. I just ... kind of ignore her? When no one is around, I talk to her. She's funny."

"Do your friends make fun of her?"

She shook her head, her face pink. "No, not my friends. Some of the other girls."

I glared at her. She looked like she might cry.

"If I talk to her when the other girls are around, they will start picking on me," she said quietly.

I frowned. She was right. I had known that when I was the isolated loser. There were some people who were nice to me when no one was around, and I always felt like they were decent people. I knew why they ignored me other times. "Okay, if you are nice to her when no one's around, she'll understand. But Isabella, if any of your friends says something mean to her, you need to stand up for her."

She paused, considering it. "Okay, I will."

"It's just like with me, here. It's about doing what's right, even if you have to risk something to do it. Sometimes you have to think of how you will feel if you *don't* do something. Like regret and guilt." I felt guilty for having upset Isabella, so I got up to hug her.

She hugged me back. "I'm not mean."

"I know. I'm sorry for thinking that even for a second. I don't think it now. But I think school politics are probably nastier than national politics right now, which is really saying something."

"Yeah."

I wondered what she knew about national politics. I was completely oblivious at her age. Actually, I was rather oblivious until last semester.

I was not oblivious anymore. And now, I was taking part in politics. But I had no idea what would come of it.

Sunday, I woke up early and read for a couple hours, until Isabella got home after spending the night at a friend's. We sat down to draw at the dining room table, the place I had spent so many hours creating that pencil dragon drawing that that P.o.S. kid, Logan, had ruined when he was at our house hanging out with Caleb last year. He'd poured coffee on the drawing right after I'd finished it. It still hurt to think about, although I had somewhat salvaged it by dyeing all the paper with coffee so that it looked kind of like antique paper.

Isabella was drawing a unicorn, but it was actually pretty good. She was working off a picture from the Internet, and she had the perspective fairly accurate.

I was thumbnailing for the third project for art class because I hadn't been able to grab the piece I'd been working on for Project 2. That one was going to be in color, and I was assuming that I'd be able to finish it when I got back.

If I got back. I frowned and thought about how bad it would be if I couldn't go back. It made me sick to my stomach. I couldn't face Emerson High again.

I looked back at my sketchbook, trying to keep my thoughts on the more positive idea that I'd be going back. The new piece would be black ink, no color, and it had to be a self-portrait. But my thumbnails so far were not interesting. I'd found a few pictures of me that Mom had sent. I didn't really do a lot of selfies. I really had no idea what I could do that wouldn't be just another headshot self-portrait.

Ms. Mangal had said that I could do it with or without props or background stuff, and it could be full body or headshot. Last semester I'd done one of me salsa dancing, which was supposed to be ironic or something—the assignment was to put myself in a situation I would never be in, and there was no way in the world I would ever be caught dancing in front of other people.

Was there anything that made me unique besides being agender? I didn't want to make everything about that.

Right after I had that thought, my phone chimed with a text.

—*How are you? Everybody here is pissed*— Sophia texted.

I was surprised for a second. We had never texted, although we'd exchanged phone numbers last summer, before moving in together as roommates in August.

—Not great. I missed my art mentorship yesterday. But what are people saying?— I really was curious. I hadn't actually given much thought to what everyone else would think. I'd been so focused on myself.

Dots appeared so I knew Sophia was typing.

Clearly, as far as things that made me unique, getting suspended was definitely one of them.

—Rachel is of course gloating, and she has her regular posse, all those "good Christians"— Sophia added an eye rolling and laughing emoji. *—But everyone else is so mad. People have looked up free speech and you guys didn't do anything wrong. The school has no right. Someone started a petition. Ms. Patton seems nervous because she knows people are bordering on revolt. —*

—Wow— I texted. A petition? I'd never thought people would be on our side like that. But Sophia wouldn't lie about this. I was guessing she was exaggerating and it wasn't "everyone," but some people must be mad.

My heart swelled. This was so different from how things had been at Emerson, where I was certain nobody would have supported me, if only because it would have destroyed their reputations.

—Yeah. Honestly, I was surprised at how many people were so vocal, just because I didn't know how many people even knew about your TikToks. I think for some people it really is just about free speech, but people don't mind that you're talking about LGBTQ rights. And everyone has watched your TikToks now. You've gotten more followers in a month than I did in a year— She added three laughing emojis.

I shook my head and I looked at Isabella. She was

focused on shading the horn, her tongue sticking out in concentration.

It made me smile.

Everything was so weird right now, but some of it was in a good way.

—*That's amazing*— I texted, still smiling.

—*Yeah. So what are you guys doing next?*—

—*Our parents are working on it. Mack's and Jenna's dad both have lawyers. We all met yesterday and they are planning for the Board of Trustees meeting next Friday. I think they may want us to give our own statements, which is scary, but they said we could read off something*—

—*That's good. I've heard some kids are planning to go to the meeting if they can*—

—*That would be great*— I tried to imagine a bunch of kids I barely knew coming out to support me. It was kind of crazy. —*Jenna also emailed the Oklahoma ACLU. It would be so much better if they could help or something*—

—*I've got to go*— Sophia texted. —*But I'll let you know if there's any news*—

I thanked her, and then I looked back at my sketchbook. Even though my mind was spinning, I shouldn't obsess about things. I thought about texting my friends, but I decided to take a break from all the stress.

I needed to figure out the self-portrait. Celebrating getting suspended probably wasn't the best idea. But it had been books and TikTok that led to the whole thing. I could show myself reading a book. I could get Isabella to take a picture of me sitting in a chair in the den.

She was working on shading the unicorn body right now. Her left hand was spread out, her friendship bracelet around her wrist. That was new since Christmas break.

Then it hit me—I should do the drawing of me on a

TikTok video, like I was on the screen of a phone, which I'd draw.

This was perfect. I started going through the videos I'd been on, sound off, until I found a few I liked, which I took screenshots of. I already knew which one I wanted to do, but I would have to turn in a bunch of thumbnails, so I went ahead and did them.

Once I had the thumbnails done, I studied them, especially the one I'd decided to go with. My mouth was slightly open and I was holding my finger up for some reason—I didn't remember why I'd done that, but it looked more active than static, so I liked it.

But I was emotionally beat down. I didn't feel like working anymore. Actually, what I wanted to do was go take a nap. Mom was at work and Dad was working on something in his office, so I figured I could get away with it. Our parents never let us take naps. They said it made it impossible to fall asleep at night. But I was just beat.

"Isabella," I whispered.

She looked up.

"I'm going to go sneak away and take a nap."

"A nap?" she asked, surprised.

"Shh." I put my finger to my lips. "You know they'll be on my case if they know. Don't tell them."

She laughed and whispered, "Okay."

I headed upstairs, wondering if the world would be different when I woke up.

Who was I kidding? Of course not.

Monday morning, I finally had adjusted to being back at home. Isabella and Caleb were at school, and Mom and Dad were at work, so I started the day off by working on physics at the dining room table. I was hoping Tiana would be willing to tell Jacob and me what the homework was as it got assigned. There was a test next week, so if we weren't back by then, we'd miss that. I had no idea how those things would be handled if we did get back.

I worked on the first two problems, which weren't too hard. But the third one stumped me right away.

I leaned back in my chair. How was I going to get through this without Tiana's help?

What an incredible mess. I never thought I'd be in this situation. Had I made a huge mistake? Should I have followed their orders and stopped filming?

I honestly didn't know. It was hard to feel so brave when I was all alone, away from my friends.

I stared at the third physics question some more, panic building.

My group text chimed.

—*I think we should start posting again*— Jenna said. —*My dad pointed out that we are fighting for our ongoing right to free speech, not just to be forgiven for previous free speech they didn't like*—

—*hmm*— Mack texted.

I thought about it, closing my eyes for a second to calm the panic that had flared at the idea. I really didn't want to end up back at Emerson. Maybe I shouldn't post again.

But that made me feel sick, too, because then I was letting the bullies win—again. This really was one of those big moments in life, where I had to decide what kind of person I was going to be.

—*I'm willing to post more*— I texted, a shiver going down my spine. —*But not everyone has to. We'll be posting individually, so they'll know exactly who is posting*—

—*Agreed*— Jenna said.

—*I'm leaning towards doing it*— Mack said. —*but I still need to decide*—

—*I'm going to do it*— Jacob said. —*Even though I may regret it*—

I couldn't blame him. I felt like my decision was a little crazy.

—*It's okay, both of you*— Jenna texted. —*We won't think less of you if you don't want to take the risk*—

—*I agree*— I said.

—*What are you thinking we should post?*— Mack asked. —*Anything specific?*—

Jenna responded right away. —*I think anything where we talk about what's going on now, or something about our experience of things. We probably should stay on topic since that's what our followers expect from us*—

I nodded to myself. I could do that.

—*I do think we should spread it out*— Jenna said. —*I can post today*—

—*I can do tomorrow*— I texted.

—*I'll take Wednesday*— Mack said, obviously having made up his mind.

—*I'll do Thursday*— Jacob said.

—*btw*— Jacob started. —*I heard from Tiana. She said the same thing Sophia told you yesterday, Nic, and she also said she'd send us the physics homework*—

—*Great!*— I texted, relieved.

—*What are you all up to today?*— Jenna asked.

—*Homework*— Jacob and I texted at the same time.

—*Same*— Mack said.

—*Yeah, me too*— Jenna texted.

There was some more chatty back-and-forth, but then we all got back to our homework. I worked for a while longer, skipping that third question, before moving over to my TikTok self-portrait. I did my value studies, which took a while, then got back to homework. Chemistry wasn't bad, and then I read for English.

Then I actually remembered the art club contest, which I kept meaning to get to—Ms. Mangal said it wasn't due until late April. I had no idea what to do for it, but they did have an ink category, so I'd do something there.

It all felt mundane, like a regular school day, except it wasn't.

I started writing up a script for my video, at least as a rough guide. It was easier with a plan for what to talk about. I'd write it up and record it today, edit it tonight, and post it tomorrow.

I was curious what, exactly, Jenna was going to talk about, but she hadn't posted yet.

I was definitely going to talk about missing the mentorship, and how we risked falling behind by missing lectures. All because the school's board was mad that we weren't mindless, obedient little creatures.

Once I had the TikTok written—at least an outline—I decided to work on a statement I might say at the meeting with the Board of Trustees. At first I'd told Mom there was no way I'd do it, but I'd rethought it. This was something that mattered to me, and it mattered for other people, too.

Friday afternoon, Mom and I were driving to Oklahoma City for the Board of Trustees meeting that night. We were quiet for the first part of the drive, which left me to my thoughts.

I'd waited until Tuesday morning to film my TikTok. I

watched Jenna's so I could build on some of her points, instead of accidentally repeating them. Her video had gotten a lot of views and likes, and so did mine. Mack's and Jacob's—he'd decided to go for it—had, too.

Jacob talked in his about how scared he was, but how this mattered to him, even though it was a risk. He even mentioned how he felt it was riskier for him, because of the way Black people always had to be so much more perfect than white people just to be considered acceptable, and their mistakes were often punished more.

I hadn't thought about that, but he was right. It was also a little like that for girls, though not as much. It was that way for Mack, too, even though it wasn't as obvious that he was Latino as it was that Jacob was Black.

With all our new TikToks, our followers were skyrocketing again.

By Thursday, my friends and I all had written our statements for the meeting, and we'd all met Thursday night to go over everything, parents and kids. Everyone read their statements as practice, including the parents. It was so nerve-racking, but I think it was good because it made me want to change one part.

I stared out the window at all the cows we passed on the interstate. There were a lot of them. Oklahoma was a beef state, so it made sense. Beef and oil. And hate, lots and lots of hate. And indifference to the hate.

That last part was what we were fighting. We had to get people who didn't care about LGBTQ+ issues, because they thought they had no stake in them, to start voting the hateful politicians out. Since so many of the laws were already passed, it would take a while to undo the damage—those laws had to be repealed, after all—but if people cared enough, it could happen.

"Do you want to practice your statement again, honey?" Mom asked in the car, interrupting my reverie.

"Sure." Although I felt awkward reading it, I knew practice was good for me. So I read through it.

"It's such a good speech, Nic. You might try to slow down a little. It's easier for people to understand if you are pausing in some places and going slower, because they have time to process what you're saying."

"I did race through it, didn't I? I could barely breathe at the end."

We both laughed, even though I was nervous.

"Do you want to try again?" she asked. "You could even make notes in the moments you want to pause."

"Do you have a pen?"

"In my purse."

It was crammed next to my feet, taking up what felt like half the footwell. I rifled through it until I found a pen, and then read through the statement to find good spots to pause. I put a star in each spot.

"Can I try again?" I asked.

"Of course. I'm all ears."

This time, I slowed down and didn't run out of breath so often, and I timed my pauses on the stars. I also practiced looking up periodically without losing my place.

"That's so good. Those pauses make those statements more powerful."

"Yeah."

She went quiet and I saw her wipe a couple tears from her eyes.

I looked away, feeling awkward about the crying, and also knowing it was probably my fault.

"Sorry, honey," she said, voice thick. "I'm just so proud of you. You're a completely different person now. I loved you before, but I always worried about you. But now—now I'm not worried. You're going to do big things, things that matter."

I blushed. "Not if I get kicked out of school."

"I don't believe that. You're strong and have convictions, and you're not afraid to stand up for what's right. But also, we're fighting it. I think we have a strong case here—especially with the lawyers."

I was so divided about this. I knew she was right, but even though I was only seventeen, I was already jaded. Right didn't always win. I'm sure Mom knew that, but she was hoping it would this time.

But I also knew she was nervous about her own statement. "Do you want me to read yours to you? Just for more familiarity?"

"Oh! I hadn't thought of that. That's a good idea. You can help me find moments to pause and mark mine up, too."

"Okay." I pulled it out of the folder in her purse and we started going through it. It was good and nearly made me cry, because I loved her so much for going out of her comfort zone to support me, even though she and Dad had asked me to not come out as agender last semester. They'd thought it was too dangerous.

I didn't think they were wrong, but it seemed so important to me at the time. It felt so amazing to finally recognize what had always been true. And Mom went with it when I said I wouldn't hide anymore.

We found some spots in her statement where she could pause, and I dutifully marked it up. Then we were quiet for the rest of the ride in. She found a parking spot and we sat there for a moment.

"Ready?" she asked.

"Ready," I said, with confidence I wasn't sure I really had.

But it sounded convincing, and that's what would matter here.

Mom and I walked up the steps to the building we were meeting in. Someone ahead of us—a man in a blue suit—held one of the large wooden doors open for us. Mom thanked him, but I silently judged him. He looked like one of the bad guys.

As soon as we were in the foyer, I could hear the hum of voices on the other side of two glass doors. My stomach twisted. I'd been okay in the car, but this was about to get very, very real.

I pulled one door open, and the hum got louder. There was a handwritten sign on a metal post that read *OAMS Board of Trustees Meeting*. We followed the arrow on the sign and found a large room where the rumble was coming from.

There was a wooden table that ran nearly the width of the room against the front wall, with six men sitting behind it, one lone woman at the end. The man who'd held the door for us moved past us and took the one empty seat behind the table. Every one of them was white.

My blood ran cold when I saw who was in the third seat from the left—Rachel's dad.

There were chairs facing the front of the room, eight seats across with an aisle down the middle, with five rows. There were people standing around everywhere, probably almost as many as there were chairs.

I realized Mom and I had just been standing there for a minute. Finally I noticed Jacob waving at us from the front two rows on the left, right when Mom noticed, too. We started walking over there. Jacob was in khakis rather than his normal jeans, and he had on a button-up shirt rather than another graphic t-shirt.

Mom had made me dress up, too. Slacks and a blue button-up shirt like Jacob's. I only agreed because neither was really feminine.

"We're holding these rows," Jacob's dad said when we approached. I was surprised at how tall he was, given how short Jacob was.

"Thank you," Mom said. They shook hands and started talking about something.

"Is your mom here?" I asked Jacob.

"Yeah. She's in the bathroom. Are you scared?"

"Flipping terrified," I said, making us both laugh.

"Me too. What if this doesn't work?" He said the last part quietly.

"I know."

He looked over my shoulder and waved. "There's Jenna."

I turned around and saw her and her dad, with Mack and his dad right behind them. Another man came in behind them and said something to Mack's dad. Probably the lawyer.

We all waved awkwardly at each other

"I've never seen you in a skirt, Jenna," Jacob said.

"My dad insisted." She self-consciously smoothed down her sweater top. "I figured he probably wasn't wrong. It's one of only two I own. One at each apartment."

"Actually, the rest of us all look the same," Mack said, motioning at Jacob and me. It was true—Mack also had on pants and a decent shirt.

We laughed nervously. I still felt like I was in a costume, but at least I wasn't the only one.

There were about ten minutes before the meeting was supposed to start. The four of us snagged the rightmost chairs in those rows, with Jenna and Mack in the front and Jacob and me in the second row. We were chatting and not paying too much attention, though out of the corner of my eye, I was watching the board members at the front of the room. They were talking and laughing like they hadn't just tried to destroy four kids' lives.

The whole thing had me completely on edge. Jenna kept nervously giggling, and Jacob wasn't saying much. Mack was a chatterbox, even though I couldn't tell you what he was saying. I was too distracted. My heart was already beating faster than normal and I felt on the verge of sweating. It was a stressful cocktail of nerves and excitement.

"Let me squeeze by," a woman said.

I looked up to see Jacob's mom. She smiled as she moved past me and sat on Jacob's other side, squeezing his shoulder when she sat down. That was where he got his height. She was shorter than he was.

Mom was down at the end of the row and waved at me. I smiled and waved back.

Then there was the sound of a gavel, like a rifle shot, and I jumped, then blushed bright red. We all looked toward the front. A burly blond man who looked like Toby Keith started talking, first about the minutes from the last meeting. There was some discussion of some parts, and eventually they approved them and moved on. We were the only topic tonight, since this was a special meeting.

"We are here to address the recent suspension of four students and determine if we will proceed with expulsion," the man explained.

My heart was beating like crazy and my stomach was roiling. I was glad I hadn't eaten in a while. Jacob looked at me and we shared a moment of terror. Jenna and Mack did the same.

"These four students"—then he listed all of our names —"repeatedly disobeyed school rules and have been temporarily removed through suspension." Repeatedly was a total lie—Ms. Patton had told us one time. The man gave some more twisted and fabricated info, with a bunch of outlandish claims about the content of our videos, claiming we were targeting other students and were therefore bullying, disparaging the school with lies, and disregarding school rules about leaving campus.

Jacob looked at me, his mouth in a tight line. "Assholes," he mouthed.

I nodded. But how could they tell such blatant lies? Anybody who looked into any of the claims would know it was all untrue.

But then I realized—nobody would look into it, so they could get away with it.

I thought I would throw up in that moment. Fortunately, I retained control, but God. We were screwed.

I was in a daze. It didn't matter what we did. All these people here were going to believe we were these horrible kids.

I obsessed for a bit on that while he kept going, saying some more crap about us. But then he said he was opening it up for us to speak, and then after that, they would allow comments from the public. We were the only kids there, so everyone in the room turned and looked at us.

We'd had to sign up to speak in advance, so we had a set order. Mack's dad would go first, so he went up to the microphone that was in front of the chairs, facing the board members. Mom and I were going last.

My mind was spinning because of all the accusations, and I was trying to decide if I should go off script to address those false claims.

But then I realized that Mack's dad was doing that. He talked about a lot of things and it sounded really good. Then Mack went and emphasized how we'd followed the rules, and that we were being targeted for talking about LGBTQ issues. He sounded so confident, but not combative, just like an earnest kid. And that was even with Rachel's dad staring him down, looking like a total douche.

The room was otherwise quiet while he talked, even though there was an occasional cough.

Jacob's mom and Jacob went next. His mom focused on how all of us are good kids, just trying to set ourselves up for productive lives in a world where we can feel safe.

Jacob's voice was a little shaky at the beginning, but it got stronger and he got through his whole statement, talking about how great OAMS was academically, but how it had old-fashioned views of gender and sexuality.

He'd been so hesitant to break the rules once they'd told us to stop making the TikToks, but then he'd ended up being the first one to say we should start again, and he never lost that new conviction.

He finished with, "Please don't take us back to the last century. If you really want to 'protect the children' and 'let kids be kids'"—he made air quotes—"then why don't you protect them from all the efforts to punish them into being some other kind of kid than they actually are? I'm being exactly who I am, and you have punished me for it. You're not letting this kid be a kid."

He was so right, and he sounded so confident and sure of himself by the end. His confidence and conviction were right there in his speech. He'd changed a lot since I first met him last semester. We both had.

When he sat back down, I touched his shoulder so he turned to face me. He had a deer-in-headlights expression.

"You did so great," I mouthed, and his eyes relaxed and a tiny smile appeared.

And then Jenna's dad went, then Jenna. When she went up to the microphone, her voice was thick at first, but she was amazing. You could tell she was a poet because she was so good with words. She reiterated that we had followed the rules except for the illegal one that forbade us to make content.

Mom got up and went to the microphone, and my stomach was doing flip after flip, for both her and for me. She sounded unsure of herself at first, but then she got on a roll. "Nic struggled in our small town, and coming to OAMS has changed their life. It would be completely wrong to take that away simply because they said some things you don't agree with, as is their legal right."

This was the very end so my heart was going crazy. It was literally seconds before I had to go up there.

Mom finished, "Please don't overstep your authority. It is wrong." Then she gave my shoulder a squeeze and went to sit back down.

"Take us home, Nic," Jacob whispered to me.

I pressed my sweaty palms against my pants to push myself up.

I don't remember how I got there, but I found myself standing in front of the microphone, speech in hand. I cleared my throat, which of course echoed throughout the room and scared the crap out of me. But everyone else had done their speeches, so I knew I could, too.

I held my paper up and started reading it. My voice was shaking like crazy and I knew I sounded way too flat, like I didn't even care about what I was saying. I got to the first pause and leaned back to take a steadying breath.

"I've always been one of those kids who follows all the rules, except the ones about how to dress and exist. I know those things are directly related to why we are here tonight. All the people in this country who claim they love and deserve freedom are doing everything in their power to take away the freedom of people they don't agree with. This is the antithesis of freedom." My heart felt open and big, but also raw.

Pause. "My friends and I all knew we were taking a risk. But we have a legal right to say what we want as long as it doesn't harm the school or other students, and we were careful to do neither of those things." My voice was still shaky, but I wasn't so terrified. I felt good because I was doing the right thing, even when it was scary. "We described real things that happened, which I guess the school didn't like people finding out about. But if you're making decisions that impact other people's lives, everyone should know about it. If you can't stand behind your decisions, then you know you're doing something wrong. Please end this suspension and let us return to school. Thank you."

I turned around to head back to my seat, and that's when I spotted Ms. Mangal and Clee in the back, both giving me thumbs up.

I was so surprised and scrambled back to my chair. Jacob gave me a big smile and it immediately calmed me. I couldn't believe Ms. Mangal and Clee had come to support us.

Then the board chairman called some other guy, who had a MAGA hat on.

Shit, I hadn't even thought of that. We were allowed to speak, which meant other people could, too.

MAGA Man opened his big hairy mouth. "If you don't shut these abominations down, you are failing this state. We are under intense threat from the left and you have to stop it."

That hit deep. *Abomination.*

There was more of this from other people. From the way they talked, I didn't they had anything at all to do with OAMS. But since it was public, anyone could come.

After a few people, Jacob actually reached over and took my hand, which should have been weird but was perfect. Then a woman spoke on our behalf, pointing out that gay and trans people are still actually people, then there were some more MAGA heads, and another supporter, and then some more morons with bunk to rant about.

I just wanted them to shut the fuck up so we could hear what the board would decide.

Finally, the last person finished and the board said they were going to another room to discuss the issue, and would be back shortly. They left through a door at the front of the room.

As soon as they were gone, one of the MAGA trash guys started shouting stuff about abominations again, and hateful words started popcorning around. Jacob and I both ducked instinctively, trying to be smaller.

My three friends and I all sat there, heads down, stressed beyond belief. Jacob and I were squeezing each other's hands for support. But Mack's dad yelled back at the asshole, and then there was more yelling all around. Russ stood up and there was movement from the other side of the room.

I glanced over and there was the original MAGA guy standing in the aisle, another man holding him by the shoulders because it looked like he was going to come over to our area and—I don't know—punch Mack's dad? Was this really happening?

There was more yelling, and King and Thomas stood up.

"You guys, remember our training," Jenna whispered.

The self-defense class. Would this turn into a brawl? It was insane. My heart was still beating like crazy and I was also on the verge of throwing up. Jacob and I were still holding onto each other's hands for dear life. But I was glad for the training we'd had in those classes. I felt safer.

Someone from the other side of the room yelled, "You cunts!" Some people echoed it and others told them to shut up.

Then the board members abruptly returned and it stopped some of the yelling, but there was one guy who was still going on. All our dads sat back down and weren't even looking at the guy who was still carrying on.

The chairman of the board motioned at someone behind us, and two security guards came in to pull out the crazy guy, who was still yelling about how the LGBTQ agenda was destroying this country.

Once it calmed back down, the board members took their seats and my pulse was going so fast I thought I might have a heart attack.

The chairman spoke into his microphone, saying, "We have decided we need more time to discuss this. We will reconvene two weeks from today."

Two *weeks*?! We all looked at each other, shocked faces all around.

And that was that. They adjourned the meeting and we were free to leave, still completely in limbo.

Our whole group looked at each other and Mack's dad's lawyer said, "This is an intentional stall. They know if they keep you away from the school for long enough, you won't be able to catch up because the school is so rigorous."

No joke.

"They want you to give up," he concluded.

"We are *not* giving up," Mack said.

The rest of us agreed.

"Good," the lawyer said. "I don't think you should. I am going to try to get them to move this up."

On our way out, Ms. Mangal and Clee waited for us.

We stopped and I introduced my mom to them. She shook hands with them both and then put her arm across my shoulders. I had that discomfort that always came up when my different worlds met—now school and parents, and mentorship and parents.

"I'm so proud of you, Nic," Ms. Mangal said. "I know speaking up must have been hard for you."

"You all did so well," Clee said. "Including the parents." She smiled at Mom.

"I'm so sorry for all the hateful people here," Ms. Mangal said.

"It's not like you brought them," I said.

We all laughed, even though it was awkward. I looked out in the foyer and saw that Jenna was waiting for me. We'd figured out a way for me to get to the mentorship, after all.

"I think I need to go," I said. "I'm staying with my friend tonight so I can go to the mentorship tomorrow. They're waiting for me."

"No problem," Ms. Mangal said. "We wanted you to know we support you."

We all moved into the foyer and I hugged Mom, thanked her for being amazing, and left with Jenna and her dad.

I'd hoped we'd know what was going on after tonight,

but they were playing dirty. We just had to figure out how to turn this around.

Jenna dropped me off at the studio late, so I scrambled to the back room.

"It's our resident hero!" Devin said when he saw me.

I immediately blushed, but everyone was smiling at me except Briana, who was focused on whatever she was working on.

"I'm not a hero," I said, going to sit with Addison.

"Oh, but you are the definition of heroic," Devin said. "You have been doing the right thing at great risk to yourself."

I grimaced. "I hate the risk part."

Lily shook her head. "Everybody knows they're just trying to delay things for you so you will have a hard time catching up when you come back. They don't have a legal leg to stand on."

I pulled my art out of the portfolio I'd brought. The only watercolor I had was one I'd done with Isabella's elementary school pans in the cheesy white plastic container. It was an okay rendition of a pot of flowers Mom had on the kitchen table.

"Do you even want to go back there?" Devin asked. "I mean, if they treated you this bad."

"I will die if I have to go back to Emerson," I said, groaning at the thought. Jenna and I had stayed up late talking about what we would do. She said she looked into online school, and it was a thing. She'd go back to her high school. It wouldn't be fun, but she'd survive. But she knew it was different for me.

"A lot of the kids go to OAMS to get away from their small towns," Lily explained.

I nodded. "Especially kids who don't fit in, or just want a chance to start over."

Briana had been quiet, but she looked up at me. "Can I ask a question?"

"Okay." I was wary.

"Why do you have to make such a big deal about all this when it's going to get you in so much trouble?"

She didn't say it in a nasty way. I assumed she really didn't understand.

Everyone looked at me, curious what I'd say.

"Well, I'm not sure exactly what you mean. What got us into trouble was talking about the anti-LGBTQ+ legislation, despite the fact that we truly have the legal right to talk about it. Even underage students have legal rights."

She was looking at me, still waiting for the rest of the answer.

"But if you're asking why we wanted to talk about anti-LGBTQ+ legislation in the first place, it's because it's a perversion of the legal system. They are making laws that are taking basic human rights away from people. It's wrong."

"But why do you have to use pronouns and all that?" She tucked the colored pencil she was holding behind her ear.

Devin laughed. "We all use pronouns, Briana."

Briana's brow furrowed. "You know what I mean."

Why was this so hard for people? She was obviously genuinely not understanding, so I was going to answer, but it was going to go flying over her head.

"I assume you're comfortable being a girl. You don't feel like your body is all wrong, desperate to be in a different one, right?"

"Of course."

"Well, I never felt like that. Every time somebody called me sir, which happened all the time, I hated it. But every time somebody said I was a girl, I just felt empty. I knew I was supposed to be a girl, but it always felt off. It was like I had no idea how to live the way I should have been born knowing. But I didn't feel like a boy, either. I finally realized that I'm neither. So both she and he are wrong. They/them makes much more sense."

She was frowning and sat there for a moment before simply saying, "Okay."

She turned back to her art and started drawing again. We all got back to our own work, and when Clee came in, Briana jumped at the chance to go first.

Addison and I did some more planning on the group project and she showed me what she'd gotten done last week. I got started on one of the panels.

Briana came back and Lily went with Clee. We all worked quietly.

After a while, my phone dinged and I had a text from Sophia.

"Nic, you know what the punishment for not muting your phone is, right?" Devin asked in a mock condescending tone.

"No, what?" This was a totally made up thing. He must be in a funny mood.

"You have to read the text to all of us."

Everyone laughed.

"Okay, well, let's see what it says." I looked at the text. "Looks fairly mundane. *Have you heard of Jack Petocz or Javier Gomez?*"

I had no idea who either of them was and nobody else seemed to, although Devin had one eye closed and his head tilted up, an exaggerated thinking-hard expression.

"Do you know, Devin?" Addison asked.

"It's familiar." His face went back to normal. "Let's ask Google."

Of course we all did that, and a bunch of ahs went around the room, except for from Briana, who was still working on her piece.

These were kids in Florida who organized and led school walkouts across the state in protest of the Don't Say Gay bill.

What Sophia was trying to tell me didn't click right away. But then it was obvious. I looked at Lily. "Sophia thinks we should organize a walkout."

Just saying it had my pulse picking up.

Lily cocked her head to the side. "You could."

"You should," Devin said, pointing at me with a paintbrush.

"I agree," Addison said. "That would be awesome."

"How?" I asked.

"You could just ... look up what these Jack and Javier guys did," Devin said. "How that all worked. There were some other kids, too—it wasn't only them."

I felt stunned. Could we really organize something like that? Would anybody support us? How would we do it?

I fired off a text to my friends. We agreed to get on a call tonight to discuss it all.

Even though I'd only just learned about it a few minutes earlier, this idea had taken root in my head.

Mom picked me up straight from the mentorship. When I was leaving, Devin encouraged me to do the walkout thing. He said he'd participate and get some friends to, as well.

Addison said she also would, and Lily said of course OAMS kids would do it. She and Sophia would make sure.

I got in the car and Mom smiled at me.

"What, no Isabella?" I asked, disappointed.

"She's spending the night at a friend's. So how was your day?"

"Great. Our group project is really cool." I told her about it as she pulled away from the curb and headed toward the interstate.

"That sounds like a lot of fun," she said once I finished explaining it all to her. But then she joked, "Some people will find meaning in the cross-shape."

I laughed. "Yeah. We decided to make sure that we have the same number of panels on the top and bottom parts, so the bottom won't look longer. We don't want it to look like a cross."

We were quiet for a moment, until I broke the silence with, "Mom?"

"Yeah?"

"Can I run a crazy idea by you?" I was already nervous about mentioning this, but I found that I did want an adult's opinion.

"I'm wary now, but sure."

But first I needed to backtrack. "First, I wanted to say thank you for supporting me last night. I know that was uncomfortable for you."

"Of course I did, Nic. Parenting is never easy, but I would do anything for you."

Tears immediately formed. "Thanks." My voice was already thick.

Then she sniffed and laughed. "I'm just so proud of you, honey. I know none of this is easy for you. And at first I thought this might be a phase, but I now know you know what you're talking about. Only you can really know how you feel."

"Thanks." A couple tears fell and I sniffed. "I do actually have a question. You might not like this idea."

"Okay, I'm wary again." She said it lightly, so I knew she wasn't too worried.

"Have you heard of the Don't Say Gay bill in Florida?"

"I think so, but I don't know anything about it."

I nodded. "So, Florida passed a law that meant that nobody could say the word 'gay' or other similar words in school—teachers, students, or anybody. So, like, even a gay teacher couldn't have a picture of their spouse on their desk and couldn't talk about being gay at all. And kids couldn't talk about being gay to anyone."

"Okay," Mom said.

So I continued. "It's stupid and one of the many hate-inspired laws. Florida is pretty much the worst for all these laws, but Texas is close behind, and of course Oklahoma is doing its best to chase after or one-up Texas."

"That old inferiority complex. It's definitely bad for women in Oklahoma."

"Yeah. So there were these Florida kids, Jack Petocz and Javier Gomez—and some others, too—who organized some school walkouts all over Florida in protest of this law. There were a lot of news stories about it, all over the country. We're talking about trying to do that here."

"Oh, wow." She sounded surprised, and nervous. "That would be a big deal."

"Yeah. Do you think it's crazy?"

"I ... don't think so." She said it uncertainly.

"You don't sound convinced."

"You know how I am with conflict. It's all very nervousing." She glanced over and smiled at me, using our favorite family word that wasn't a real word.

"Yeah. Some of the kids in the art mentorship said they would participate. Lily said she and Sophia would make sure it happened at OAMS."

"Your old roommate Sophia?" Mom asked, surprised again.

"Oh, yeah. I guess I haven't kept you up to date with everything that's been going on." I dialed things back and basically explained all the major stuff from the past two semesters, including Rachel—Mom hadn't known who her dad was last night—always trying to cause trouble for me, Lily ending up on my side, Sophia helping us, and everything. I even told her about the whole mess with Mack, but I did leave out the kiss.

"Sophia was the one who texted me the Florida guys' names, which is what made me look them up. I texted my friends and they're all on board with trying this."

"What would it involve?" she asked.

"We're not quite sure yet. We're going to get on a call tonight to talk about it. Everybody is doing research right now. Except me. I'm soliciting adult advice." I laughed.

"Well, you know I never would have had the gumption to do something like this at your age—or possibly at this age." She smiled wryly. "But no, I don't think it's crazy to try. It might not work, though."

"Yeah, I know. But I think not trying because it might not work is just wimpy."

"And you definitely aren't a wimp," she said.

"Not about this stuff."

"Well, keep me informed once you've talked to your friends, please. I'm going to talk to your dad. I'm wondering if we might need to talk to a lawyer. Or maybe Mack should have his dad ask their lawyer. I just wonder if you encouraging students to miss school might count against you."

My stomach twisted. Was she right about giving them ammunition? I wasn't sure. "I'm talking to everybody tonight. I'll ask Mack."

"There was something I wanted to talk about," Mom said in a confident subject-change tone.

"Okay, now I'm wary."

She laughed, but then got serious. "We need to talk about what happens if they do expel you."

I frowned. She was right, of course, and I knew this was actually a likely outcome. But still. "Jenna said you can do online school. It's like real school, not a GED."

"I did look into that, too. We can think about it. I know going back to Emerson High would be hard for you."

I snorted. "That's the understatement of the year."

Mom nodded. "I really hope they come to their senses fast. If they delay again in two weeks, I'm going to be so pissed."

"Yeah."

She didn't say anything else. Was this the whole conversation about the backup plan? Did that mean she was on board with the online school idea?

I was worn out, and the darkness outside made me sleepy. I felt bad taking a nap here, leaving Mom to her thoughts. I should just ask her.

"So does that mean you're okay with me doing online school?"

She blew air out of her mouth. "I think so, but we need to look into it in more detail. I'm not sure how everything works. Would you have to do the whole spring semester over? I don't know enough. But honestly, I don't want you back at Emerson High. It was not a good place for you."

That made me smile. I'd still vastly prefer staying at OAMS, but at least the worst case scenario wasn't really the worst possible thing.

But it was almost two full weeks before I would know anything more.

I logged onto the Zoom Jenna had set up through her dad, and everyone else was already there.

"Nic, I can't believe we didn't think of doing a walkout ourselves!" Jenna said.

"Yeah," I said. "Honestly, when I first met Sophia at the beginning of last semester, she was kinda horrible. And now she's like the best thing that happened to us."

"No joke!" Jenna said. Jacob and Mack laughed.

"So now, we've got something to figure out," Mack said. "I was doing some research."

Jacob and Jenna both said, "Me too," at the same time.

"I didn't," I admitted. "I was going to in the car, but my mom and I ended up talking. She said I won't have to go back to Emerson High if we get expelled. Thank God."

"Oh, that's great," Jenna said. "Online?"

I nodded.

"I should do that, too," Mack said. "Though I really, really hope it doesn't come to that." A big frown appeared as he looked off somewhere over the camera.

Nobody said anything, because we got it. It would really suck for him to not graduate from OAMS. He had less than three months left.

"Anyway," he said. "Let's plan."

Everyone nodded, but then it seemed like none of us knew how to start.

"Well," Jenna said. "Um. I guess this is new territory for us. But I guess the first step is to figure out exactly what we are asking people to do."

Mack nodded. "Yeah, like, what exactly is a walkout? From the articles I read, it sounds like they basically picked a time and announced it on social media. But then I think each school kind of had someone who led it. There was chanting and stuff. We might need to tell people what to chant. And signs."

"Also, this may seem obvious," Jacob started, "but what exactly are we protesting? Is it about us specifically, or freedom of speech for students in general, or about the anti-LGBTQ+ laws, or a specific one, or what?"

That was a good point. We all frowned in unison.

"Hmm," Jenna said, rubbing her chin. "We do need to clarify that. Will kids in Elmore City, OK, give a crap about four kids at another school? It doesn't impact them at all."

"Yeah," Mack said. "We need to make it about LGBTQ+ rights in general."

"But also, don't forget the free speech angle," Jacob pointed out.

"Oh, yeah," Mack said, leaning back in his chair. "Hmm. I guess it's that combination?"

Jenna pointed at the screen. "You haven't said anything yet, Nic."

I laughed. "Yeah. Everything you all are saying makes sense. I haven't read all about these protests like you all did. But I do think we need to be clear about what the protest is about."

Everyone nodded.

"Okay, here's a thought," Mack said. "If we want this to have an impact on our Board of Trustees, it needs to be about us. But we need to make it about something bigger so more kids will join in. But it should really be about the fact that LGBTQ+ people should be able to speak up."

"How do we frame that?" Jenna asked.

Mack grimaced. "Not sure."

"Should we think of some stuff to put on signs?" I asked. "There could be multiple slogans, and they can choose which ones to use. Or come up with their own."

We brainstormed for a bit and googled some, and came up with a few, some of which could be chants, too. The first one was about us—*Let them back in!* Then we had two more generally about LGBTQ rights to speak out. Two we came up with were pretty simple—*Our voice is loud!* and *Student rights are human rights!*

After that, we talked about how to get the message out. We hadn't yet released anything about the meeting last night, and that was going to be step one. We decided to do a joint video with all four of us on the screen, taking turns speaking. This was going to involve using some specific video app on the phone, but we figured it out and planned to all share our videos with Jenna, who'd put it all together and post it tomorrow.

Then we were each going to make separate posts about the walkout, and post one per day from everyone.

We picked Friday at eleven for the walkout.

Now we had to wait to see if it would really go down like we wanted.

Thursday night, we all convened at Jenna's dad's apartment. It was pretty crazy, because it was a two-bedroom place and Jenna's room had only a single bed. We'd all brought sleeping bags, and Jacob had borrowed three of his family's sleeping pads. We were spread out in the living room and Jenna even ended up sleeping on the couch because we were up late planning.

But we were so excited because our videos had gone viral. Tons of people posted on TikTok and commented on our posts, saying they'd be doing the walkout. The really crazy part was this wasn't only in Oklahoma, which was incredible. We hadn't even meant for anybody outside of Oklahoma to participate, but other states obviously had similar problems, so that seemed to be the draw. It made me so happy to know that people were standing up for themselves all over the place.

Friday morning, Mack woke up first, but he quickly had us all up because he wanted us to practice some chants. He really seemed much improved. I think having this purpose of fighting for our rights so we could keep doing a worthwhile thing had made his depression fade.

Jenna's dad had left early, so we had the apartment to ourselves. We practiced and put final touches on our signs. Jenna had bought everything we needed, and we'd made them the night before.

We talked strategy while Jenna made some scrambled eggs for us all, even though we'd already planned everything down to the minute. Being part of something that needed all this planning was so cool. I felt grown up, like I had the power to change the world. We scarfed our eggs, grabbed our signs, and left at ten.

We spent the twenty minutes driving through the suburbs to get to Burnside—an Arby's here, a Braum's there —practicing the two chants we'd settled on. The first was, *We are proud and we are loud!* A second one was longer, *Student rights are human rights ... Trans rights are human rights ... LGBTQ rights are human rights.* We were laughing, and yelling and I was almost getting high off the excited energy in the car.

There was a moment in the midst of all that where I suddenly felt taken out of the middle of everything, like I was observing myself. And I was almost unrecognizable. And it was good, so good. I accidentally made eye contact with Mack in that instant, and he looked reflective, too. I felt so connected to him right then, like we both knew ourselves and each other completely.

Then Jacob and Jenna started chanting again, and we joined in. The moment was over, but nothing was lost.

Once we got close to campus, Jenna found a parking spot behind one of the shops near the corner. We grabbed our signs and headed onto the OIT campus, setting up to wait on the other side of the parking lot that was adjacent to the OAMS dorm.

And we waited as quietly as we could to avoid calling attention to ourselves. We were planning to not step on the lawn in front of the dorm, even though that's where all the OAMS kids were going to be, but we knew there was a chance that they would kick us off even the OIT campus.

"I'm so excited," Jenna said, bouncing on her feet as we stood in the spot.

There were college students moving all around, presumably trying to get to ten-thirty classes. Nobody was paying much attention to us, other than giving us a few curious glances. A girl with perfect makeup, pink sweats, and fuzzy clogs walked by and I wondered what fashion rules applied there.

But then I was back to staring at the dorm and classroom building, which we could see from where we were. By this point, it was barely after ten thirty, so there was nothing to see yet. Behind us was another one of the white brick buildings of campus, and in front of us was the sea of cars we'd walked through every day for the last six months. The sun was out so light was glinting off all the metal on the cars, making me squint.

Everything was familiar, but everything was different.

My mind and stomach were all over the place. It was cold, but it was the kind of day that would get hot in the afternoon, when the jacket we needed now would be a burden later.

Why was I thinking about the weather? We wouldn't be out here long enough for the afternoon to heat up.

I couldn't focus.

Mack and I sat down to lean against the building, but Jenna was pacing, and Jacob leaned against the wall, but stayed on his feet. He looked tense, too.

How could time move so slow?

Soon it was ten forty-five. Still no activity, but I was too antsy. I stood up and started rocking on my feet. I had so much energy in my legs, but my stomach was hosting a butterfly rave.

"I'm so nervous and excited at the same time," Jacob said. "My brain is about to explode from confusion."

Mack got up and started moving around, too. "Same." His face was tense.

"I know, right?" Jenna said. "It's almost time."

"What if nobody comes out?" Jacob asked quietly.

"They will." There wasn't an ounce of doubt in Jenna's voice.

"Lily and Sophia both told me they had a bunch of people on board," I said. Although Sophia had said she couldn't help us before, she'd been willing to help this time since it was a bunch of people, not just her and us.

"To be fair, Tiana told me the same thing," Jacob said, sounding more convinced.

I checked my phone. "Ten fifty-five. Should we start over there?"

"I think so," Jenna said. "But let's keep our signs down."

We stepped into the parking lot and started crossing, all of us taking steps so strong it was like we were stomping. We were all in sync again.

Jenna pulled her phone out and started recording a video showing the classroom building as we crossed the parking lot.

We reached the edge of the parking lot, the sidewalk the only thing between us and the OAMS lawn. We stood in a line facing the classroom building, our shoes touching the side of the curb. It was weird to be back here, knowing we weren't supposed to be here. I felt unstoppable.

Ten fifty-nine. "Oh, my God, I'm freaking out," I squeaked out.

"I know!" Jenna said.

We all stared at the classroom building front doors, and I remembered the first time I'd gone through them—last year, when I was still at Emerson. My mom drove me down for the interview. I'd been so scared going through those doors, only to be welcomed. And now I had been tossed aside, and it would be people coming out of those same doors who would make me know I still belonged.

Light glinted off the metal door handle. Then the door swung open and two kids came out.

My heart nearly stopped.

One kid held a rolled up poster. I didn't know either of them, except as fellow students.

Jenna grinned and looked at each of us. "See?"

Then the other door opened up, and Sophia stepped out

to hold it open, and kids started streaming out, many holding rolls.

"Oh, wow," Jacob said.

Sophia waved at us. More kids came out. Lily and Tiana both appeared. Both waved at us.

I was so touched that tears welled behind my eyes and I fought them off as I waved back. I did not want to cry now—this was a powerful, beautiful moment that didn't deserve tears.

I won the battle with my tear ducts, and eventually the flow of kids slowed, but there had to be more than thirty of them, maybe even close to forty. There were only around a hundred and fifty kids at the school.

They started walking toward us, holding up their signs. We finally all came to our senses and started holding up our own signs. I heard a car go by behind us and twisted around to look. It was a local news van, something I hadn't even considered.

Once everyone got to the sidewalk, we were all holding up our signs. Mine said *Our voices are human voices* and I'd painted the Pride flag behind the letters. Jacob's said *Proud and loud!* Jenna's said *We say gay!* And Mack's said the old standby, *Trans rights are human rights*.

"Face the camera!" Jenna said. We all turned around because they were filming us.

Then she faced the other kids again and shouted "Student rights are human rights!"

Most of the kids repeated her words and then she cried, "Trans rights are human rights!"

"Trans rights are human rights!" the crowd repeated back.

"LGBTQ rights are human rights!" Jenna yelled, and the crowd responded.

This was surreal. My heart was beating like crazy at how intense this was. All these kids were out here supporting me and my friends. It was obviously bigger than us, too, but this, right here, was for us. I took a step back and took some photos of everything. That's when I saw Ms. Patton walking toward us from the dorm.

I stared. Jenna was still facing the crowd, holding her sign to face the camera, but she couldn't see past the crowd, and Mack and Jacob were facing forward, so I was the only one who watched her approach.

Jenna was mid-chant when Ms. Patton reached us. "You need to leave. You can't be on campus."

Mack looked at her, his back ramrod straight. "We're not on OAMS campus."

"You're on OIT campus, and campus police have been called."

Jenna missed all this, but Mack and Jacob were looking at me. We shared a grim expression, but none of us was willing to give up.

Once Jenna finished her round, Jacob touched her shoulder and whispered in her ear.

Another news van showed up and some college kids had arrived to watch us. I was buzzing from the energy so much that my body was confused, almost like it was having a panic attack, but I felt good.

Jenna kept leading chants and we decided to stick around until they made us leave.

"Who's that?" Mack asked.

I turned around and saw a group of maybe twenty-five people walking toward us from the direction of the cafeteria, holding up signs. College kids here to help us, not to gawk. This was crazy. Mack, Jacob, and I watched them and as they got closer, I could see that there were some Pride shirts and many of the trans-rights-are-human-rights signs, some with Pride flags drawn on, and one guy waving an actual Pride flag.

"Hi!" one of them said, a gender neutral-looking person. "We're from the OIT LGBTQ Student Alliance, and we're here to join you!"

"Awesome!" Jenna said. The new people spread out and faced the news van, holding their signs up high. Someone started a chant and everyone joined in, except for us.

The alliance member who'd first spoken said, "I'm Orion, they/them."

We all introduced ourselves and Orion said, "I've seen your videos. We've been rooting for you."

Then two golf carts pulled up and two people got out— campus cops, based on their blue uniforms and badges.

"They're supposedly kicking us off campus," I said to Orion, who looked confused.

"They can't do that," Orion said. "We all have the right to protest so long as we don't disrupt classes, which we obviously aren't."

"They were probably just hoping we wouldn't know better," Jenna said. "Seems to be the way authority figures operate around here."

"Okay, let's go," said one of the cops. Ms. Patton watched from a distance.

The cops crowded us. "You need to leave campus. You can do so on your own, or we can escort you."

The crowd had gone quiet and Jenna looked at all of us. Her face said that nothing would stop her.

"You have no legal right to kick us off campus," Orion said. "We aren't messing with classes. You're just being bullies."

The two cops looked pissed, but they didn't say anything.

Jenna started leading another chant.

"Actually," Orion started, "if you all want, we can go to Burnside City Hall. We actually got a permit. One of our members has a mom who works there. We even got a permit to march there from here."

"Really?" I asked. Mack and Jacob looked surprised.

"Should we?" Jacob asked.

Mack stood close to Jenna and when she paused to catch her breath, he got her attention and she turned around. We explained and her eyes lit up and she said, "Let's do it!"

Then she called, "March to city hall!" She pointed at Orion. "Lead the way!"

"Yes, ma'am," Orion said, laughing. "Or sir, if you prefer."

Jenna laughed and we started walking toward the edge of campus, Orion and the other alliance members leading the way. I had no idea where the city hall was. But I didn't need to know, because someone was helping us. This was turning out to be amazing.

Emerson Nic would never have imagined I'd be involved —and even kind of leading—something like this.

As we headed away from the parking lot, I looked back to see that, amazingly, the whole group was following us. The golf carts also drove along beside us. I wondered if Orion was right and they were just trying to trick us into stopping. Sort of like how the Board of Trustees didn't have a legal right to stop us from posting our videos, but they were trying anyway.

What if Orion was wrong and they could arrest us? That added a twist to my already raging stomach. Could college cops do that? Would my mom be so understanding if I ended up in some kind of jail?

Maybe. I hoped it never came to that. But we were in the thick of it, and we were seeing this through, whatever it turned into.

We reached the edge of campus and the golf carts stopped, but they waited until the light had changed and we all crossed the street. The whole group didn't make it across before the Walk sign went away, and they just kept coming. The drivers at the intersection all looked confused, but we carried on.

As we marched down the street, Jenna had some people chanting, and others were talking excitedly. I'd never been part of such a big group before. It was incredible. Every step felt important and powerful. My voice was tired from all the yelling, so I'd started checking what else was on social media. I posted a quick video I'd taken early on to our TikTok channel with the caption, "It's really happening!!!!!"

We'd created a hashtag for all social media and I searched it. There were already a dozen videos on TikTok and several posts on Instagram. I couldn't see where all were located, but one had snow in the background. There wasn't snow anywhere in Oklahoma right now, so that meant it really was bigger. My heart was about to burst from happiness.

I started looking closer. There was a video of a small group of kids in Durant and another in Oklahoma City. Then one in Lawton. Oh, my God! That was Addison holding a sign about LGBTQ rights. There weren't that many kids, but it was not zero.

The march lasted for four long blocks, almost a mile and a half, before we got to the city hall. Some office workers were standing outside the gray building, arms crossed, watching us. A Fox News van was waiting there and the two that had been on campus had followed us there, filming the march.

We got onto the lawn in front of the building and faced the news cameras that were still around. We held our signs up and Jenna started a round of "Let them back in!" We'd never talked about that one, but it made sense.

Some police cars pulled into the parking lot, which nearly made my heart stop. Now, these people *could* arrest us.

Except Orion said we had permission to be there. The college students had spread out, mixing with us.

But I kept looking on social media while holding up my sign and chanting along with the crowd. Instagram yielded photos from Tulsa and Norman. Then three kids in Elmore City, which was hilarious since Jenna had specifically called that town out, even though I'd never heard of it. There must be somebody at OAMS from there—was that how most of these schools were getting kids to come out? Because people here told them about it? Every time I searched, I got more results on our hashtag.

Oh, my God, this was fucking insane.

One of the newscasters approached me, but I didn't see him until he was right in front of me. He asked, "What's this about?" even though he must have known, and shoved a microphone in my face.

Somehow I managed to not feel too shocked. "Students have the right to say what they want if it doesn't hurt anybody—even if they're LGBTQ," I said. My voice was high and fast, obviously excited. The newscaster asked someone near me why they were here, and I focused back on the protest.

We kept going, moments of relative quiet mixing with

chanting, and then three other people showed up with signs. They were all adults, and at first I thought they were going to join us.

But then they raised their signs. One read, *Trans is a fad*. Another said, *Kids need protection*, and the last one read, *Let kids be kids*. These were stupid, and probably recycled from some anti-LGBTQ rally. It was again the extreme right saying words and then going completely against what those words actually mean.

I stepped away to get more video of the whole scene. So many kids. Some were singing, and everyone was holding up their signs. Three office workers still stood in front of the building with their arms crossed, obviously pissed, and the counter-protesters were waving their signs and saying something I couldn't make out.

Well, screw you, hateful people.

Something caught my eye, and I watched about twenty more kids come around the corner of the building. They saw us and cheered. Then we cheered. I checked their signs, and they were obviously on our side so I filmed them approach us across the lawn.

One of them had a megaphone and they were doing the multi-part human rights chant.

One kid with a black mohawk came up to me. "Are you guys from OAMS?"

"Yeah." I had never seen a mohawk in person, and I was distracted by it because it was very cool. But then I came to my senses. "Where are you from?"

"Burnside High." He—I was guessing—pointed in what I assumed was the general direction of their high school, though I had no idea.

"That's amazing. Thanks for coming!" I sounded

completely ridiculous and the kid and I gave an exuberant laugh.

"Oh, I see you have some trash here." They nodded toward the counter-protesters.

"Yes, the 'let kids be kids' battalion that keeps telling kids they can't be who they are."

"Makes so much sense. Ooh, I love your sign. I'm Liam, by the way. He/him."

"Nic. They/them." I looked at his sign, which read, *Trans rights are human rights*, and I nodded at it and said, "A solid choice."

"They're starting a chant!" he said. "Let's join in."

So we did.

The Burnside kids had completely integrated with us. There had to be more than sixty now, maybe even a lot more than that. This was bananas.

My phone dinged with a text from Isabella. It was a selfie with her and some of her friends, standing outside in front of the elementary school.

My heart nearly stopped. Isabella was protesting? I was shocked. She was still in elementary school. She shouldn't be doing that. Her friends' parents were all going to think she was a bad influence.

But oh, my God—my little sister was the best. She knew this could put her at risk of being bullied, and she did it anyway.

—*Isabella, I never thought you would participate! You're going to get in trouble!*—

—*I know I don't care. Emily, Priya, Sarah, and Maggie are here too!*— She sent a picture of four girls, the first three were friends of hers I recognized, but then there was a short and chubby girl who looked like she might be somewhat confused about why she was there, but she was trying to smile.

Maggie was the girl everyone picked on, and the one Isabella told me she was afraid to talk to in front of other kids. Apparently, she'd moved beyond that. I hoped this whole thing didn't cost her any friends.

Liam looked over. "Is that an elementary school?"

"Yeah. My sister. She's in fifth grade." I giggled, a little hysterically. I really hoped Mom wasn't going to be mad at me for Isabella taking part.

She probably wouldn't. She knew Isabella was old enough to make her own decisions about a lot of things.

I sent Isabella some of the pictures I'd taken, showing so many of us, and then joined in another chant, and shaking my sign.

Then I went back to searching the hashtag and finding more and more posts.

This was big. It was real, lots of kids were taking part, and it felt like this could be the beginning of something huge.

People were really out there supporting us and standing up for their own rights. I couldn't believe I was a part of this.

It was barely after noon, so I had no idea where else this was going to go. I also didn't know if it would make a difference in our situation, because as incredible as this whole thing was, we still needed to be let back into school.

But I was feeling more positive about it now that I knew people believed in us. It would be another week before we found out.

The wait was killer.

In the meantime, I had a protest to chant for, and a big sign to hold high in the air.

Devin and Addison whooped when I got to the back room at the mentorship session the next day. Lily and Briana weren't there yet. But every one of them—well, except Briana—had been in one of the protests. I'd seen bits and pieces of both of them. And Lily had been with us.

"You're amazing," Devin said.

I shook my head. "Not really—I was just trying to assert my rights. You all were the amazing ones, helping with nothing specific to be gained."

Lily walked in and grinned at us. "Hey."

"Thank you all so much," I said to everyone.

"It was actually fun," Addison said. "I never get in trouble so I was nervous, but there were about ten of us, which honestly surprised me. I handed out Pride flags. But I only had five."

"I saw your protest on TikTok—I even saw you," I said. "I loved it. Did you get in any trouble?"

Addison shook her head. "Nope."

"Nic and I marched together to Burnside City Hall," Lily said.

"How many?" Devin asked. "We had about twenty."

Lily sat down at her table. "Did you count, Nic? I got up to thirty-five from OAMS, but everyone was moving around so much. But I think more kids joined after that. Ms. Patton was so stressed."

"Yeah, there were thirty to forty OAMS kids, and then the OIT LGBTQ Student Alliance showed up, and *then*, when we got to the city hall, the Burnside kids showed up, and we were definitely over sixty." I said. "I was so shocked that so many people came with us."

"Yeah, I was impressed, too," Lily said.

"How did you get everybody to go?" I asked her.

"Sophia and I mostly organized it—well, more Sophia than me, honestly. But Tiana was going around that morning encouraging everyone, too. Rachel was trying to convince everyone they'd get in trouble." She laughed at the last part.

"Who's Rachel?" Devin asked.

"My and Mack's archnemesis." I gave him a wry look.

He raised an eyebrow and Addison looked at me with curiosity. Lily chuckled.

"So, it's actually convoluted." I summarized with the high points, starting in Texas and ending at OAMS, with her dad inserting himself into everything so he could wreak as much havoc as possible.

Devin shook his head.

"What do people get out of doing this crap?" Addison asked.

"I guess a sense of power?" I said.

"It's just that these people want to tell everybody how to live their lives," Lily said. "Like their way is the only way."

Clee came in, so we all turned to her. "Morning everyone. Briana can't make it this morning. Who wants to go first?"

Was Briana missing because of the walkout? It didn't really make sense, but it seemed quite a coincidence.

Nobody had said anything yet, so I volunteered to go with Clee. I hadn't gotten anything done so far, and now I was all fired up.

"Congratulations on yesterday," Clee said as soon as we got to her studio.

I blushed, as per usual. "Thanks. I'm still in shock."

She smiled at me and sat in her chair. "I have a good feeling about this. The fact that kids in other states joined in is such a good sign. We need a youth movement to save this country."

I sat next to her and put my two pieces on the table. "Do you think that can really happen? That the country can be saved?"

"I do." She clasped her hands together and rested her chin on her fingertips. "We will have to undo a lot of damage, but I believe things can get better. Your generation is truly more open-minded. Even mine isn't bad. We've still got a lot of Boomers in politics, but they're slowly working their way out. Then we'll have more of those Gen Xers, who are all over the place politically but are still an improvement, if not perfect."

"I hope so." I looked back at my work, curious what she would think. I was thinking about how most of the state-level politicians weren't really old. They were often even Millennials. But I didn't want to talk politics right now.

She turned in her seat and looked at my work. "These are both nice."

For the ink drawing, she'd asked me to find an image of a bird in flight, and I'd chosen a bald eagle.

"This angle is really powerful. And I love that you chose the most American bird there is. Did you do that on purpose?"

I looked at her in confusion. "Not really."

"I just mean, it feels like you're making a statement about our country, maybe subconsciously."

"Definitely subconsciously. I didn't even think about how it's an image used so much by conservatives."

"Sharing a rack at Walmart with those evocative wolf and full moon t-shirts."

I laughed.

"Anyway, I love it." She gave me some tips on some areas

I could have done differently, but it was still a successful piece.

The watercolor was of a stack of fantasy books, but I had done only the colors and not the titles, which made her chuckle.

"Lettering is so hard to get right," she said. "You have one more week at home, right?"

"Yeah." God, I hoped it was the last one.

She turned sideways to face me. "For the watercolor, see if you can do something else in the house, something mundane and homey if possible. But I'm really happy with your development in the medium. I think you've got the basic knack for it, and the more you paint, the better you'll get. If you want to try adding ink to this week's watercolor, give it a shot."

We finished up, and I returned to the back room and started working with Addison on our pieces.

Everybody was serious now, and there wasn't much more chatting for most of the rest of the day. But when it was time to go, everyone wished me good luck with the next Board of Trustees meeting. Devin and Addison said they might even try to go, though they weren't sure.

Isabella came with Mom to pick me up this time, and we ended up reminiscing about some funny family vacations and just having a light evening, a nice break from all the intensity.

But I couldn't forget that everything still hung in the balance, and there was no way to know which side it would land on—but it would be right or wrong, not in the middle.

Mom and I drove to the board meeting Friday night.

I was still in a daze. The national news had picked up the story of the protests because they happened at a lot of schools in Oklahoma, even in small towns, which surprised a lot of people. And there were the ones in other states, especially in the south, so it was being called a national protest. Liberal media was wondering if this was the start of a youth movement, just like Clee had said, and conservative media was complaining about entitled groomers.

It was crazy that I'd been a part of that. And I really wondered if it was going to fizzle out, or if we had really started something. Only time would tell. And my immediate concern was this meeting, starting in ten minutes.

We'd claimed the same area of the chairs as last time—front left. I was sitting next to Mom this time. None of us—kids or parents—were speaking at this one. Only the two lawyers.

I had my arms crossed in front of me and had been staring at the floor to try to calm my nerves, but it was getting really loud in there, so I turned around to see what was going on. The place was crammed full. I was sick to my stomach, like the last time I was here. All the chairs were taken and there were people lining the side walls and filling the back of the room. There were two different news cameras in there and two other photographers moving around the room, snapping pictures.

I quickly faced the front again, sweat breaking out across my forehead and neck. But then I had this slow realization that I'd seen something. I turned back around and this time, Addison and Devin waved at me, his septum piercing making him stand out in a mostly stuffy crowd. Ms. Mangal and Clee were there again. There were also some other kids—I assumed in high school—standing in the back, holding up Pride flags, and one had a poster that said *LGBTQ people are people too*. I didn't recognize any of them.

This was crazy. I'd been so unpopular at Emerson, and now I was inspiring kids to stand up for my and my friends' rights. I'd been so isolated, and now I was surrounded by support.

Obviously the walkout, and the unexpected success of it, had brought attention to our situation.

I looked at the trustees sitting behind their table at the front of the room. Rachel's dad looked unhappy, with a pinched and angry face. The others were mostly just sitting there, and none of them were talking like they had been last time.

Then, the chairman hit the gavel on the table like last time, sharp and loud, and he called the meeting to order. I thought I was going to throw up. I closed my eyes to try to settle myself.

There were a few unrelated things they talked about at the beginning. The minutes and whatever. But then the chairman said, "We're here to talk about the four students who have been suspended. We want to first say that OAMS is a special place, providing an opportunity for bright students from all over the state to excel and develop in ways their schools may not be able to support. It exists because of state lawmakers' and donors' benevolence, and it must be a place where students feel safe and able to focus on academics, because that's why they're there."

Some rando hooted from the back of the room.

I was queasy. This sounded bad. Mom reached over and squeezed my hand, which actually made me feel worse because it meant I'd read this man right.

He continued. "The welfare and success of our students is paramount. But we understand that kids have lives outside of academics. As long as they are able to maintain academic success, kids are allowed to do extracurricular activities."

I wasn't sure where he was going with this.

"The Board of Trustees has made the decision to rescind the suspensions and allow the four students to return to the Oklahoma Academy of Mathematics and Science."

My mouth fell open and my friends and I all gasped, and much of the room cheered. There were some boos, but Mom squeezed my hand again and then leaned over to give me a hug. "We won," she whispered. "I'm so proud of you."

The chairman continued, "They may return to the dorm Sunday evening and go back to attending classes Monday morning." He started listing our names to be recorded in the minutes. "This decision is final, but we are allowing comments from the public."

I was in shock. It had happened so fast. Was it because of the walkout? All the bad press? I looked at my group, and caught Jenna's eye. She was smiling, but I could tell she was in shock, too.

Some people did go up and comment. Some thanked them for making the right decision. One said that they hoped they would continue treating LGBTQ kids as people, since that's what they were. Then there were the detractors, who slammed the board for bowing to pressure from the left and giving in to woke culture. Some of them got pretty heated and I wondered if we'd have another near-fight, but I wasn't paying full attention because it was just too much emotionally.

Mom must have been able to tell I was overwhelmed, because she held my hand the whole time, and afterward, we hugged goodbye before I left with Jenna. She said, "I was thinking of having you pack everything in case this happened so you could just stay here, but I didn't want to jinx it."

"I think that was the right move," I said, finishing the hug.

We parted ways and I followed Jenna and her dad to their car.

What a crazy ride this had all been.

Sunday night, Mom parked near the dorm, and then she and Isabella helped me get all my stuff inside. I was happy to be back, but still all nerves. I didn't know what other people were going to be like.

As soon as we were through the front door, several kids who were at the front tables stared, and one girl I didn't really know waved, which was new. I tried to remember if I'd seen her at the walkout.

I checked in at the desk, with the older RA greeting me with a smile. He was nice, even if he had thought I was a boy when I first got here last semester.

I started up the stairs, Mom and Isabella behind me.

"I know where your room is!" Isabella said.

"That you do," I said.

We headed down the hallway and I unlocked the door and pushed it open. Mack hadn't gotten here yet.

We still had to share a room. The lawyers had said that was an issue that was probably not winnable, especially in the short term—as in, Mack's last two months before graduating. We decided to let it go for this year. Mom promised we'd look into it over the summer and try for mine next year.

I dragged my suitcase in and dropped my backpack on

the desk. Isabella set my portfolio next to my desk and Mom put my duffel on the bottom bunk.

She sat on it, barely missing hitting her head on the top bunk. "Well, you're back. What do you think, honey?"

I sat in my desk chair. "It's going to be tough to catch up. Especially physics. I missed a test and I'm hoping she'll give us some time before we have to take it. Jacob and Jenna both have to make it up, too."

Mom nodded. "I really believe in you, Nic. But let me know if you need me to talk to somebody if they are not giving you a fair chance. But we should get going so you can get back to studying. I know you've got a tough week ahead of you, catching up."

"Okay." I looked at Isabella, who was staring out the window even though it was dark outside. "You're being quiet, Isabella."

She frowned and looked at me. "Now you're back here and I have to get used to you being gone again."

"I know, it sucks being apart. But I'll be back in a couple months, for the whole summer. Give me a hug." I put my arms out and she walked into them and we had a nice long hug. I stood up to hug Mom, and they left.

"Oh, hi Mack," I heard down the hall. Mom talked to him for a second, and then he came in.

I smiled at him. "We're back."

He returned the smile, even though he looked stressed. "We are. I saw Jenna coming in and she texted Jacob. We're going to meet downstairs in ten and head over for dinner."

We both started unpacking our suitcases. He looked a little serious.

"Are you okay?" I asked him.

"Huh?" He looked at me. "Oh, I'm okay. I just—there's a lot to do. I'm scared about getting caught up."

"Yeah. We all missed a physics test, and you know she hates Jacob and me."

He nodded, and we ended up having to do the awkward sorry-I'm-in-the-way dance trying to get to our closets at the foot of the beds. But we managed it.

Then we went back downstairs. We found Jacob and Jenna standing behind the couch in the TV lounge area, a couple people talking to them.

Jenna saw us and said, "Hey!" Jacob turned and they both came over. We were all smiles, even though we'd just seen each other.

The two kids they'd been talking to waved and said they were off, but I got a definite starstruck vibe off them, something I would never in a million billion years have thought could have been inspired by me.

"It's almost like things are back to normal, but not," Jenna said.

I nodded. "Yeah, nothing will ever be the same."

"We're going to have to continue to toe the line and be really careful," Mack said. "They'll be looking at any excuse to punish us now. Retaliation. Hopefully, if we can last this year, Rachel's dad's obsession will end and you'll be good for next year."

"Should we go?" Jacob asked.

We all nodded.

"Let's go," Mack said.

I looked at the front desk as we walked by and I wondered what kind of looks we were going to get from the other RAs. Mack was right about us needing to be careful.

But as long as we were careful, we would be okay.

We would be okay.

EPILOGUE

It was absolutely baking outside, the first Saturday of June. Jenna, Jacob, and I were unofficially attending Mack's graduation. The ceremony was in front of the Oklahoma state capitol, the graduates standing on the steps and going down to a stage in front of the steps to pick up their diplomas. The official guests were all in some black chairs opposite the stage.

Mack had only been allowed to invite two people, so it was obviously his parents. So we were standing off to the side on the lawn. Some of the school administrators made us move further back, and we'd found a tree for a little bit of shade.

There were actually other kids from the school scattered about, but not many. They were using a microphone, so we could hear bits of the commencement speech. The speaker was some lady from a butter company. Nobody knew why.

"Oh, my God, I'm dying," Jenna said, pulling her shirt away from her front. "Those chairs must be nuclear hot. And oh, my God—those robes."

"No joke. Our tree is a superior spot, for sure," I said.

Jacob grunted in agreement. He'd surprised us both by wearing tan cargo shorts. We'd literally never seen him in anything but long pants because of his burn scars all over his legs.

I was trying to listen to the speech, but I kept mentally fixating on Jacob's burns. He'd told me about them months ago, but they were way worse than I'd imagined. I hadn't really thought about how bad they must have been for him to be in the hospital for months.

I just kept imaging little Jacob falling on a campfire, and his family desperately trying to put the fire out that engulfed his pants. When I'd told Jenna about it one time when it was just her and Mack there, Mack told us that Jacob's brother and mom both had burns on their hands from trying to help him, but it was his dad who'd finally stopped the fire. It's just so weird that you can think you know someone, but then not know about major things in their lives. I guess that was something we all did to keep from dwelling on the past in a bad way.

A bit of a breeze blew by us, and I pinched my shirt out to get a bit of air flow. The speaker's voice got louder. "—can do it. Only you know who you are and what you can become. Strength comes from inside, but you have to give yourself permission to use it." But then we couldn't hear the rest.

Was she making a reference to us? Who knew. Maybe she lifted that from some other commencement speech. But she might have known about us even if no one specifically told her. Because after the walkout, I found out a lot of things. One was that Briana had missed the mentorship session the Saturday after the walkout because she'd participated with a few other people at her school, and her parents punished her. She'd told me their reaction made her better understand why we felt like we had to do something. We got along well after that. I really appreciated she'd made an effort to understand me—and LGBTQ issues in general—something a lot of her church buddies wouldn't have done.

Then we also found out how we'd managed to go viral—Lily had a cousin in Hollywood, and they'd shared some of our early videos with people, and somehow it had gotten to exactly the right people who could blow it up. She'd actually not told me—but she'd told everyone else at the mentorship, and when Lily went back for her time with Clee, Devin had told me.

But then the truly craziest thing had happened—we'd been featured on the cover of *People* magazine after everything got so big, with the national walkouts. Thinking about the photo shoot made me smile. We'd all been so uncomfortable. But the picture had been cool—we were in the middle of laughing at something, so we all looked happy. And somehow we also looked like a cohesive unit. I didn't know how the photographer had done that, but she had.

The other crazy thing that happened with all that was that the piece I'd entered in the art club contest actually won first place, which was so shocking. I'd ended up doing an ink drawing of a scene from the protests as the self-portrait for class. It showed us at the city hall, with Jenna and me visible, along with a bunch of other people. It was a shot from a great video. Jenna had a megaphone one of the Burnside kids had given her. Pissed-off officials stood in the background, and they were part of what made the piece so perfect—the contrast between old and young was really clear.

The truly extra part of the whole thing was that *People* also published it with our story.

I shook my head, trying to clear memories of all the

unexpected fame—I guess that's what you had to call it. It had already faded fast, which I was glad for. We got recognized a few times on campus, and Jacob and I were so awkward. Jenna and Mack took it in stride.

But back to the present. I glanced back at Jacob, who was looking down.

When he'd told me about his burns, I'd said he shouldn't feel like he had to hide his legs. But I understood his fear. Every one of us knew what it was like to have some visual cue that made us obviously different from other people—well, maybe not Jenna quite as much.

I glanced over. She didn't do Oklahoma girl exactly like she was supposed to, but she did wear a little makeup, and she wasn't really unfeminine, so she wasn't that different. She still managed to pull off cute with her spiky blonde hair. I'd never been able to do cute, even when I was still confused about my gender and thought I was a girl.

The speaker finished, and then the president of the school got up to give some kind of speech herself, but it was short, and soon she was calling graduate names.

"Let's get closer so Mack can hear us when we cheer," Jenna said.

"Good idea," Jacob said, even though he might be as uncomfortable as I was at the idea of cheering.

I just wasn't a whooper.

We got close enough that some of the parents looked over at us, but we stood there watching them get through the As, the Bs, and the Cs, waiting for the Ds.

Mack was the first one. "Mackenzie Davis," the president said.

Mack got up and starting walking down the steps to the stage.

"When he gets handed the diploma, woo really loud, okay?" Jenna said quietly.

We'd asked him if hearing his deadname would bother him, and he said he didn't consider his legal name his deadname—his deadname was Kenzie, because that's what he'd always gone by before. I only knew it because Rachel called him that to be horrible. Mack said he actually liked his legal name. I could relate to that, sort of—I liked Nic, but not Nicole. I was going to get that legally changed some time.

Mack was almost there. He reached his hand out and the second he touched it, I yelled "Woo!" so loud that I almost stopped out of shock.

But Jenna and Jacob were still going, and Mack looked over at us and smiled, then headed back up, so we quieted down, and the president called the next D.

I was so proud of him, so glad I'd met him, and Jenna and Jacob. We all looked at each other, grinning.

Apparently I *was* a whooper.

I was a lot of things Emerson Nic would never have believed possible. I think Mom might have been right—I probably could do almost anything I put my mind to. If it mattered, I would do it.

THE END

KELLY VINCENT

ACKNOWLEDGMENTS

As always, there were many people who helped me bring this book to fruition. There are of course my regular writing partners: Anne Shaw, Shari Duffin, and Vicky McDonald. Gwen Sharp has done many a beta read for me, and she squeezed this one in before a trip so she could get the feedback to me quickly (then had a great trip, so a win-win all around). I also had some new beta readers this time, and they are very much appreciated: Teylor Black and Jeff Elmore. I also used the services of a couple of sensitivity readers primarily to look at Jacob and how he interacts with the world and the rest of the group. moukies editing and Kayla Dunigan (BlackSensitivityReader.com) both did a great job of making sure I represented Jacob and Tiana as authentically as possible. Finally, my editor, Monique Conrod, was the best, as usual.

AUTHOR'S NOTE

Those of you who have read the earlier books in the series know how far Nic has come in their development. Nic in the first book would never have imagined the things they would do the next year. This whole series is a hugely personal one. *Ugly* is largely autobiographical. Most of the things in that book happened to me (in the 1980s and 1990s, not the 2020s), and when I started writing the story in November 2018, it flowed out of me like blood from a sliced carotid artery. Before the end of the month, I had 80,000 (about 350 pages), and then I was physically and mentally exhausted. But the story was out of me, ready to be cleaned up and shared with the world.

Almost everything in *Uglier* and *Ugliest* is fiction. It was kind of a thought experiment for me, where I imagined how different my life could have been if I'd known back then what we know about gender nowadays. I grew up in Tulsa and went to the "real OAMS"—the Oklahoma School of Science and Mathematics in Oklahoma City—for my last two years of high school. But my struggles there were different from Nic's, because it absolutely is a different time.

When I was growing up and in my 20s in Oklahoma, my mere presence in public was offensive enough for people to comment, or at minimum give me judgmental looks. And not conforming to the gender standard was worthy of punishment in some people's eyes. Teachers told me that if I'd wear makeup, kids would stop "teasing" me (that's what we called bullying and harassment in those days). My parents' friend told me I should draw flowers instead of dragons. The message was clear—I was living life wrong and it was my fault for choosing to be different.

But it never felt like a choice. I just wanted to be free to exist—the dream was to go through the world without friction. But other people—teachers, peers, strangers—weren't going to let that happen. One time I was waiting to cross a street on my college campus wearing a fun, colorful hat, and a guy in a passing car yelled, "What are you?" I was coming back from a pizza delivery run once and a guy in the parking lot yelled, "Is your name Pat?" (a reference to SNL's Pat sketches, where nobody could figure out which gender the person was). These comments felt like slaps in the face out of nowhere and always threw me for a loop.

The incident in the book where Nic throws the coke in the kid's face actually happened—the first time I ever fought back against this stuff, as I usually cowered in discomfort. One time when I was sitting in a Taco Bell, some college-age guys came in and caused a big scene while ordering, just being generally loud and dickish, and when they left, they slipped a note into my driver's side window (it was open a crack because of the heat). The note was filled with anti-LGBTQ hate, including the words "fucking dyke bitch" and "1-800-KILLURSELF." I'd had literally no interaction with these guys, not even accidental eye contact, yet my mere existence was that offensive to them. It was actually a little scary. Fortunately, they were gone by the time I found the note. Just being out in public meant being a target.

Of all the places I've lived, including some other fairly conservative places, Oklahoma was the worst in terms of intolerance for difference, especially in gender presentation. I don't know why that is. I was misgendered as male several times a week, every week, for years, starting in high school. Nowhere else I've lived has it been that common. And in other places, people often apologize when they realize their mistake. No one ever apologized in Oklahoma—because they viewed it as my fault. Back then, it drove me crazy, because I still thought I was woman—just a deeply defective one—since it was the only option, and I knew I wasn't a man. Getting misgendered reminded me how hard I was failing at being a woman.

But the truth is that in some ways, things are better now than when I was growing up. I don't go back to Oklahoma very often, but I went a couple of times recently for some family things. I picked up my laptop and headed out into the world to work—usually at a bagel shop near my hotel in south Tulsa, where I spent hours every day. Normally whenever I do something like that there, I'm tense and on guard, waiting for somebody to say something mean.

In October of 2023, I sat there tensely eating my pizza bagel waiting for a nasty look or comment. But I spent hours there every day, and no one ever said anything or gave me dirty looks. Eventually I realized that nobody actually cared about me, at least in Tulsa (Tulsa County and Oklahoma County, where Oklahoma City is, actually went blue in the governor's race in 2022, but the rest of the state is unabashedly MAGA country). People in Tulsa didn't care that I looked different. This felt amazing at first, so freeing. I didn't have to be constantly waiting for a judgmental comment to be thrown at me. I could just be.

But then I realized this was actually a false relief. All was not perfect. Most people don't care what I do or how I look, which is great, but not enough of them care about what the politicians do, especially in regards to anti-LGBTQ legislation. Some do care about human rights—I think the main issue that drove the blue in Tulsa and Oklahoma Counties in the 2022 governor's race was abortion rights, as Governor Stitt had signed one of the most draconian anti-abortion laws in the country at the time (as always, trying to out-do Texas).

Most of the politicians taking away the rights of LGBTQ people are also the ones taking away women's rights, so a vote against restrictive abortion laws is a vote against anti-LGBTQ legislation. But it isn't enough for people in Tulsa and Oklahoma Counties to vote against the politicians driven by hate. We need the rest of the state, and this dynamic is true in most red states. We need people in the cities to convince the rest of the counties in their states to vote for human rights, too. It probably sounds impossible to convince Republicans—it really isn't only MAGA people— to vote for a Democrat. But a Democrat in Oklahoma is not the same kind of Democrat as one in Washington state. They could start by finding all those rural and small-town women who were shocked when they learned they could no longer get an abortion, or get rid of a dead fetus. I think it's possible to get through to enough people about the many other rights that are being taken away from them to change things. But it's hard work, and it's not fair that people in the cities have to do the work of convincing people to stop voting against basic rights. But I don't know how else to go about it. We've tried a top-down approach, but people just plug their ears with their fingers and close their eyes. This has to be grassroots, person-to-person.

One of the reasons this matters so much is that some people still do hate us and feel entitled to judge us, and worse. In a lot of places, it's simply not safe right now. Violence against trans and other LGBTQ people has increased across the US, but it has increased almost four-fold in states that are passing the anti-trans and anti-LGBTQ legislation, including Oklahoma and most red states. Politicians are giving permission for people to target trans and other LGBTQ kids. Kids like Nex Benedict.

Nex's story came to light right before my last trip to Oklahoma. I arrived the day before the vigils were held for him. Nex's story completely broke my heart. Any time a trans kid is bullied to death is awful, but Nex's story feels so much more personal to me because Owasso is only fifteen miles from the house I grew up in. My guess is that most of the kids at Owasso High School ignored Nex and left him alone, but a handful targeted him and made his life hell.

In places like Oklahoma, Nex and kids like him get no support from most of the adults around them—in my experience, those adults are likely to side with the bullies. They say, *If you just conform, they'll leave you alone; everything is your fault.* It's very much a blame-the-victim mentality, and it's simply not true. I did try to conform, and got mocked for my efforts. Also, in my experience, a lot of high school teachers are as desperate to be liked by the popular kids as other kids are. Since it's the popular kids who are tormenting the kids who are different, it doesn't take a genius to realize it's pointless to reach out to an adult for help. More likely than not, something hurtful will come out of their mouths.

I hope that Nic's story will help people understand that trans people really are just people, and keep real kids like Nex from being targeted and punished for being different. These are the stakes—it's truly life and death.

RESOURCES FOR TRANS AND OTHER LGBTQ TEENS

Below are some of the resources I know about so it's US-focused. But Google will lead you to additional resources if you're in a different country.

Mental Health Support

The Trevor Project (https://www.thetrevorproject.org/) has several resources for young LGBTQ+ people (by young, they mean up to age 24). Its main focus is suicide prevention and crisis intervention, and they have help available 24/7 every day. You can reach out by phone, online chat, or text. The phone Lifeline is 866-4-U-TREVOR (866-488-7386); Trevor-Chat and TrevorText can both be found at https://www.thetrevorproject.org/get-help/.

Trans Lifeline (https://translifeline.org/) has a hotline for trans people in crisis. One of their big goals is to avoid police involvement because it's so unsafe, so they do not call the police. Unfortunately, the hotline (https://translifeline.org/

hotline/) is not available 24/7 but at the time of writing, they are hoping to expand their hours. The US hotline number is 877-565-8860 and the Canada one is 877-330-6366.

Advocacy and Support

The Trans Youth Equality Foundation (https://www.transy outhequality.org/) supports and advocates for trans, nonbinary, and gender nonconforming youth and their families. They have resources for kids and teens (https://www.transy outhequality.org/for-youth).

Stand with Trans (https://standwithtrans.org/) is another advocacy group for trans people. They have a resources page (https://standwithtrans.org/trans-lifeline-library/) that includes some for kids and teens.

The Human Rights Campaign (https://www.hrc.org/) fights for LGBTQ+ rights with a focus on trans rights. They also have a resources page (https://www.hrc.org/resources/lgbtq-youth) for youth.

GLAAD (https://glaad.org/) is a media advocacy group focused on LGBTQ rights and also has a resources page for transgender people (https://glaad.org/transgender/resources/).

News

The single best source of news about trans and LGBTQ rights in America is the blog Erin in the Morning (https://www.erininthemorning.com/) with Erin Reed. This is the blog Mack shares with all the kids in *Ugliest* because Erin posts about laws and rights related to trans people mostly in the US, almost every weekday and some weekend days. She has a subscription fee for the blog but also has some free content. She also posts to Twitter and TikTok at @erininthemorn and Instagram at @erininthemorning.

Another good source of news about LGBTQ people and issues is Them (https://www.them.us/).

THE ART OF BEING UGLY SERIES

Want to see just how far Nic has come, from a bullied small-town Oklahoma artist to a youth movement leader? Check out the first two books in the series.

ALSO BY KELLY VINCENT

Finding Frances

New Girl

Binding Off (prequel)

Always the New Girl

The Art of Being Ugly

Ugly

Uglier

Ugliest

ABOUT THE AUTHOR

Kelly Vincent wrangles data weekdays and spends the rest of their time with words. They grew up in Oklahoma but have moved around a bit, with Glasgow, Scotland being their favorite stop. They now live near Seattle with several cats who help them write their stories by strategically walking across the keyboard. Their first novel, *Finding Frances*, is a fine example of this technique, also winning several indie awards. Their most recent release, *Ugly*, was selected as the Honor book for SCBWI's Spark Award in the Books for Older Readers category for 2022. Kelly has a Master of Fine Arts in creative writing from Oklahoma City University's Red Earth program.

Made in the USA
Monee, IL
17 October 2024

67924080R00166